WHACKED!

WHACKED!

A ROMANTIC SUSPENSE

AMY CORWIN

FIVE STAR
A part of Gale, Cengage Learning

GALE
CENGAGE Learning®

Detroit • New York • San Francisco • New Haven, Conn • Waterville, Maine • London

GALE
CENGAGE Learning·

LIBRARY OF CONGRESS CATALOGING-IN-PUBLICATION DATA

Corwin, Amy, 1956–
    Whacked! : a romantic suspense / Amy Corwin. — 1st ed.
      p. cm.
    ISBN 978-1-4328-2588-1 (hardcover) — ISBN 1-4328-2588-7
(hardcover)
    1. Single women—Fiction. 2. Vacations—North Carolina—
Fiction. 3. Murder—Investigation—Fiction. I. Title.
PS3603.O7865W43 2012
813'.6—dc23   2012028910

First Edition. First Printing: December 2012.
Published in conjunction with Tekno Books and Ed Gorman.
Find us on Facebook– https://www.facebook.com/FiveStarCengage
Visit our website– http://www.gale.cengage.com/fivestar/
Contact Five Star™ Publishing at FiveStar@cengage.com

Printed in Mexico
1 2 3 4 5 6 7 16 15 14 13 12

ADDITIONAL COPYRIGHT INFORMATION

CHAPTER ONE

Uncle Frank was notorious for his unpredictable excursions into left field, and as Cassiopeia Edwards eyed their family home, she decided he'd finally escaped from the ballpark entirely. The once staid, gray house was now purple, and as the late spring sunshine glittered over the fresh coat of paint, the color blossomed with near-blinding intensity.

She blinked but the view didn't change. The rambling farmhouse rose majestically toward the cerulean skies with all the subtle elegance of an overgrown pitcher of grape Kool-Aid.

Her appalled gaze shifted upward to the second story. Newly painted shutters sang in a vibrant, poppy-orange hue that left blue after-images when she closed her eyes. But despite the psychedelic glow generated by Frank's latest burst of creativity, an involuntary grin spread across her tired face.

The paint job was so like her uncle. It was so *Frank.* Her smile widened, dimpling her cheeks as the years away from Peyton faded into the dust. Like a tired child dragging her feet around a corner and catching her first glimpse of home, a sense of profound relief warmed her.

Even if home was now shocking purple instead of the soft, dove gray.

Rubbing away sudden, emotional tears, she grabbed her duffle and the crumpled fast-food bag from the front seat of her car. Her unwelcome response came uncomfortably close to confirming her doctor's diagnosis that she was a basket-case badly in need of a long, quiet vacation. Thankfully, house-sitting for her aunt and uncle qualified for a restful, perhaps even boring, break.

She shouldered her bags and clattered up the steps, only to be confronted by one last horror: a vivid red door. Uncle Frank had not stopped at painting the shutters orange and exterior purple. He had given the door a new coat of brilliant crimson, too. With a sigh, she selected an old, tarnished key from her key ring and opened the door. She held her breath as she peered inside, tensing with anticipation at the thought of a similar, jarring paint job within.

Pale peach walls with barely a breath of warm color graced the wide entryway. A narrow, deep blue runner, slightly frayed along the edges, stretched across the oak floor toward the stairs in soothing, restful harmony. She dropped her bags on the pine bench next to the door and relaxed. The knot in her stomach eased.

Then she took a deep breath and gagged. The thick odor of burning rope mixed with the sweet, cloying scent of sandalwood joss sticks filled the air.

Someone was smoking an illegal substance and burning incense to disguise the smell. Cassie's shoulders tightened as she glanced around the foyer uneasily, wishing she had never agreed to come to Peyton. She could have let the doctor sign her into a sanatorium, instead.

She shivered and rubbed her arms, trying to suppress the disquieting memory evoked by the unpleasant smell. In the silent confines of the house, she could almost hear the echoes of her aunt's angry accusations that Uncle Frank's weakness for marijuana would ruin them someday.

And despite her years away, and her relative maturity, Cassie realized she hadn't escaped from the desperate, unhappy certainty that she was the real reason for the tension between

Frank and Sylvia, and Frank's need for "better living through chemistry."

"Frank?" Cassie pushed her fingers against her breastbone to relieve the knot of tension. "Uncle Frank? Are you here?"

Nothing.

Wary, she pulled out her cell phone as she wandered toward the living room, following the smoky trail.

The room was empty.

An open mason jar sat on the low, maple table in front of the sofa. Inside the jar, a sandalwood incense stick burned slowly, sending a thin, mocking spiral of cloying smoke drifting toward the ceiling. A metal lid rested next to the jar. A few crumbled, blackened ashes smeared the bottom of the brassy lid.

She stiffened and tilted her head to listen, but there was only silence and the familiar creaking of the old house. A ripple of uneasiness coursed through her as she glanced around. Aunt Sylvia and Uncle Frank were supposed to be on the road, driving to West Virginia to visit friends while Cassie took care of their house.

Had something happened?

"Aunt Sylvia? Uncle Frank, are you here?" With a sharp gesture, Cassie picked up the incense and ground the stick into the bottom of the jar. She screwed on the lid and set the container abruptly on the table. "Uncle Frank!"

In the distance, she heard the steady buzz of a fly trapped inside the house.

Maybe Sylvia and Frank had gotten a late start—really, really late. Leaving minutes before she'd turned into the driveway. Seconds really, judging from the half-burnt incense.

Her glance hung on the ashes in the Mason jar. Her hand moved from her chest to her roiling stomach. A final, thin spiral of smoke dispersed into the air. In a decisive move, she strode to a window and opened it to let in some fresh air.

Then she searched the house. When she didn't find anything alarming, she returned to the living room but was too restless to relax. So she shoved her cell phone into her pocket and walked back outside. She stared at the wide expanse of lawn and took a deep breath, contemplating the joys of two weeks in the country.

The air was crisp and cool as the afternoon sunshine spread across the beautiful North Carolina countryside. The Outer Banks and deep gray Atlantic Ocean were only a few miles away. Everything was going to be great. There was nothing to worry about.

Her uncle and aunt had clearly left according to plan.

And left incense burning? Don't think about it.

Maybe she should take the pill she'd neglected earlier that morning. The one for stress so she could unwind and enjoy all the . . . green. She glanced around. Grass and more grass, undulating toward the road in virulent Technicolor. She frowned and rubbed her tired eyes, already longing for the soothing gray and black of city streets.

Then she straightened and leapt down the steps, heading around the house toward the backyard.

A little exercise like I promised the doctor and then dinner. She could be normal. It wasn't that hard. And she didn't need prescription drugs to do it.

Behind the house, thick woods encircled the wide backyard like a lover's arm. A curving dirt trail plunged through bracken and cinnamon ferns under the trees at the far edge of the lawn. Chin up, she walked through the dim opening between two ancient sweet gums. With each step, a plume of rich, organic scent arose from the pine needles and old leaves blanketing the ground. Her left foot sank into the spongy earth. She tripped over a gnarled root. Fortunately, one of the rough-barked pine trees broke her fall.

Something about the resulting splinters in her palm reminded her of her job in Raleigh. Then, no matter how much she tried to concentrate on the crisp scent of pine and unfurling beauty of the ferns brushing her legs, her mind raced uncooperatively back to the office in an endless loop of worry.

She picked another sliver of wood out of her palm as her stomach twisted, reminding her once more that she hadn't taken her ulcer medication.

I should go back. Now.

If she took enough anti-anxiety drugs, she might even stop thinking, just like a regular human being. But after a longing glance over her shoulder, she continued forward. Ahead, the sound of water frothing over the rocks beckoned with seductive whispers. Sun-dappled shadows threaded through the tree trunks. A swarm of late spring insects flitted through a shaft of grainy, golden light in random spirals of joy. For a nanosecond, the sight broke the cycle of her unproductive, racing thoughts. Then, despite the sparkling beauty of the insects' translucent wings, her unease returned.

A feather-light touch tickled her leg. She stooped and scratched her shin, thinking about bugs in general and ticks in particular.

When she straightened, the woods around her felt vaguely hostile and foreign, full of rustling, secretive creatures. She could hear unseen animals moving through the underbrush. The twisted branches of the trees surrounding her moved ominously, clattering in an unfelt breeze. The thick, mossy trunks effectively hid whatever lurked nearby in the oppressive gloom.

Out here, no one would hear her scream. She was as isolated as the unhappy visitors to Shirley Jackson's Hill House.

She ran forward and staggered to a breathless halt at the edge of a stream, her chest tight. With a start, she realized she wasn't quite alone after all.

"Frank?" she called hesitantly.

Her uncle sprawled lazily in a decrepit lawn chair next to the water. A whitish-blue trickle of smoke rose and then settled in a fluffy halo around his head. The haze filled the air, trapped beneath the overhanging branches of the huge trees. She sniffed and then gagged at the sweet-bitter scent of marijuana.

Trying not to breathe too deeply, she edged closer, aware of a swirl of complex emotions. He failed to respond or notice her, even when she loomed over him. He seemed to be all long, bony arms and legs, and slightly deaf. This sudden, sharp evidence of his advancing age tore at her conscience. She should have come sooner.

"Uncle Frank?"

"H-eey," he called, catching sight of her. He flapped a heavily veined hand through the air. "Hey!"

"What are you doing here?" She glanced around uneasily, hoping no one else was taking a walk through the woods.

"Who?" He glanced around. Then, oddly, he stared down at the water on his right.

"Uncle Frank," she said, speaking in slow, clear tones. "I thought you and Aunt Sylvia went to West Virginia."

"West Virginia?" His head swiveled around on his thin neck. "Who?"

"It's me, Frank, your niece, Cassiopeia."

"Sorry. Cass isn't here. Lives in Raleigh. Too bad." He shook his head before taking another deep drag of his twisted, lumpy cigarette. He held his breath for several seconds before the smoke dribbled out of his nose in two thin spirals. As the gray air wafted upward and threaded through the tree limbs, he stared across the stream in an unfocused daze.

"I'm Cass, your niece. Cut it out, will you? Quit fooling around." She stared at him suspiciously. Something was out of kilter, even for him. She'd seen him stoned before, but never incoherent. She glanced down the trail. She had to get him out of here and sobered up before anyone else found him.

"Relax," he said with a peculiar smile that appeared almost bitter despite his overly relaxed attitude. "Want a hit?"

"No! I don't smoke—you know that." She sniffed and backed away. She could get high standing downwind of him and there was another, more deeply unpleasant scent in the air that she could not identify. "Uncle Frank—*Frank!* What are you doing? I can't believe you're sitting here in the middle of the day, totally *whacked!*" She stared past him. What if a nature-loving cop wandered by? Or worse, what if Sylvia found her husband in this seriously becalmed condition? She'd be furious.

Then she'd blame the first responsible adult she located. Who in this case would be Cassie.

Her heart sank. "You're lucky I'm the one who found you—if Aunt Sylvia knew—where *is* Aunt Sylvia?"

"It's cool." He lolled in his seat, leaning his head back as if it was suddenly too heavy for his thin neck. His eyes rolled up to gaze at a patch of glimmering blue sky, visible through the black tree branches overhead. The aluminum frame of his chair creaked, adjusting to his weight. "Here man, take another hit." He dropped his right hand toward the stream.

Cassie edged around him and looked down.

A man lay in the stream, next to Frank. Her uncle gave her another peculiar, mellow smile. Then he held the lumpy roach to the man's gaping, blue lips. *Dead lips.*

The pie and ice cream Cassie ate earlier hit the back of her throat. She gagged.

Dashing down the path a few yards, she stumbled into the unyielding solidity of a thick oak. She stopped and leaned against it, resting her head briefly against her forearm.

She should never have left Raleigh.

And she should have taken *both* her stress and ulcer medications.

Finally, she prayed it was all a mistake—a drug-induced illusion caused by inhaling too much smoke.

Another prickling wave of heat flashed over her, leaving her skin damp and cold in its wake. Her mouth filled with saliva. She swallowed convulsively and locked her arm around the tree as a second flush swept over her. Finally, she leaned over and surrendered. Throat burning, she emptied her stomach, trying to ignore the streaks of red and sharp, metallic taste burning her lips.

When she stopped gagging, she wiped her face on her sleeve and spit a few times. Shoulder pressed against the tree trunk, she fought for control, but a chill sluiced through her, slipping cold, clammy fingers under her damp cotton shirt. She shivered despite the pale rays of sunlight breaking through the pale green leaves overhead.

Finally, she straightened and took a deep breath.

I should have taken my meds. Well, it was too late now.

She pulled out a roll of antacids and peeled one off with shaky, uncooperative fingers. Her feet stumbled over the broken twigs and depressions in the path as she paced, but gradually she regained her balance. Then she concentrated on bringing order to her incoherent and irrational thoughts.

Unfortunately, there was nothing rational about her uncle giving hits of marijuana to a dead man.

And while she knew her gentle uncle well enough to know he was innocent of any crimes except pot and stupidity, no one else viewing the scene would believe it.

She stopped, took another long, shaky breath and held it, willing her body to relax. She had to take care of her uncle— that was the most important thing—right after she figured out what had happened.

After one more mint, she forced herself to return to the stream. She gazed down at the body, striving for objectivity and hoping she had been mistaken.

The man was definitely dead. His partially open eyes were flat and dull under heavy lids. His mouth gaped. Cassie had the uncomfortable feeling that if she watched too long, his eyelids would move with unfortunate evidence of insect life.

Unable to look away, her stomach curled and gurgled when a ripple cascaded around his eyes and mouth. Flies buzzed his head and landed. The insects tap-danced over the gray skin, their hind legs rubbing together with glee over their appetizing discovery. Then the man's lips moved as if in silent protest at this final outrage.

She glanced away hastily and caught her uncle's gaze. He reached down and held his roach to the corpse's lips.

"Stop that!" she yelled.

"What?" Frank jerked his hand away and stared at her.

"Stop—he's dead! What the hell happened to him?"

"Who's dead?"

She pointed, her hand shaking. Another prickling flush of nausea flared through her. "He's dead. Pay attention!"

"Naw—he's just really, really relaxed. We shared a hit or two—nothing major."

"What's wrong with you? He's dead!" A slight breeze curled over the stream, carrying the nauseating smell of putrefaction. She pressed icy fingers to her mouth and gulped.

"He can't be dead. See? He's waving," her uncle said. "He's just chillin'."

The dead man was, indeed, waving. His right hand, floating in the rippling water, flapped up and down in a jaunty movement. Someone completely insane might think the corpse was gesturing, "Hit me again, dude!"

Coughing, she turned away. She wrapped her arms around

herself in a desperate bid for warmth and clutched her elbows with icy fingers. "He's dead, Uncle Frank. Get up—we've got to call the police."

"Police, hey, no. No police."

"We've got to call them. You should go back to the house. Now."

Frank could not face the authorities in his current state. And if Sylvia caught him, it would be the end of their marriage. She had threatened divorce before—this would be the final straw.

Cassie's childhood panic surged inside her, vivid as a nightmare. Sylvia and Frank were her only family. If anything happened . . .

That thought panicked her almost as much as her innate fear of the police, bred into her by long years of exposure to Frank.

"Where's Sylvia?"

"Sylvia?" he echoed.

"Your wife! Oh, never mind."

He eyed her expectantly. Then he stretched his long limbs and rose to his feet. His joints cracked and snapped as he straightened. Weaving awkwardly, he towered above her, his gray hair fluttering around his lined, drooping face.

The grayish-white strands clung to his ears and a few hairs caught on the stubble shadowing his pointed chin. He looked like a very old, very sad bloodhound that had inadvertently walked through a spider web. Brown splotches marred his scalp and she found herself worrying over the age spots as a welcomed distraction.

She reached out to steady him, alarmed at the fragility of his wrist. Her hand tightened as he leaned on her briefly. He looked vulnerable, sweet, and frighteningly frail.

And completely whacked on weed.

"Please, go back to the house." She pulled her cell phone out of her pocket. Three bars. She started to dial nine-one-one and paused. She did not want to hang on the line and talk to someone who would ask a lot of intrusive questions and tell her to remain where she was.

There was no way she was going to remain where she was with a dead man making obscene gestures at her.

And her mind snatched at the first flimsy excuse she found. What if her cell phone connected to nine-one-one in Raleigh instead of Peyton? Now that she stopped to think, it seemed possible that she wouldn't connect to the right nine-one-one service. After all, she hadn't listened to the salesperson's spiel, so how did she know? She latched on to the problem, spinning out all the technical ramifications of roaming nine-one-one service.

How did nine-one-one work if she was traveling?

Who knows?

It was all the excuse she needed to avoid talking to the officious folks at the emergency call center.

Relieved, she dialed her best friend.

"Cassie? Is everything okay?" Anne asked, her voice sounding distant and distracted. "Did you get to the farm okay?"

"No—yes, I'm here, but it's not all right. Call nine-one-one. I'm at the stream behind the farm. There's, uh, been an accident."

"An accident? Are you hurt?"

"No—no, not me. It's someone else." She glanced down at the dead man. The left eyelid rippled in a ghastly, insect-induced wink. She squeezed her eyes shut and turned away hastily. "A stranger. I think he fell. He's dead."

"Dead?" Anne's voice rose. "Oh, my God, are you okay? What happened?"

"I don't know. I took a walk and found him. Can you call nine-one-one and tell them to come here?"

"I'll call my brother."

"No! Don't call your brother. Call the cops or nine-one-one."

Anne sighed. "My brother *is* the cops."

This isn't going to be good. Not for anyone. Cassie focused, trying not to think about Anne's older brother, James Fletcher. The cop.

As a kid, she'd had the obligatory crush on her best friend's gorgeous brother. Back then, he'd wanted to be a writer. That creative goal made him even more romantic in her young eyes. Unfortunately, he was also the guy she threw up on after her senior prom and he hadn't even been her date.

It had been one of the most humiliating experiences in her life.

"Call nine-one-one." Cassie hung up and realized Frank had ambled away.

She ran a few yards and glanced around. With a sigh of relief, she located him beyond a bend in the path. He stood in the middle of the trail watching her. Spanish moss hung down around his ears like a goofy gray wig. His brown eyes were bloodshot and he seemed lost and confused, despite the tension implied by the stiffness of his shoulders.

She repressed the urge to pat him on the head and tell him everything was going to be all right. She couldn't lie, and she was fairly sure everything was *not* going to be all right. Instead, she went over to him and gave him a quick hug.

He had always done the same for her, despite his occasional mental absences.

He'd always been there for every scraped knee, every bruised ego, and every bad grade on her report card. After one particularly terrible day being bullied at school, she remembered coming home to find him in the kitchen. She'd burst into tears. After one look, he'd wordlessly held out a pan full of brownies. She ate half of them before he gave her a hug and suggested she take a long walk in the woods.

Uncle Frank was weird, but he tried his best.

Now, it was her turn. She had to make sure he didn't get into trouble with Sylvia or the police.

"Are you okay? Can you get back to the house?"

"Sure." He nodded, staring blissfully at the dimly lit path.

"Are you going to go now?"

"Sure, sure." After a few more seconds, he took a tentative step.

"Please wait for me at the house," she said in an encouraging voice. She gave him a gentle nudge.

He flapped his hand at her and continued forward at a snail's pace.

Shifting her feet, Cassie watched him go, unsure if she should accompany him or return to the stream. Finally, she hurried back to ensure no incriminating evidence remained. And the first thing she noticed was the sagging lawn chair. Hands shaking, she folded it up and ran down the path. Frank hadn't gotten far.

She caught up with him and thrust the chair into his hand. "Take this, too, Uncle Frank. I'll be home in a few minutes."

"You hungry?" He scratched his scrawny belly. "I'm hungry. Maybe I'll bake something."

He looked as if he hadn't eaten in weeks. His worn, faded T-shirt hung limply off sharp collar bones, skimming over his ribs. Then she noticed the barely legible print on the front of his shirt. Her lips trembled, almost smiling despite her incipient panic.

"Use horticulture in a sentence: You can lead a whore to culture, but you can't make her think.—Dorothy Parker." Uncle Frank might be a flake, but he was a firm believer in the power of deep thoughts.

"Great, Uncle Frank. I love your cooking." Cassie swallowed

the lump in her throat. "Just stay at the house. I'll be there soon."

Humming to himself, he wandered away, the chair bouncing against his thigh.

Once more, she ran back to the stream and studied the area, trying not to look at the dead man. Unfortunately, her eyes kept straying toward the water, drawn there by the ghastly remains.

He lay face up with his head and bulky shoulders propped up on the bank. Fine, dark hair plastered his head in lank strands. His heavy eyebrows frowned over a bulbous nose and created the brutish appearance Hollywood favored for film noir goons who got killed in the first scene. And the body had either started to bloat or the water had shrunk his shirt because the garment was taut and only half buttoned. The saturated fabric gaped, exposing his chest. Black curls of wet hair starkly shadowed the mottled flesh, continually dampened by shallow ripples.

And although the murky, brownish water covered his legs and feet, the stream wasn't deep enough to hide his upper thighs and thickened, middle-aged waist. He looked arrogant and mean, even in death.

Cassie drew back, uncertain. Nothing suggested an obvious cause of death.

Had he wandered into the woods and had a heart attack? Fallen and hit his head? There were no rocks nearby, only mud and damp, twisted roots. She couldn't see how a fall could have killed him.

Then she noticed the ashes from her uncle's "special cigarette" and the long, narrow grooves in the mud from the chair where her uncle had been sitting, giving hits of marijuana to a dead man.

The crime scene investigators would have a field day. She shuddered as the thought released a new set of horrors.

What if he was murdered?

The cops might pick up enough evidence to conclude her uncle had killed him—which was obviously not true. If he had murdered him, Frank would not loll around in a lawn chair, sharing a smoke with his victim.

Even Frank was not that crazy. But how could she explain that to a cop? Especially a cop like Anne's brother who probably had nothing but unpleasant, embarrassing memories of her.

He would never believe Frank Edwards had been too whacked to realize what he was doing. Even *she* had problems believing it. He'd arrest Frank. And he'd lock him up and intimidate him until he extracted a confession so he could close the case quickly and with minimal effort.

And he'd have flakes of marijuana on the lips of the dead man, laced with her uncle's saliva and DNA, too. How was she going to explain that? How was *Frank* going to explain that?

How could any sane person explain that?

She stepped on the nearest depression marking the chair's location and hurriedly scraped leaves over the area with her heel. Then she paused. DNA evidence was more important than mysterious grooves in the ground. She turned to the corpse. Her hands flew behind her back and twisted together in mute protest as she considered the situation.

She couldn't bring herself to touch the flaccid body.

Maybe there wouldn't be any evidence on his lips. Leaning closer, she searched for brown flakes. The plump, lower lip moved and a gust of putrid air blossomed in her face.

She stumbled back, nearly losing her balance on the slick Carolina mud.

No way.

Then she thought about her uncle.

Yes, way.

She scooped up a handful of water. She could wash the

mouth and flush away any incriminating traces of marijuana. Her uncle would be safe.

Behind her, a twig snapped.

The water slipped through her fingers, splashing over the corpse's face. She stood up hastily and wiped her damp hands on her jeans. Then she rotated her shoulders to ease her tension while trying to assemble an expression of suitably appalled innocence before she turned.

A huge cop stood two yards away, watching her, eyes hidden behind a pair of silvered sunglasses. He crossed massive arms over his chest. Her lungs squeezed shut, leaving her gasping for air like a hooked fish.

The sudden fear of unreasonable arrest strangled her.

Intimidation. Long hours of questioning without access to restrooms or water . . .

The blood left her head. Her stomach burned while her skin flushed hot and then damply cold in a prelude to another bout of deep sickness. She pressed her hands against her belly, praying not to faint or vomit.

"Thank God," she said in a strangled voice, trying to hear over the frantic beating of her heart. She forced herself to appear honest and glad to see him. He was, after all, Anne's brother. "There's a—there's a dead man. In the stream."

"Are you the one who found him?"

"Yes. Cassiopeia Edwards. I—" She swallowed convulsively. She was going to faint. Or throw up. She didn't trust him, even though he was Anne's brother. He made her nervous.

Police made arbitrary decisions based upon circumstantial evidence that destroyed people's lives. Innocence . . . guilt . . . What did they know?

All she knew was that when the cops showed up, anyone around was basically—and royally—screwed.

The only person safe from persecution was the dead guy.

She glanced down at him.

He waved at her and smiled.

CHAPTER TWO

Sheriff James Fletcher contemplated Cassie Edwards' wet hands. She'd been bending over the stream when he arrived.

Washing away evidence?

"What were you doing?" he asked.

Behind him, he could hear the emergency crew and his deputies arriving. It sounded as if they were trying to plow through the trees instead of simply walking down the open path. He almost winced when he heard someone—or something—fall, followed by the sounds of wood cracking and a lot of muffled swearing.

"I-uh, I was sick." She waved in the direction of the trail. "I was washing off my hands."

He studied her damp hands briefly before he dropped his gaze down the long line of her jean-clad legs. Then he noticed her shoes. They were scuffed with mud and leaves—fresh and moist. And the area on the bank nearest the body was disturbed.

So much for his crime scene.

"Go wait over there," he ordered, watching until she moved away.

Her hands nervously rubbed up and down her thighs. Her eyes darted around, refusing to focus on him. A sheen of sweat glazed her pale skin. Her dark hair was damp around her forehead.

She looked scared and ill. And guilty.

"There are traces of blood back there, Jim," one of the EMTs said. "About ten feet away, at the base of a Sweet Gum. Could be where the actual, uh, accident occurred."

Jim stared at the body and surrounding area before walking back to the Sweet Gum. To his surprise, Cassie Edwards stepped between him and the tree. Her face paled so dramatically he held out his hand, thinking she was going to faint right there and fall into what little uncontaminated evidence he had left.

"That's mine," she said. "I'm sorry."

"What's yours?" He studied her, striving for a dispassionate but firm air of authority when he wanted to pat her on the shoulder and reassure her.

"I, uh, threw up. I was upset. I've never seen a dead man before. I got sick."

"Right." A sudden memory flashed into his head of his younger sister's best friend and a prom night he wanted to forget. He almost sighed. "Understandable. You've always had a weak stomach."

"I had the flu, for God's sake! It wasn't my fault!"

"You have the flu?" He took a step back. That's all he needed, a murder and the flu.

"No! Not now. At the prom, ten years ago. When I threw up on you—you're Jim Fletcher, right? Anne's brother? I had a fever of a hundred-and-two. I didn't even have a glass of punch. All I drank that night was water."

That explained the mystery of why she felt like a banked fire against him when he drove the four kids home from the prom. It didn't endear her to him, however. It had taken him nearly six months to get the smell out of the car. And he'd had to get rid of his most comfortable pair of jeans.

"So what about this? How do you explain the blood?" he asked, gesturing toward the base of the tree.

"Peptic ulcers. I have a prescription if you want to check. Call my doctor. I'm under a lot of pressure at work—stress. I'm on vacation now so I can rest."

"I'd appreciate getting that information," he said. *Enough stress to make you go crazy and kill a man?* He examined her pale, tense face.

Definitely possible.

She stared back at him, her blue eyes wide and wild. "Can I go now?"

"Where are you staying?" he asked. "I'll need to take your statement when we finish here."

"I live in Raleigh. But for the next two weeks, I'm at the farm. You're probably parked in our driveway."

"You're at the Edwards place? Aren't they gone?"

"Yes, it's my place, too, you know. At least, I used to live there."

She replied defensively, her hands hidden behind her back. He didn't think she was holding anything, but the nervous gesture made him thoughtful.

"Listen, can I go now?" she said. "I'm really not feeling well."

"How well did you know the victim?" he asked, ignoring her request. Her nervous discomfort might encourage her to provide more information than she would reveal in a calmer, less harassed state.

"I don't know him at all. I have no idea who he is, or why he's in our stream."

"This is your property?"

"My family's property. I guess, technically, it's Uncle Frank's place. I'm not exactly sure where the property line is, though. He owns about fifty acres, give or take."

"And you've never met the victim?"

"No. Never. I have no idea who he is. I just got here a couple of hours ago. Ask Anne. I stopped at her diner on my way."

"Then you haven't been in the area recently and you've never met—"

"No. I haven't been here since I graduated. You know that." Her voice sounded increasingly brittle. "Or you should know. I mean, have you seen me around? I live in Raleigh, now. I've been there for the last six years—ever since college. Ask Anne."

"And your uncle?"

"Frank? What about him?" She shifted her feet and fixed her gaze on his left shoulder.

Her actions indicated she knew more than she was telling. His attention sharpened, focusing on her posture and awkward movements. He studied the rigid tension in her body. Her fingers brushed imaginary lint off her jean-clad thighs.

Subconsciously brushing away guilt?

"I thought you said the Edwards were gone. Is your uncle here?" he asked in a deceptively mild voice, hoping to lull her into an admission.

"He's at the house."

"Then I'll need to talk to him, too. On my way out." His gaze rested thoughtfully on her face, and he remained quiet. Most people could not stand silence. Some folks would even begin talking, just to create noise. And they often revealed more than they intended because of their nervousness.

In Cassie's case, it didn't work. She remained stubbornly silent, and he had the distinct impression she was diligently avoiding the truth. Not lying, precisely, but bent on omitting important details.

"Can I go?" she asked at last, a hostile tone hardening her voice. She crossed her arms over her chest.

"Back to your uncle's house? Yes."

He watched her wobble away. She kept stumbling and catching herself on the trees lining the path.

Either she really was in shock, or she was drunk.

And the sight of her dredged up a few more random memories. She'd been a skinny little big-eyed kid who hung around with his younger sister. A budding tree-hugger and general whacko, qualities that made him uncomfortable despite the attractive swell of her hips and the curve of her waist as she staggered away.

The entire Edwards family was nuts. Her crazy uncle and aunt were certifiable, even if they both had their PhDs. The rest of the scientific community might hold them in awe for their contributions to the horticultural sciences, but Jim's interest was purely professional.

In fact, he suspected Frank Edwards might have a small role in the current upswing of drugs. Maybe not the hard stuff, but certainly weed. He had the credentials to cultivate it and the perfect place to grow it.

Jim sniffed. Then he pulled out a large, white handkerchief and sneezed.

Hell, even the air smells like marijuana. With a sigh he turned back to watch his team painstakingly work the scene.

The coroner, David Bolander, stood next to the body, eyeing it as Bill Meyers fussily snapped a few photographs.

The coroner stepped closer, studying the corpse dispassionately. Bolander was a tall man with a weathered face marked by brown age spots and white scars where skin cancers had been removed over the years. Stoop shouldered with a bit of a paunch, he looked more like a farmer—a man who had worked outside most of his life—than a coroner who spent his days bent over stainless steel tables under fluorescent lighting.

However, a lot of Peyton women seemed to think the widowed coroner's thick, white hair made up for his face. And they diligently made sure he never had to suffer with his own cooking.

The rumor in Peyton was that Bolander didn't even know how to cook and had nearly died of starvation after his wife passed. That was before the ladies in town got him under their

gentle but inescapable control. Jim knew how that felt. He had
to work with increasing fervor to stay out of female clutches,
himself.

When Bolander took a step away, Jim stared at the body with
a shock of recognition. The corpse was Nick Gracie, the
bodyguard for the wealthiest man in their county, Howard
Butler.

And here he thought Butler was crazy to hire a bodyguard.
Maybe someone really had been out to get him.

"What have you got, Dave?" he asked at last.

Bolander rubbed his chin. "Don't have a thing, yet. Except
this boy's been dead at least a day, maybe more. Surprised he's
lasted this long without some critter gnawing on him."

"Insects have been at him, though," Jim replied, breathing
through his mouth as a particularly ripe gust of air curled
around them. "Can you tell how he died?"

"No sign of any wounds—can I roll him over?"

Jim nodded, taking a step back.

With a grunt, Bolander pulled the body over onto the bank.
The black hair was matted with blood. Bits of bone and brain
tissue showed through the crushed skull, and the wound was
alive with insect life.

"Can't tell you one hundred percent, but looks like blunt
force trauma. Someone hit this boy on the back of the head
with something. Hard."

"Not an accident, then?"

"Look around. Soft mud and a few tree roots—nothing that's
going to cause this amount of trauma unless he fell out of an
airplane."

Jim smiled grimly. "Possible, but unlikely."

"I'd say unlikely. However the way some of these yahoos fly,
it might not be entirely out of the realm of possibility," the
coroner said dryly. "There was that damn fool who ran his

plane into a tree trying to take off outta his field."

"Yeah. Well, then we're looking at murder with some kind of a heavy weapon. And he didn't walk here after getting his brains bashed in—someone dumped him. There's no blood or evidence to suggest he sustained his injuries in the immediate vicinity."

"I'd say that was pretty accurate," Dave commented before giving orders to the EMT team to bag the body.

"Wait a minute." Jim bent down and looked at the ground along the bank near Nick Gracie's corpse. Gracie's pallid fingers seemed to be pointing to several long depressions. "You see these?"

"What would make those marks? Maybe whoever dumped the body here used some kind of a wheelbarrow to drag him."

"Those aren't from a wheelbarrow." The sheriff brushed aside the leaves and found one more marking. When he stood up, the depressions formed parallel lines, but one of them was smudged and nearly gone. Several leaves were crushed into the mud.

He remembered Cassie Edwards' dirty sneakers and her guilty expression.

But what the hell would make grooves in the clay beside the stream? It looked almost like the marks a lawn chair left on a sandy beach. Which didn't make much sense.

Drag marks he could understand. Even tire treads or something else that could be used to convey a two hundred and twenty-five pound body, but not a chair. Unless the killer was a lot odder than even Jim could imagine.

"Take a picture of these depressions, will you, Bill?" He stood up and snapped off his rubber gloves. "And get some samples and a casting. Then make sure you go over this area again and pick up anything you find."

Bill's lips thinned in irritation but he nodded. Jim backed off, sensing Bill's resentment at being told his job. The man tended to be overly sensitive and took offense so easily that Jim wouldn't be surprised if he found a silver bullet etched with his name in Bill's desk.

Pausing again, Jim eyed some fine gray ash near the edge of the stream. Water had washed most of it away and even as he watched, a ripple snagged a few more flakes and swirled them downstream. Pulling a plastic bag out of his pocket, he carefully scooped up the remaining ash with the blade of his pocketknife before handing the bag to Bill to place with the rest of the evidence.

"You coming back with us?" Dave asked, stripping off his gloves. As always, he tucked them into a plastic bag and added it meticulously to the stack of evidence bags.

"No. I'm going to stop at the farm and talk to the witness."

"That young woman looked like she was about to faint. Scared to death."

"Or guilty as hell."

Dave chuckled. "You're too cynical, Jim. Isn't she a friend of Anne's?"

"They went to high school together, but she hasn't been back in years. So, no. Not that friendly."

"No conflict of interest, eh?"

"No more than with anyone else in this town. I've known most of them my whole life and all of them a lot more recently than Cassie Edwards."

He hadn't seen her since the disaster of her prom night.

And yet at strange moments, he still remembered how her long body looked draped in her pale blue prom gown. And her dark hair knotted at the base of her neck. Even though she had been too young and wacky to really interest him, he'd noticed the slow, sensuous way she moved. And the heat of her thigh pressing against his when he drove her home that night.

"I hope Frank Edwards isn't involved, poor old guy," Dave said. "Despite that fancy degree, he can't find his ass with both hands. But he's never bothered anyone before." He chuckled. "And to hear him tell it, his grandmother was a Teach and that makes him one of the last surviving descendants of Blackbeard."

"Yeah, right." But in spite of himself, Jim smiled. "Anyway, long lost relative of Blackbeard or not, the body's on Frank's land. His niece found it. You tell me."

"And there's the odor of burning weed everywhere. Or hadn't you picked up on that?"

"I noticed."

"Drug deal gone bad?" Dave moved toward the path. "Maybe Frank is growing more than orchids."

Jim followed. "Maybe. The girl's up from Raleigh—"

"Just arrived today, though. And Nick's been dead a lot longer than that."

"Frank Edwards has been here. It's getting on toward supper time." Jim glanced at the darkening sky. The techs had already resorted to flashlights under the spreading forest gloom. They walked beneath the rustling canopy of trees as the last of the daylight faded. Nearby, a Barred Owl hooted, calling, "Who cooks for you—who cooks for you all?" A sharp pang of hunger reminded Jim that he'd skipped lunch.

Signs were good that he could forget about dinner, too.

"When will you have a report?" he asked.

"Tomorrow afternoon. Come by tomorrow afternoon. Thank God we don't have many murders 'round here. I only have one ahead of him."

"Thanks, Dave."

"Hey, I live for this," the coroner replied.

Jim thought about Cassie Edwards' pale face and long legs and sighed. "Yeah, right. We all do. Just live for this. Right."

CHAPTER THREE

When Cassie got back to the house, she snagged her purse and ran to the kitchen. She needed a tranquilizer for her nerves and a Zantac for her stomach.

And a relaxing, recuperative vacation that she apparently wasn't going to get.

In the kitchen, Uncle Frank was washing up some dishes in the sink. He stacked the clean bowl in the dish rack and aligned all the utensils heads up, in separate compartments. Spoons with spoons, knives with knives. In some ways, he was even more of a stickler about how to do things than Cassie. She patted him on the shoulder on her way to the refrigerator.

"Have we got any milk?" She spied a cluster of bananas on the counter. "Or better yet, cream?"

"Both. Always have both." Her uncle stacked the last bowl in the rack next to the sink and dried his hands.

She wasn't sure how her stomach would react, but maybe cream would settle it. She grabbed a banana and sliced it into a bowl. Then she poured a liberal amount of cream over it before adding a sprinkling of sugar.

"Reminds me of your mom," Frank said. A goofy, sappy smile lit his face at the thought of his sister. "She loved her bananas and cream."

"Food of the Gods." Cassie took the first spoonful and closed her eyes with pleasure as the rich cream slid over her tongue. Then she waited, spoon poised over the bowl while she swallowed. The cool, creamy concoction slid down her burning stomach in a soothing wave. Encouraged, she ate another bite and paused again. Her stomach didn't object. With a sense of relief, she downed the rest of the bowl. By the time she got up to wash the dish, the rich scent of dark chocolate filled the kitchen.

"Are you baking something?" she asked.

"Brownies. They're almost ready. You want some?"

Her heart thumped. The cream in her belly curdled slightly as she remembered the sheriff was coming soon.

"Are those your *special* brownies?"

He chuckled. "All my brownies are special—I bake them all from scratch."

"The police are coming. What are you doing baking at a time like this?"

"They can have some." He stared at her with a hurt look in his eyes. His sagging cheeks wobbled.

"No, they can't—are you crazy? You can't offer them your special brownies."

"But—"

"No, I mean it. We're in enough trouble, and I've got to talk to you. Sit down, Uncle Frank. This is serious."

"What's wrong? You can tell your Uncle Frank. You're not in trouble, are you?"

"I'm not in trouble—you are."

"Me? I may be a descendant of Blackbeard, but I'm an old man. It's only me and Sylvia, now. You know I've never looked at another woman—"

"No one is accusing you of cheating—"

"You said—"

"I said you're in trouble with the law! They're coming here. They found that dead body."

"What dead body?"

"The one by the stream. You saw him."

"Whoa, you'd better ask that other guy 'cause I don't remember anything about any dead body."

"Trust me, there's a dead body at the stream. And the cops are coming here to question us. We've got to get our stories straight."

"Not me. I didn't see any dead body."

She reached out and flung her arm around his thin shoulders. She hugged him and wondered if she could coax him into taking a shower and changing clothes. He smelled like sandalwood, cocoa, and ever so faintly of burning rope.

He was in big trouble.

"When will the brownies be done?"

His face brightened and he moved over to pull open the oven and check on the progress of his brownies. "Ten minutes, give or take."

"Good, then maybe they'll come, interview us, and leave before the brownies are ready."

Her uncle gaped at her, his expression fuzzier and more confused than usual.

"Never mind," she said, pulling out one of the wooden kitchen chairs. "Sit here for a few minutes, okay? Now, when did you go to the stream today?"

"Oh, this afternoon. I went to see if the fish were biting." He blushed and glanced over his shoulder. "Your aunt's away. Don't tell her I went fishing. She hates fishing. Bad karma to fish." He waved his large hands as if shooing the bad vibes away.

"I won't tell her," Cassie assured him. "So you went there around . . . when? One? Two? I got there around four. Were you there very long before I arrived?"

"Not long."

"How long? An hour? Two hours?"

He shrugged. "Just set up the lawn chair and fished for a

while. Might have dozed off."

"And you smoked—"

"Seemed the neighborly thing to do, once I realized Nick was already there, relaxing."

"Nick? You knew him?"

"Sure. Never much cared for him, but hey, we're neighbors." He shrugged. "Shared some weed with him."

"Who is—was—he?"

"Works for that rich kid you used to date. Never could stand him." He studied her under lowered brows. "Is that why you're here? You're not still seeing him, are you?"

"No. And please try to focus, Uncle Frank. He works for. . . ." *Who was that guy?* Damn, she couldn't believe she had forgotten all about him, including his name, after he had taken her to the prom.

Maybe it wasn't so surprising. After she threw up on their driver, Jim Fletcher, her unmemorable date refused to kiss her goodnight. Even the prospect of taking her virginity in the time-honored tradition of prom night hadn't been enough to convince him.

Good old Howard Butler. Or "Howie-the-butt" as Anne used to call him.

An unfortunately accurate moniker when you caught sight of him from the back. Howard had a decidedly pear-shaped physique with hips that any strong peasant woman would love to call her own.

"The dead guy works—worked—for Howard?"

"Howie-the-butt," her uncle confirmed.

She groaned and rubbed the bridge of her nose. Nothing had been secret in the Edwards house. *Nothing.*

"So you knew this Nick guy?"

"Sure. You know it's not like Raleigh here. We're a small town. You get to know everyone."

"No kidding. Were you two friends or something?"

"Not really friends," he replied slowly.

"You didn't fight, did you? Argue?"

"Hey, no—no way. You know me."

"Okay, so you didn't argue with him, but—"

The house reverberated with the sound of someone knocking at the front door. The cops. It sounded like they were using a battering ram.

Rubbing her icy fingers over her jeans, Cassie walked into the hallway. She moved slowly, with great dignity and confidence, despite her shaking hands. She took a quick mental inventory in front of the door. To her surprise, she didn't feel too bad. Her stomach felt fine. She was almost calm except for her clammy skin.

Then, opening the door, she almost lost it.

The sheriff had taken off his silvered shades, but he had on a pair of rubber gloves. Uncle Frank's lawn chair dangled from his long, blue-covered fingers. A small clot of damp mud, stuck to a withered leaf fragment, fell off one of the legs as she watched.

"Oh," she said, trying to sound innocent, but not too cheerful. It was a fine line. "Hi!"

"You want to tell me about this?" he asked. His eyes were very dark gray, she noted. Very cold. Not at all like the warm, intellectual gaze of the budding novelist she remembered.

"It's a lawn chair," she said. "Where did you find it?"

"On your porch."

"Oh, good. Well. You can leave it there. Thanks."

"You want to explain it?"

"Explain what?" Her stomach gurgled uneasily. She covered it with a frozen hand.

"It was used by the stream. Today. Near to where the victim was discovered. By you."

37

"Oh, no. I didn't use it." She smiled, although she couldn't feel it. Her face was numb.

"Do you have a plastic garbage bag?"

"Yes, I—"

"Bring me one."

"Sure, ah, no problem." She let go of the front door. It started to swing shut in his face. Cassie grabbed it. "Sorry, the door . . ."

He stuck a booted foot out, propping it open.

"Thanks," she said, sprinting for the kitchen.

As she skidded to a halt in front of the sink, Frank was opening the door to the oven.

"Hey—I think they're done."

"Great," she gulped, yanking out a black, plastic trash bag from a drawer. She glanced around distractedly. The delicious aroma of warm brownies filled the air. She sniffed but couldn't tell if a more herbal odor underlay the fragrance. "Just great."

She fled the kitchen. When she got back to the front door, the sheriff was still standing there, his face devoid of any helpful expression. She handed him the bag and watched as he put the chair inside.

"I'll be right back," he said before returning to his patrol car, parked a few feet away. Another officer waited at the car, and the sheriff handed the wrapped chair to him.

She waved weakly at the second officer and smiled.

The sheriff strolled back up the driveway and suddenly stopped near her car. Her heart fluttered, but she couldn't think of anything in her vehicle that would interest the police. Nonetheless, he slowly walked around it. He glanced at the house and then eyed the car again.

When he finally approached the front porch, he asked, "Is that your car? The electric-blue one?"

"Yes."

"Figures." He looked up at the house and shook his head.

"Guess you picked out the paint for the house, too?"

"No, I did not!" she replied, stung. "Why would you even say that?"

"Electric-blue car, purple house . . ." His voice trailed off as he shrugged. "Looks like the same genes at work to me."

Cassie flushed but refused to comment. He was obviously trying to get under her skin to make her say something she shouldn't. It wasn't going to work. "So, are you coming inside, or what?"

"Inside." He edged past her and entered the house. "I'd like to speak with you, first. Then your uncle. He's here, isn't he?"

"Yes. He's in the kitchen."

The shadow of a smile brushed his lips. "I thought I smelled something. Brownies?"

"Yes, but I don't think they're done yet. Sorry. Can I get you anything to drink? Milk? Coffee? Water? Blood?"

"Nothing. Why don't we go sit down." He turned toward the living room before he seemed to notice her luggage, still piled up against the wall. "Did you just arrive?"

"Yes. I thought I told you that."

On top of her duffle was the crumpled fast-food bag. He picked it up and stared at the receipt stapled to the gaping top. "I'd like to hang on to this, if you don't mind."

What the hell! "Knock yourself out. My trash is your trash."

Pulling out a baggie from his pocked, he dropped the paper sack inside and sealed it. "How about the living room?"

"How about it?" She flapped her hand. "Take anything you want. You need some more garbage bags? Baggies? Rubber gloves? I'm sure there's dust in the vacuum cleaner if you're interested."

He eyed her. She flushed and glanced away, trying to control her nervous reaction to his presence. This was a murder investigation. She wasn't at some sleazy bar trying to fend off some no-neck loser. She needed to cooperate so he'd leave Uncle Frank alone.

Be polite.

Blushing, she smiled and tried to look as normal as possible under the circumstances. Unfortunately, her mind kept circling back to Uncle Frank in the kitchen baking his *special* brownies. What if he brought a plate out for them? He'd be arrested. It would kill him.

While she stood in the doorway, shifting feet, the sheriff parked himself on the edge of the sofa. He pulled out a pad of paper and pen. Her heart fell down to her suddenly wobbly knees.

"Please sit down." He glanced up at her.

Grateful, Cassie sat on a huge, olive green footstool roughly the size of a loveseat. She pulled her feet up and rested her chin on her knees, wrapping her arms around her shins. The room still smelled of incense and weed. She shifted, feeling like the caterpillar in *Alice in Wonderland,* sitting on a huge mushroom, puffing on a hookah.

Slowly, the alternating flushes of hot prickles and clamminess diminished to a slight, warm glow. Everything was going to be all right. She shook her head to clear it. Then she realized the tranquilizer was working. Now, she only had to look calm. She smiled, crossed her legs under her, and stared back at the sheriff.

Damn, he's changed. She frowned.

Where was the slightly nerdy, skinny guy who always had his nose in a book? This man looked like he chewed rocks for breakfast and could yank the engines out of small, foreign cars with his bare hands. He'd put on weight, and it was all muscle judging by the way his shirt stretched across his shoulders. He moved his arm to take out a small notebook. She watched the heavy ripple of muscles under his tan sleeve. Her mouth went dry.

"Why don't you tell me what happened?" he asked.

She blinked and tried to focus. "Well, uh, I already told you I got here this afternoon, sort of late. Sometime around four. I was tired from driving so I thought a walk would do me good. I went down to the stream."

He nodded, making a few notes.

"And, well, I found the dead guy, Nick."

His head snapped up. He studied her, frowning. "You said you didn't know him."

"I don't know him! I've never seen him before in my life."

"But you know his first name?"

"Uncle Frank told me his name, just now!"

"Your uncle? I thought you found the body. Were you with your uncle?"

Her stomach squeezed tight. "Yes—no, uh, I talked to my uncle when I got home. I described the, uh, man. He said it sounded like this guy, Nick."

His gaze intensified.

"I swear, I've never seen the guy before. I haven't been back here in six years." She ran a nervous hand over her shin.

"People do travel," he commented in a dry voice. "And folks from Peyton have been known to go to the big city of Raleigh. Are you sure you never met him in Raleigh?"

"No—never. I work almost eighty hours a week, most weeks. I work weekends." Her voice rose. "Why do you think I've got ulcers? I work all the freakin' time. I don't meet anyone except the people at work. Computer people."

"Well—"

"Don't tell me he was a computer person? Out here?"

"Believe it or not, we have heard of them. Even out here, Miss Edwards." He watched her with that half-scared, pained expression men get when they're around a woman they think is going to get hysterical.

41

Cassie took a deep breath, feeling some of her anxiety turn to annoyance. "Sorry. And what's with the Miss Edwards stuff? You know me. I'm the girl who got sick on you after the prom."

"After your prom."

"What?"

"It wasn't *my* prom. I was in college at the time. And working nights so I could buy gas to drive kids home from the prom so they wouldn't kill themselves."

"Talk to Anne about that. It sure wasn't my idea."

Irritation passed briefly over his rock-like face. Then he resumed his bland expression with a practiced ease she envied. "So, you went to the stream and found the body. What exactly did you see?"

"Just that *guy*. Lying half in the water." Pressing her fingers against her mouth, she burped and tasted bananas. She stopped for a moment to take a deep breath and pray for her stomach to settle. "Then I got sick—well, you know that. And I called Anne and asked her to call nine-one-one."

"Why would you call Anne? Why didn't you make the call yourself?"

"Because I wasn't sure if I dialed nine-one-one from my cell phone, which nine-one-one it would call."

"What do you mean, 'which nine-one-one'?"

"Well, would it call the Raleigh nine-one-one, or the Peyton nine-one-one? My cell service is in Raleigh."

"It calls the local nine-one-one. It wouldn't be worth a damn if it called the Raleigh nine-one-one, would it?" He sounded exasperated.

Her back tightened. "How would it know to do that? It's registered in Raleigh."

"Because it's got to connect to a local tower to get a signal. So nine-one-one goes to the closest call center to that tower."

"Which could have been anywhere! It could have been the

next county over or something. Who knows which call center it might have decided to use?"

"There's only one call center in this area."

She could have sworn he was grinding his teeth. While she was perfectly aware she sounded completely insane, she couldn't stop defending her admittedly lame excuse. It would sound much worse to explain she simply hadn't wanted to hang on the phone while the nine-one-one people asked her annoying questions and repeatedly assured her that everything was peachy-keen when it clearly was not.

Besides, there was the evil fascination of torturing the sheriff.

Cassie smiled at him, resting her chin again on her knees. "Well, it was faster to call Anne."

"So you called Anne," he repeated. "Then what happened?"

"I, uh, waited for the authorities."

"You didn't remove anything from the scene?"

"Remove anything?"

"Like that lawn chair, for example."

"Oh, that—I thought I told you."

"You never mentioned the lawn chair. Are you sure the dead man wasn't sitting in the lawn chair? Are you sure you didn't push him out of the chair into the stream?"

"Of course I'm sure! I thought I told you." She took a deep breath to ease the tension in her chest. Although it was nice to annoy the sheriff, it was difficult to suppress her increasingly desperate wish for the sheriff to stand up, announce that he was satisfied and knew her uncle was innocent, and then leave. The longer he stayed, the more likely her uncle would do or say something that would land him in jail. Her palms dampened at the thought.

"Then tell me again." The sheriff settled into the cushions with the comfortable air of a guy happy to stay where he was for hours, if not days.

"The chair was there, by the stream. Next to the dead guy. I didn't touch the dead guy."

"But you did something with the chair."

She widened her eyes, feigning innocent agreement, and nodded.

"Didn't you wait by the stream after you called Anne?"

A leading question meant to uncover the mystery of the moving chair. She moistened her dry lips. The sheriff's gaze focused on her mouth for about two milliseconds. Distracted, she almost gave in to the urge to throw back her shoulders, stick out her chest, and yank her shirt tighter.

"Hey, Cassie, they're ready," Frank called, walking into the living room with a plate piled high with warm, fresh brownies. "Take one. Oh, man, company!" His head swiveled toward Jim Fletcher. "Oh, man, the cops—"

"It's the sheriff, Uncle Frank," she replied in an overly bright voice. "But I've already offered him refreshments. He didn't want any. Why don't you take those back to the kitchen?"

The room filled with the evocative scent of warm chocolate. Cassie's mouth watered. Even the sheriff's nose twitched.

"Oh, sure Cassie, sure. I'll be in the kitch—"

"I'd like to talk to you, Mr. Edwards," the sheriff interrupted.

"They're only brownies." Cassie stood up hastily and grabbed the plate. "I'll take them back to the kitchen for you." She avoided looking at Jim Fletcher, who by now was studying the plate with an odd expression on his face.

"What do you want to talk to me about?" Frank asked, his voice rising plaintively as he eyed Fletcher. His gaze kept drifting down to the firearm at the sheriff's side.

"It's about Nick Gracie, the man Miss Edwards found at the stream this afternoon."

"Hey, I told her to leave him alone—the dude was just tired." He shook his head and moved a pile of seed catalogs from the seat of a tattered armchair to the floor. Then he eased down to sit with his long legs sprawling out in front of him. "Nuisance call. Well, sorry, man. But you know these young women. Always panicking over something."

"You told her . . . were you present when she found the body?"

"I forgot he was there. I'm sorry," Cassie answered hastily. She placed the plate of brownies on a narrow table near the doorway. Then, she pulled the stool near her uncle and resumed her seat, hoping to keep her uncle from incriminating himself. When the sheriff glanced at her trembling hands, she shoved them under her thighs. "I've never seen a dead body before. It scared me to death."

"Are you scared now?" Jim asked. He had clearly recognized her tension. He studied her face with a dispassionate gaze that seemed to note every nerve twitching in her body.

"Of course not."

"But you still didn't think you should mention your uncle's presence at the stream?"

"It was a detail, an unimportant detail. And now you know, so no damage done." Cassie eyed him and smiled with stiff lips, silently urging him to move on to another line of questioning. There was no point in answering the same things time and time again. Her hands fluttered to her knees, and she rubbed her cold fingers against the denim, trying to warm them.

"Sure, man. I was fishing, like Cass said," her uncle said.

She caught the sheriff's gaze and flushed when he said, "She didn't say that."

"I forgot to mention it," she said. "I have a very poor memory, and I'm under a lot of stress. At work."

"You did mention that."

To Cassie's discomfiture, he paused to write in his small book. The silence lengthened intolerably until she could hardly sit still. She shifted and glanced at her uncle. His head was leaning against the top of the chair back. As she watched, his mouth dropped open. A loud, sonorous snore vibrated past his lips.

"Were you sitting in a lawn chair to do your fishing, Mr. Edwards?" the sheriff asked.

Cassie kicked the side of her uncle's chair.

"What?" Uncle Frank straightened and glanced around. When he caught the sheriff's gaze, to everyone's surprise, he said, "Sure. A lawn chair. It's right out front, on the porch. You can borrow it if you want to do some fishing, yourself."

"Thanks. While you were fishing, did you notice Nick Gracie?"

"Not at first. But then he waved to me."

Hastily rising, Cassie skittered over to her uncle. She draped a protective arm over his sloping shoulders, wishing she could gag him without Jim Fletcher noticing. She glared at the sheriff.

"It looked like he was waving, because of the water." Cassie swallowed to clear her throat. She could barely breathe. "Frank was confused."

"Because of the water?" the sheriff asked.

"The hand—that man's hand—it was, well, floating. It looked like he was waving."

Her uncle stared up at her with an expression of surprised interest. He appeared to have no idea what she was saying, or going to say next, and was thrilled to hear whatever it might be.

"I see." Jim wrote a few more incriminating comments in his book. "So you didn't realize Mr. Gracie was dead?"

"He wasn't dead, just very relaxed," her uncle insisted with a benign smile. He seemed to think the sheriff and Cassie were simply being obtuse.

She could have cheerfully slapped a large piece of duct tape over his mouth.

"When did you go to the stream today, Mr. Edwards? Or do you prefer Dr. Edwards?"

"Call me Frank. No one calls me Mr. Edwards anymore. And I'm not a medical doctor."

"Fine," the sheriff said. "When did you get to the stream?"

Frank glanced at Cassie. Then his eyes sort of rolled back in his head as he considered the question. "This afternoon?"

"What time this afternoon?"

"Before Cassie came. Right before she came."

"Around three? Three-thirty?"

"The sun was still over the trees, so more like two. Or maybe two-thirty. Of course, it could have been as late as three, but not four. Definitely not that late." He paused to smile. His gaze landed on the table near the door. "Would you like a brownie?"

Writing assiduously, the sheriff glanced up and caught Cassie nervously studying him.

He examined her for a moment before shaking his head. "No, thank you. So you got to the stream around two. What happened then? Did you notice anything?"

"Well, I started out down at the big maple snag. But the fish weren't biting, so I went upstream. Say, Cassie, I left my pole, there, near that snag." He stood, agitated. "If Sylvia comes back and finds it there—"

"Sylvia?" the sheriff asked.

"My wife."

"Where is she?"

Uncle Frank glanced toward the door and then waved his hand. "Said she wanted to visit some relatives . . ." His voice drifted off.

Cassie's gaze jerked toward him, suddenly sensing something wrong. Or rather more wrong than sharing a smoke with a dead guy. Frank looked sadder than ever, his lips working as he stared at the door.

"How long has she been gone?" Cassie asked, chilled. Her gaze lingered on the empty doorway.

"A couple of days. She left Saturday." He shook his head. "Or maybe it was Friday. Sorry, man."

"That's almost two days," Cassie said. "Did she go to visit someone? What about your plans for your vacation?"

"Not sure—she said something." He shook his head. Thin strands of gray hair floated around his ears, creating an air of aging fragility that made Cassie's heart clench. He smoothed back the fine hair from his forehead with an unsteady hand. "Can't remember, exactly."

"She must have told you." Cassie gripped his hand.

He shrugged and stared at the floor.

"So you've been here alone?" the sheriff asked, dragging everyone's attention back to him and his little black book. "Since Friday or Saturday?"

"Cassie's here now." Uncle Frank's grip tightened briefly on Cassie's fingers before he let go.

"Right. So let's get back to this afternoon. You went fishing around two." He plucked the radio from his belt. "Milt, go back to the stream and start walking south. See if you can find a fishing pole propped up against some kind of a snag—"

"Maple tree—"

"An old Maple tree—"

"Stump sprouting," Uncle Frank added. "Damn Maples. They grow like weeds around here."

"Maple snag," the sheriff repeated into the radio. There was a violent surge of static after which he mumbled a few more commands before shoving it back into his belt holster. "Milt will find your fishing pole."

While her uncle beamed, Cassie eyed the sheriff's bland expression. "Thanks. I appreciate you sending someone to get it."

"Evidence," the sheriff replied, squashing her nascent gratitude. "So you walked upstream, and then?"

"Well, I was getting a little tired, so I stopped and sat down."

"In a lawn chair?"

Frank nodded, the unsuspecting chump. "I always bring it. Fishing can be tiring."

"So you were fishing, and?"

"I noticed Nick Gracie. He'd gotten there before me, and he was already dangling his feet in the water. But he didn't seem to mind me joining him."

"And you didn't notice anything peculiar about him at the time?" the sheriff asked.

Frank shook his head. "A little quiet, maybe. But when I spoke to him, he waved like I said. So we both settled back to enjoy a little quiet."

"And?" The sheriff let the word hang in the air.

"And?" Frank asked, perplexed.

The sheriff studied him. "You just sat there?"

"Well—"

"You forget that I arrived right about that time," Cassie cut him off, afraid he would mention sharing a joint with the corpse. "When I saw Nick—the corpse—I told Uncle Frank to go back to the house. And I called Anne. That's it."

"You're both sure?"

"Well, I—" Frank said.

"Of course we're both sure," Cassie interrupted. Her icy, restless hands rubbed the seams of her jeans. She couldn't seem to stop fidgeting, even when the sheriff's sharp eyes followed—and noted—her movements. "I called the police, er, Anne, immediately."

"And you'd never met, or seen, the dead man before? Even in Raleigh?"

"No, never. I didn't even know his name until Uncle Frank

told me when I got back to the house."

"You two will need to make formal statements." He eyed them as if suspecting they were both incapable of performing even that simple task. "At the sheriff's office."

"No problem. We'll come to the station tomorrow." She felt limp with relief. All they had to do was sign their statements and they were done. Frank would be out of danger.

"You sure you don't want some brownies?" Frank asked, sniffing. "They're best when they're still warm from the oven."

When the sheriff hesitated, Cassie could have happily strangled her uncle.

"I'm sure you're busy." Cassie waved toward the door. "He's got to get back to the station, Uncle Frank. He doesn't have time to eat anything." *Especially brownies laced with your extra-special ingredient.*

"I'm not that busy—"

She stepped between Frank and the sheriff and began herding him in the direction of the front door. "And Milt—you did say the other officer's name was Milt, right?"

"Yes, Milt Singleton."

"Milt could probably use some help finding that fishing pole. If you don't mind looking for it. Now that it's dark," Cassie said, stumbling over her words in her anxiety and increasing desperation to get the sheriff out of the house and out of their lives. "That is, I'd hate to leave it out overnight and have it stolen. Or have some animal get tangled up in it."

"We'll find it. If it's there," he promised.

She got the strong impression that a chuckle lurked in the back of his throat. His gaze drifted from her face to the plate of brownies and back again. He knew what was in those brownies as well as she did.

And he thought it was hilarious. Probably because he was

about to arrest them both, anyway.

What were a few "special" brownies in the face of a murder?

CHAPTER FOUR

After closing the door behind the sheriff, Cassie turned back to her uncle. She struggled to appear calm and suppress the chilling anxiety that her uncle was one step away from arrest. "Are you sure there's nothing in these?" She eyed the luscious, warm brownies. Despite the bananas and cream she had eaten earlier, she couldn't resist the distraction of a crumbly, melting brownie sundae.

As if reading her mind, her uncle got two large stoneware bowls out of the cupboard. Rummaging through the drawers, he pulled out a large spatula. Then, with a practiced turn of the wrist, he scooped two huge chunks of brownies out of the pan and deposited the warm squares in the bottom of each bowl. He grabbed a carton of vanilla ice cream from the freezer and a container of fresh whipped cream from the refrigerator. Finally, he pulled a bag of bittersweet chocolate morsels out of the cupboard.

"What?" he asked with a conspiratorial wink before nuking the chocolate morsels in the microwave until they melted into a thick, smooth goo.

"The brownies. There aren't any illegal substances in them, are there?" She leaned over her bowl and breathed deeply. God, the intensely chocolate aroma smelled good. "You didn't put any . . . weed in them, did you?"

"Of course not!" he replied, staring at her. "Would I have offered them to the sheriff if I had?"

"I don't know. To be honest, you might have thought they would mellow him out."

He laughed and shook his head. "I know you think I'm not all here, but I'm with-it enough to know you don't hand a cop a brownie laced with an illegal substance."

"Thank God for that." She grabbed her bowl and layered on the ice cream, a few spoonfuls of the chocolate goo, and two big dollops of whipped cream. When she caught her uncle's twinkling eye, she smiled back. "This isn't dinner, you know."

"Dessert, first, then dinner."

"Curried chicken? With cream sauce?" By the end of her two-week vacation, her arteries were going to be begging for mercy. But despite medical opinion to the contrary, she always found that cream—real cream—soothed her stomach better than any medicine.

When they finished eating dessert, Cassie cleaned up the dishes. Feeling much happier, she went through the fridge, pulling out the ingredients for the chicken. Uncle Frank sat at the kitchen table, leaning back, contentedly watching her.

"When will Aunt Sylvia be back?" she asked as she threw strips of chicken into a frying pan with a few diced shallots. As it cooked, she uncorked a bottle of dry white wine to deglaze the pan after the chicken lost its pinkness.

Silence.

She prodded the chicken with a wooden spoon. "Uncle Frank?"

Glancing over her shoulder, she was horrified to see Frank's long face crumple. His goofy act vanished, leaving behind the sensitive, serious man he kept hidden in hopes of avoiding the desperation of real life.

"Don't know," he said. "She didn't say."

"She is coming back, isn't she?"

"I don't know!"

"Did you two have a fight?"

"I—I think she left me!"

"Oh, Uncle Frank!" Cassie pulled the pan off the stove and bent over to hug her uncle. "What happened?"

He shook his head. His lips trembled as he rubbed his hand over his face. The raspy sound told her he hadn't shaved in a couple of days, which was unlike him despite his long hair. He always kept his face clean-shaven because Sylvia hated kissing a man with facial hair. And she complained that his gray whiskers aged him.

If he stopped shaving, it meant Sylvia really was gone.

"What did she say? She must have said something—she wouldn't walk out without a word."

"She said she couldn't take it anymore. She was disappointed in me."

Her heart thumped erratically, making it hard to breathe. Each time she thought about her uncle and aunt separating, she could barely suppress the overwhelming sense of panic. All the feelings she had experienced as a child after the death of her parents rushed back. The world around her was not logical or controllable. It was far darker and much more dangerous in its sheer, cruel randomness.

And she was lost and terribly alone.

"Why? Why would she say that?" Cassie whispered.

Please don't tell me you've started on the harder drugs. Please, don't.

Shaking his head, he just rubbed his jaw. "She doesn't love me anymore. After nearly forty years—"

"No, you're wrong. I'm sure she still loves you, Uncle Frank. It's a misunderstanding. You'll see. She'll come back. She probably went on vacation because she needed a break. I'll talk to her. I'll find out what's wrong. And she'll come back and everything will be fine. Just like it used to be."

"I don't know, Cassie. Things around here aren't like they once were. Not anymore. Not since Howie-the-butt brought Gracie here as his bodyguard. The whole town's changed. Lots of strangers. And it's like Howie thinks he owns Peyton now. You've been gone a long time. You don't know what it's like."

Hands stiff with cold, she caught her uncle's shoulders and gave him a little shake. "Uncle Frank, this is important. You didn't fight with Nick Gracie, did you? You didn't shove him, did you? At the stream?"

"No. I swear, Cassie."

"But couldn't you see there was something odd with him?"

"Well, he did seem a little quiet. And I wouldn't normally have thought he'd be the type to go swimming in that stream." He shrugged. "But I don't judge. I took a seat to keep him company. We smoked. I swear nothing happened. Not while I was there. Did something happen after I left?"

"No, of course not. Are you sure you didn't have a fight with him? Maybe you pushed him and he fell?"

"No, nothing like that. I'm too old to fight with folks these days. I grow orchids. That's all."

"God, I hope so," Cassie said with a shiver. "And I hope the sheriff thinks so, too."

She thought about his hard eyes and exasperated air, and wondered if she should have behaved with a little more circumspection. And perhaps she should have admitted that she was an idiot and too nervous to call nine-one-one herself, instead of compounding her stupidity by continuing to make excuses.

But in the end, she suspected her quiet vacation wasn't going to be the nirvana she anticipated.

CHAPTER FIVE

Jim Fletcher climbed into his car and glanced at his deputy sheriff.

"You don't think Frank Edwards did it, do you?" Milt asked, running a hand over his knee as he studied the house.

"I have no idea." Jim sighed. "But he spent a helluva long time down at that stream."

"Smokin' weed with a dead guy." When he caught Jim's glance, he shut up, staring straight out the windshield as Jim turned the car around. "The woods reeked of marijuana."

"It's possible he was too incapacitated to realize Nick Gracie was dead. It struck me that he had other things on his mind."

"Yeah. Like getting high."

Even Jim had to struggle to keep an appropriately serious expression on his face. The Edwards were notorious as crystal-gazing, tree-hugging intellectuals, but none of them had ever been arrested. Yet. He thought about Cassie's pinched, worried face.

His sister Anne had told him that Cassie had arrived in town today for a two-week vacation. To convalesce. And it looked as if Cassie needed it. Her skin was too pale and stretched tautly over her high cheekbones. And stress had hollowed her blue eyes, sinking them into deep shadows. She looked as if she lived on the edge of hysteria.

"Miss Edwards said she didn't know who Nick Gracie was at the stream," Jim added, trying to weigh her conflicting statements. "But when I showed up at the house, she called him by his first name. How often did Nick go to Raleigh?"

"No idea. But I don't think it was that often. It's almost a hundred-fifty miles. Even if you speed, it takes three or four hours. I doubt Mr. Butler would let him take that kind of time off. Besides, Nick's girl lives in Morehead. He's got no reason to go to Raleigh, if you ask me."

"Butler sent him once or twice that I know about." Jim weighed the scanty information before acknowledging Milt's point. "But you're right. I don't see him crossing paths with Cassie Edwards by accident."

"Didn't Bolander say Nick had been dead for a while? I don't see how she could have killed him, unless she got here yesterday instead of today."

"Yeah." He grunted. "I found a receipt for some fast food she claims she got on her way here. She stopped in New Bern."

"Then I don't see how she could have done it. Her uncle, yeah, but not her."

"Inconclusive. We don't know where she was yesterday. And she could have helped him cover up the murder."

"Murder?"

"It sure didn't look like an accident to me."

Milt shook his head. "Frank Edwards might kill someone by accident, maybe pushing him or something. That's about it. No way is he gonna be able to pull himself together enough to move the body like that."

"He's got a doctorate. He's not stupid."

"Not stupid, just not very smart, if you know what I mean."

"Yeah. But his niece could have helped him."

"No way. Not if she was in Raleigh yesterday and stopped in New Bern this afternoon for a burger."

"I'd like to know what Frank Edwards was doing, sitting in a lawn chair next to a corpse," Jim said.

"Maybe I've been watching too much television, but what if he came back to 'relive his crime'?"

"Like the Green River killer?" Jim scratched the back of his neck. "I can't see that. You have to be pretty deranged to do something along those lines."

Milt snorted. "And you don't think it's deranged to relax next to a dead guy?"

"Is it possible it happened exactly as he said? That he was going fishing and set up at the stream near Nick Gracie and didn't notice he was dead?"

"There *was* a certain, distinctive odor."

"Yeah, but the thing is, when you back up to a swamp, you often get that odor. What if he figured it was some dead animal in the underbrush? Or maybe all the smoke from his joint covered the smell. Anyone could see he was stoned."

"Sure, it's *possible*." Milt studied Jim as if trying to judge the way his boss was leaning.

"At this point, *anything* is possible."

And although he'd have to check it out, try as he might, Jim could not see how Cassie Edwards could be guilty. This simultaneously relieved and annoyed him. But what was worse, he could not quite picture Frank Edwards bashing in Nick Gracie's skull, either. And especially not sitting next to him all afternoon, afterwards, shooting the breeze. Even if it was a one-sided conversation.

As killers went, Frank Edwards would be more of a disorganized, whoopsie-daisy kind of murderer. On the other hand, his niece, Cassie, would be the sort to meticulously plan it out. She'd make sure no evidence remained behind to incriminate her. Which didn't fit the situation, either.

If only her alibi would fall apart, he could make an arrest and close the case today. He thought longingly of the manuscript scattered across his desk at home and realized his spare time had just gone to zero. Fame and fortune would have to wait a while.

"So what do you want to do next?" Milt asked.

"Go back to the station. See if Bolander has anything else to say before he does the autopsy, tomorrow. And I want to look at the evidence again."

When they reached the two small brick buildings that served as the courthouse and police station complex, Bolander had already disappeared for the day. Frustrated, Jim and Milt collected the evidence bags from Bill Meyers. Adding their own to the pile, they congregated in Jim's small office. The film Bill had taken at the scene was still being developed, but he had also taken a series of digital images, which they reviewed on the computer.

Jim stared at the images, slowly clicking through them. He examined even the smallest details, hoping to build up a theoretical scenario that could be proved, disproved, or changed as they accumulated evidence. One thing he had learned was to let the evidence show what had happened and not to try to see things that weren't there. Unlike Cassie Edwards, who seemed amazingly proficient at imagining all sorts of things, regardless of the facts.

However, no matter what stupid things she had done when she found her uncle sitting next to Nick's body, Jim could not see her in the role of killer. Much as he would like to fit *someone* in that role.

And there was ample evidence to suggest that her discovery of a corpse had upset her. Not that there weren't some killers who became physically ill when they realized what they had done. But Cassie hadn't been anywhere near Peyton when the murder occurred. That fact, when combined with her emotional distress, seemed to rule her out. Except . . .

"Milt, get ahold of the judge. I want a search warrant for

Cassie Edwards' car and the farmhouse. And Frank's car, as well," Jim said.

"Frank doesn't own a car," Milt replied. "He sold it. His vision was so bad they took his license away last year."

"Then get it for the house. And Cassie Edwards' car."

"I don't think you're gonna find squat—"

"Get it. We'll see what we find tomorrow. In the meantime, let's look at what we've got, now."

"It ain't much."

"We've got the lawn chair. And evidence that Frank Edwards was sitting in it, next to Nick Gracie, most of the afternoon." Jim stared at the photo of the mud where the chair legs had made long, parallel tracks. "What does that look like to you?" he asked, pointing to some other depressions in the muck beside the stream. He clicked through the other photos, filling the screen with the images.

Sure enough, there were light ridges in the mud, the crests growing pale as they dried. Drag marks. Old drag marks.

"Dunno. Maybe he was dragged?"

"Have someone check the vic's shoes and clothing for mud. It looks to me like he was dragged the last few feet before he was thrown into the stream. Whoever did this was probably hoping the water would wash away whatever trace evidence remained. And that animals would take care of the rest."

Going back to the picture of the impression made by the chair, he realized Frank Edwards had positioned the chair after the body had been deposited. The lawn chair's legs had broken and squashed several of the older, dried ridges. And the most superficial smears were those in the upper right corner, most likely made by Cassie.

Trying to cover evidence of her uncle's guilt? Or afraid he would *appear* guilty?

"So, we know the vic was left at the stream for several hours,"

Jim said, thinking out loud. "And there's no evidence he was killed at that location. Based on the tracks in these pictures, we know Frank sat in his lawn chair *after* the body was deposited there."

Milt's head snapped up, and he stared at Jim with widened eyes. "You don't think Frank sat there and waited for him to die, do you? To make sure he *did* die?"

Shaking his head, Jim continued through the photos. "No. Nick died at least twenty-four hours ago, considering the condition of his body. The drag marks were dry and already crumbling before Edwards set up the lawn chair. It's safe to assume Nick Gracie would have tried to pull himself out of the water if he were alive when he fell—or was deposited—there. No sign of that, or a struggle."

"Yeah," Milt said, relief lightening his face. "Sure. Frank and Cassie found the body, right?"

"It appears Cassie is innocent, although she did tamper with the evidence. Tried to make it look like her uncle had never been there."

"Can't blame her. I mean, it's crazy, that old guy sitting there talking to a dead man."

"If that's what really happened." Jim stood up. "The autopsy won't be until tomorrow, but we still have the victim's effects to go through."

Before he got to the door, Bill Meyers came in with a paper bag, carefully labeled and sealed. "Thought you might want this," he said.

The slim, fair-haired man excelled at anticipating Jim's requests to the point of occasionally coming off creepy and obsequious. "Thanks," Jim said. Grabbing the bag, he tried to include, if not welcome, Bill.

Nonetheless, he couldn't stop scratching the spot right behind his left ear when he remembered Bill's almost hysterical reaction when Jim got the position as sheriff. And while Jim spent most nights writing and fantasizing about handing in his resignation, Bill spent most of his time talking about mistakes Jim made and attempting to prove to voters that he would be a better sheriff.

To Jim, this only proved everyone was guilty of something. It was a question of which crime you were trying to investigate at the time. And there was nothing like ten years of police work to make you want to write the kind of fiction where good people existed and the bad people always went to jail. Where there was an honest-to-goodness resolution.

Carefully opening the bag, Jim pulled out the damp clothing, laying it out on the folding table in front of his desk. Everything smelled like mold and rank, North Carolina mud. Wearing gloves, each man picked up an item and examined every pocket and fold in the material.

Jim took the slacks. They were unwieldy and covered most of one side of the table, reminding him that Nick Gracie hadn't been a small man. As he turned the trousers over, he noticed discolored, worn areas and smears of mud along the back hems and calves, evidence of movement along the damp soil. However, the body hadn't been dragged very far, or the fabric would have been more frayed and abraded. Nonetheless, if Gracie had been pulled over the last few yards, that surely accounted for the dried ridges along the stream bank.

Making a note to have the soil analyzed, he worked his way toward the waistband, looking for dried blood or other evidence. Nothing. He couldn't find any traces of blood. Nothing remained on the outside surfaces except a few patches of mud.

As he turned the pants inside out, he felt the pockets. In the right pocket were a few brown flakes and a torn strip of rolling paper. Using tweezers, he collected as many of the flakes as he could and put them, along with the strip of paper, into a plastic bag. In the back of his mind, he saw Frank's lumpy, homemade cigarettes.

Something else to search for tomorrow, Frank's rolling paper.

"Have you found anything?" he asked Milt and Bill.

Milt glanced up from the left shoe he was examining. "Mud, like you thought. Looks like the heel is scuffed up, but not the way it gets worn down when you walk. More like the backs of his shoes were dragged for a ways."

"That's consistent with the markings on the cuffs and lower legs of his slacks. What about you, Bill? Anything?"

"Well, the shirt's still wet. Most of the mud has washed out, but the right elbow has some faint streaks of reddish clay that run down to the cuff."

Jim remembered the images in the digital pictures. "Did any of you notice how odd Nick looked in that shirt? It didn't fit. It wouldn't even button over his chest."

"Maybe it shrank because of the water," Milt suggested.

"It takes hot water to shrink cotton. Or polyester," Bill replied. His voice was quiet although not meek enough to hide the oily note of superiority in his tone.

Jim nodded and ignored Milt's quick glance at Bill. After twenty years as a small-town deputy, Milt had long ago learned to let the smart remarks from pissant upstarts roll over him without comment. He'd get back at him later in some minor but annoying fashion. Jim just hoped it wouldn't be too disruptive to the investigation.

After a subdued snort, Milt returned to the sneaker he still held in his hand.

Relieved, Jim addressed his next remark to Bill. "What's the label read?"

"No label." Bill frowned with exaggerated thoughtfulness.

"Custom-made? Nick Gracie had on a custom-made shirt?"

"Guess old Howie paid him better than you'd expect. Maybe

I ought to apply to be his next bodyguard." Bill laughed.

"And perhaps we'll be sorting through your things next time," Milt said, shifting a wad of gum to the other cheek.

Despite his irritation at the sound of Milt's noisy chewing, Jim didn't comment. Milt was trying to stop smoking, and the nicotine gum was his latest crutch.

"Custom-made or homemade?" Jim asked. The expensive shirt opened up an entirely new line of questions. Since Nick Gracie had been Howard Butler's bodyguard, they might be looking at evidence that proved Howard Butler actually needed protection. "We'll need to find out which. Follow up on that, Milt. Do either of you know why Howard Butler hired a bodyguard to begin with?"

"He's wealthy," Bill offered as if that answered the question adequately.

"A lot of folks around here are well off, if not wealthy," Milt said, peering inside a sneaker again. "I don't see folks like the McDougals getting bodyguards. Their own plane and airfield, maybe, but not a bodyguard."

"Drugs?" Jim asked. The other pockets contained the normal detritus: small knots of loose thread and fuzz, a black comb, a handkerchief, and a few coins. No paper money, however, and no billfold.

Milt's eyes flickered to him and then back to his examination. "Not that I've heard."

"What about you, Bill?"

Frowning, Bill appeared to give the question serious consideration. He carefully folded the shirt and placed it into the evidence bag before looking up at Jim. "I'm not aware of any connection to the drug trade, but it is possible."

"Follow up on that, Bill," Jim said. "See what you can find out. Anything else? Anyone?"

64

"Naw, we've picked him clean as a bone," Milt said. "Cleaner, maybe."

As they folded up the remaining clothing, Jim eyed his team. He considered the anomaly that had been irritating him all afternoon, if he discounted Cassie's annoyance factor.

"Did any of you find any evidence of blood?" he asked.

The two men stared back.

Milt answered first, "Naw, at least not on the shoes."

"Bill?"

Bill pulled the shirt out of the bag again, scanning the shoulders and the back. "I don't see any evidence of blood. Wasn't he hit on the back of the head?"

"That's certainly the way it appeared to me."

Bill placed the shirt down on the table so they could see the inside of the collar. "There's blood on the inside, but it's mostly washed out. He must have lain in that stream a long time. The water washed away all the evidence."

"If that's true, then the blood must have been fresh," Milt added, eyeing the damp shirt. "Weird that it's mostly on the inside."

"I'd expect to see more splatter on the collar and down the back. Let me look." Jim picked up the shirt, turning it over under a light to examine the material more closely. "Even if most of the blood washed away, there should be some on the collar." He grinned at Bill and Milt, opening up a much beloved subject within their tiny department. "Now if this were television, like in *CSI* we'd have all kinds of fancy arrays of microscopes with huge lights and spectrometers, spectrographs, and racks of equipment that could analyze all of this and spit out reports within seconds."

"Damn," Milt replied mournfully, his brown eyes revealing one of his rare moments of humor. "All we've got are brains, a little brawn, and our good old Coroner Dave Bolander's antique microscope. And a hacksaw. I'm partial to that hacksaw, myself."

Bill glanced away and said softly, "Maybe *some* of us have brains."

Although Jim was fairly sure Milt heard the quiet remark, Milt's expression never changed. However, it was sure to be one more tick in his book against Bill Meyers. One more reason for some annoying little incident, like finding your car has a flat tire on your way to work in the morning. Or that some mouse has up and died in your desk drawer.

Or worse, some snake has crawled into your boots to die.

Well, if Jim was any judge of people, Bill would move on soon enough. Peyton, North Carolina, didn't have enough big, sexy crimes to hold an ambitious man. At least, they hadn't until this afternoon.

Glancing at his watch, Jim realized with a jolt that it was almost ten P.M. A glance at the dark windows confirmed this. "Put the evidence back in the bag and lock it up, Bill. We'll get back to it tomorrow."

"You leaving?" Milt stared with intense concentration at the table to disguise his hopeful expression.

"I'm going on up to the Butler residence. You want to come?"

"I'll go with you," Bill offered.

"That's all right," Milt said. "I can go. No sense in all of us going. And you've got to lock up that there evidence."

Milt stared at Bill, waiting for him to make some comment. However this time, the younger man shrugged his shoulders and ignored the sudden burst of Southern backwoods grammar that occasionally afflicted Milt when he wanted to really piss off Bill.

Jim suppressed the urge to say the phrase that had popped out of his mother's mouth a hundred times a day while he was growing up. *Now boys . . .*

Grabbing his light jacket, Jim walked out. When he caught a

final glimpse of Bill through the wide windows, his lips were moving as he talked to himself while he closed up the office.

"With any luck, Butler will be gone, and we can turn around and get on home," Milt said, settling into the front seat of the police car. He wasn't quite fat, despite being over forty; however most people would call him large. His cannonball head rode on a short, thick neck ridged with rings of muscle and fat that appeared compressed. The slope of his shoulders gave him a humped appearance that almost disguised the deep, barrel-like chest.

He looked like a mean character, and sometimes he was. Still, Jim had a lot of respect for Milt's common sense and the way he could ease into conversations with anyone, rich or poor. Everyone liked old Milt Singleton. And after his first year as sheriff, Jim frequently sent him out to nose around on his own. The deputy frequently came back with some of the more surprising bits of information, even if he professed he wasn't always sure what it all meant.

Unlike Bill, who more and more was a plain old stick, jabbing Jim in the eye every chance he got. Bill might be smart and ambitious, but he was also an asshole.

Which probably meant Bill would be the damn county commissioner someday and make all their lives a living hell.

The Butler place was one of the newer brick homes in Peyton. The house was built over the foundations of the original building, which had burned down twelve years ago when Jim was still working his way through college. Apparently, the Butlers had good insurance, because they certainly got themselves a bigger and better home out of it. Or at least Howard had.

Unfortunately, neither of his parents had been lucky enough to survive the blaze.

"I hate this place," Milt said as they rolled to a stop in front of the house. "No porches, like they don't want you hanging around, socializing."

"Then it's a good thing we're not here to socialize." Jim eased out of the car and stared at the darkened doorway. Milt was right. It was the most unfriendly looking house he'd ever seen. Shrouded in deep shadows, the black door was recessed between two white pillars that looked gray in the moonlight, giving it the appearance of a cave. No one had bothered to turn on the lights beside the door.

A series of shallow, brick steps led up to the door. Black, wrought-iron railings lined the stairs and funneled visitors to the black doorway as if the Butlers were afraid some poor soul might stray off the straight, cement path and set foot on the narrow strip of grass on either side.

Milt cursed as he climbed out of the car, gripping the door to support himself. His leather belt creaked as he slipped his walkie-talkie and gun into their holsters. "They must've heard us drive up. You can hear a damn cricket in the next county 'round here, it's so quiet. And the damn light's still off."

"Maybe they're in bed. It's almost ten-thirty." Jim rapped on the door with his fist. After a minute, Jim pounded again. The metal door didn't even shift under his fist.

"You want me to go 'round back?" Milt asked.

"No."

The door swung open as Jim stepped back to take a look at the house and search for lighted windows.

The lights on either side of the door flicked on. "Who's there?" a woman asked in an uncertain voice.

"The sheriff, ma'am. May we come in to speak with you?"

"Now? We've already gone to bed."

Really? And Howie-the-butt let his wife get up to answer the door? Jim couldn't suppress the thought that Howard needed a lesson or two in chivalry.

When the door opened, the light in the hallway revealed a

leggy blonde wearing a white-and-pink nightgown and robe that looked like it came from a Disney cartoon. She stared at Jim, her gaze hardening before she flicked a glance over his shoulder to Milt. A highly manicured hand gripped the collar of her dressing gown, holding it closed.

"We'd like to speak with you and your husband," Jim said.

"Can't you come back in the morning?" she asked, her gaze bouncing from Jim to Milt.

"Yes, ma'am, or you and Mr. Butler can come to the sheriff's office."

"What's this about?"

"Nick Gracie."

"Nick lives—"

"No, ma'am, he's dead."

"Dead? How did he die? An accident?"

"That's what we want to speak to you about."

She released the door and gestured for Jim and Milt to come inside. As they did, her face froze into a controlled mask. "My husband has already gone to bed," she said. "He wasn't feeling well."

"I'm sorry, ma'am," Jim said. "We need to speak to both of you, but we can take your statement tonight, if it's convenient. Should we go into the living room?"

"The living room?" She sounded appalled. "We can sit in the dining room, if you'd like. And I'll get Howard out of bed, so we can get this interview, or whatever, over with. Nick Gracie dead? I can't believe it! And Howard has to know. Nick is . . . was his bodyguard."

"Yes, ma'am." Jim waited until she disappeared at the top of the stairs before he wandered into the living room, flicking on the lights as he went. Part of him expected to see damp stains, or signs of a hurried cleaning. Maybe even some flecks of blood. What he found instead was what looked like a blinding snow storm. "You've got to see this," he told Milt. "No wonder she didn't want us in here."

Milt glanced around. The he threw his hands up in front of his face. "My eyes—I'm blind!" He shook his head. "Do you think they ever use this room?"

"White leather? Sure. You can wipe off leather. Easy to clean."

"Shit, if I had a white carpet, it wouldn't last a day."

"Hardly surprising with that pack of wild dogs you have roaming through your house."

"Only a couple of Bluetick Coonhounds is all. Probably better mannered than that woman." He jerked his head toward the stairs. "And a damn sight more affectionate."

Unlike the living room, the formal dining room glowed with polish. A faint, but not unpleasant, odor of lemons lingered. There were two low hutches in pale pine, with a long, oval table made out of the same pine in the center of the room. Six straight-back, matching chairs were arrayed around the table.

Pulling out the chair at the head of the table, Jim threw his notepad on the seat, staking out the dominant position.

Mrs. Butler returned, a few steps in front of her bedraggled husband. She eyed Jim with obvious dislike. "I told Howard that Nick is dead. I'd now like to know how and where he died." She grabbed the sleeve of her husband's robe and pulled him forward.

Stumbling, he yawned and ran a hand over his balding head. Thin tufts of pale brown hair stood up like short tree snags, dotting but not hiding the marsh-like scalp, spread with pink and fungus-brown splotches. He'd obviously tried to tan and had only managed to induce peeling.

Mrs. Butler waited for her husband to take a seat. Then she sat down next to him, as far away from Jim as possible.

Interesting. She hadn't chosen the chair at the end of the table, opposite him, even though he was fairly sure she normally sat there. Unless she wore the pants in the family and occupied the spot where Jim now sat.

He nodded to Butler. "When was the last time you saw Nick Gracie?"

Butler stared down at his hands folded on top of the table, as if he wasn't entirely awake.

Mrs. Butler's narrow jaw tightened. "He lives . . . lived over the garage and didn't come into the house much," she said.

"Did you see him today?"

"It's Sunday," she replied. "Unless my husband is going somewhere, we wouldn't see him on a Sunday. Did you see him today, honey?" She gave her husband's arm a squeeze.

He glanced up, his brown eyes bloodshot and glassy. The unpleasant scent of metabolized alcohol poured out of his oversized pores. "Nick? No. Not today. Not on a Sunday."

"So you didn't go out today? You didn't need him?"

"No."

Jim hesitated, trying to get a feel for the atmosphere in the room. Strange undercurrents flowed between the husband and wife. Was their tension a natural reaction to being questioned by the police late at night, or was there something more?

"Mr. Butler," Jim started, inscribing a fresh sheet of notepad paper with the current date, time, location, and names.

"Howard," Butler said with a tired grin. "Hell, we grew up together, Jimmie."

Jim suppressed the impulse to remind the man that he was four years older than Butler, and that socially they occupied vastly different circles. "When did you last see Nick, sir?"

Butler yawned. He rubbed the top of his head, fluffing the remaining tufts of hair. After a brief glance at his wife, he shrugged. "My wife and I went to church this morning. Then brunch. Did we see him after we got back from brunch, honey?"

71

"I don't think so." She smiled at Jim, but her eyes remained flat.

"Nick has Sundays off unless I need him," Butler said, "so it's not unusual that we didn't see him. May I ask where you found him?"

"At the trout stream at the back of the Edwards place."

"The trout stream?" Mrs. Butler sounded amazed. She started to turn her head toward her husband, but stopped midway. The muscles in her thin neck stood out rigidly.

Jim decided to wait and let them determine the direction the questioning should take.

"What was he doing at the trout stream?" Butler said. "Was it a heart attack?"

"Did he have heart problems?" Milt asked.

"No. Not that I'm aware of. When a man dies all of a sudden, though, it's usually something like a heart attack. Or a stroke. So what was it?"

"Looked like it might have been deliberate," Milt said, leaning back in his chair. The wood creaked as if about to give way. At the sound, Milt shifted forward and rested his meaty fists on top of the table.

"He was murdered? Is that what you're saying?" Mrs. Butler asked.

"Yes, ma'am. We believe so," Jim said.

Butler eyed him. "Then you're not sure? It could have been an accident?"

Jim searched for signs of guilt in Butler's blotchy face. "I'd say it was definitely murder, sir. We're simply determining the circumstances and his movements at this point."

"Well, we didn't see him today. I'm sorry. Wish we could give you more information." Butler leaned back, rubbing his face tiredly.

Jim watched him for a minute before his gaze drifted to Mrs.

Butler. "You and your husband were together all day?"

"Yes," Mrs. Butler said, her voice sharp. "All day. We went to church and then brunch before returning here. Some of our friends came by later in the afternoon and we played bridge. We always have a small get-together Sunday afternoon. Then we spent a quiet evening here."

"I appreciate the information, ma'am. Where were you folks on Saturday?"

"Saturday? I thought you said Nick died *today.*" Mrs. Butler glanced at her husband and gripped his arm. "This is so dreadful."

"My wife is in shock and exhausted, Jimmie boy. Can't these questions wait until tomorrow?"

"It would be better if we could get what information you have about Nick Gracie's movements while it's still fresh in your mind."

"But we haven't even seen him."

"What about yesterday? You said he had Sundays off, what about Saturday?" Milt asked.

Furrows deepened in Butler's forehead. "I know he was here in the morning. I ran into him when I went to the kitchen to get a cup of coffee."

Jim studied his tired face. "And he was okay then? Did he seem worried about anything?"

"Same old Nick. Nothing bothered him. Or if it did, he never talked about it. At least not to me. But I was his employer, not his friend. He did what I told him to do. We got along. I don't know what else I can tell you."

"And you, Mrs. Butler?" Jim asked.

"Me?" Her hand fluttered to her neck and back down to the table, and there was worry in her eyes. "I rarely saw him. I mean, he worked for my husband, not me. He was your typical dumb jock, if you want the truth. I had no reason to talk to him."

"Did you see him on Saturday?" Jim asked.

"I might have. I suppose so. I mean, he was always hanging around the kitchen or the workout room, waiting for Howie."

"When was the last time you saw Nick?" Jim asked.

"I believe it was before I went shopping. I went out that afternoon. I met a friend, and we went shopping in Morehead. We ate dinner and got home around seven. I don't think I saw him after I left to go shopping."

"And you, Mr. Butler? Did you see him after your cup of coffee in the morning?"

"Of course," Butler replied. "I played golf—I always play golf in the morning—and I went to Max Marine in the afternoon. Then I came home. I told him I didn't need him Saturday because I was meeting some of my buddies for a few beers later. My wife was also out, like she said." He shrugged. "Never saw Nick again."

"We'll need the names of your buddies," Milt said, and everyone stared at him, as if surprised to see he was still there.

"Exactly what did Nick Gracie do for you?" Jim asked.

"He was my bodyguard."

"Why did you need one? There are lots of rich folks around here. I can't say as I know of any others who feel the need," Milt said.

"Maybe they didn't. But there are plenty who think kidnapping sounds like the perfect way to make a few dollars." Butler glanced from Milt to Jim with an air of superiority that set Jim's teeth on edge. Like Jim wouldn't understand the dangers endured by the wealthy.

"Do you have any enemies? Anyone who might want to get to you and may think Nick was in the way?"

"Now that's the question that has been worrying me. While

you've been talking, I've been sitting here wondering if someone got rid of Nick so they could kidnap or kill, me. I can't think of anyone, but I'm more than a little worried about our safety. You boys'll stick close, won't you?"

"We'll certainly keep an eye on you," Jim replied. "So you hired Nick because you thought there was a possibility you'd be kidnapped?"

"If you don't think that's a very real risk, then you're a fool. Besides, I knew Nick in college. He got in contact with me a year ago when he quit the police up there in Boston. He was out of work. He didn't know what he was going to do, so I figured he might as well come down here for a few days until he could decide. And things worked out from there."

"Why did he quit the police force?" Jim asked.

"Oh, the usual. His wife left him because of the stress of his job, and he felt he wasn't getting anywhere. He wanted a change. It suited me, too. I knew him and knew I could trust him. Seemed like the perfect solution."

In a way, Jim could sympathize with Nick Gracie's desire to leave the stress of police work behind him. Unfortunately, it seemed like being a bodyguard would be just as stressful if his presence was necessary due to real threats.

Otherwise, it seemed like a foolish waste of money. Howard Butler might be a jerk, but he wouldn't throw money away on a bodyguard he didn't need. However, Peyton wasn't Boston or New York. There were no gangs here, only a disorganized bunch of petty criminals with delusions of toughness.

And at least one murderer.

"Is that all?" Mrs. Butler's voice rose in irritation.

Jim got up. His body felt stiff with exhaustion, and his knees creaked when he moved. "Yes, ma'am. I appreciate your time, Mr. and Mrs. Butler. We'd appreciate it if you could come by the sheriff's office sometime tomorrow to give statements. And if you remember anything else, please let us know."

"We will," Butler said.

As the men left the room, Jim glanced back. Mrs. Butler remained seated, face pale, her gaze following them.

She looked ready to pass out.

Butler patted Jim on the shoulder. "We appreciate you stopping by to let us know."

"Yes, sir." Jim walked down the marble hallway.

He'd have given a week's wages to hear what Butler said to his wife after he shut the door.

CHAPTER SIX

After checking twice on her uncle, who was sleeping the deep, slobbering slumber of the seriously whacked, Cassie called Anne. Worried and depressed, she needed to talk to someone sympathetic.

"Can you come over?"

"What's wrong?" Anne asked.

"Nothing. Can't you come over?" Cassie fidgeted and stared at the darkened window above the kitchen sink. She shouldn't ask Anne to come out this late when there was a homicidal maniac running around Peyton. "Or maybe you shouldn't. It's late—"

"Sure." Then, as if she had glanced at a clock, she added, "It's ten-thirty! Some of us are working tomorrow, you know. Oh, I'm sorry."

"No, I'm sorry."

"Hey, no problem, really. You've had a rough day. I know how it is." Through the phone, Cassie could hear the grin in Anne's voice when she added, "It's not like I have some hot guy in bed with me or anything. Give me a few minutes, okay?"

"Thanks," Cassie said with a rush of true gratitude.

By the time Anne knocked on the kitchen door, Cassie had heated a pan of milk and was pouring it into two mugs already laced with cocoa and sugar. April was not exactly prime hot-chocolate-drinking season, but guilt and nerves made her antsy. She needed to do something, anything, to keep busy.

She felt as if she was sitting on a box of compressed steel springs and the slightest move would release all of them.

"Hot chocolate? What a great idea! Like a pajama party." Anne picked up one of the mugs and blew away some of the heat collecting at the rim.

Cassie smiled and stopped stirring her cup and tried to place the spoon gently in the sink. It clattered against the stainless steel, making her cringe. Her hands shook noticeably. Embarrassed at her lack of self-control, she jerked them behind her and rubbed her lower back, pretending she was tired.

"Thanks for coming," she said with false brightness.

"So, do you want to talk about it?" Anne flopped down in one of the kitchen chairs. Her fluffy green bathrobe flapped open to reveal emerald green silk pajamas. She looked like some sort of exotic harem dancer slumming it in the country.

"Not really . . . well . . . yes," Cassie stammered.

Anne eyed her over the rim of her mug. "So, talk."

"It's not that easy. This is exactly the reason I've avoided coming home for so long. Frank's always getting into trouble, and I can't handle it. He means well, but he can't seem to get it together. And I know he didn't kill that guy, but how the heck am I supposed to keep him out of jail when he acts like a complete idiot? This thing with Frank today—it's not fair!" She walked to the table and pulled out a chair. Then, instead of sitting down, she turned with a jerk and walked back to the sink. She couldn't stay still. Her fluttering hands touched the faucet and counter before she picked up a sponge to wipe them down with quick, nervous strokes. "I thought I could come here for two weeks and relax. I mean, I thought it would be like it was when we were kids. You know what I mean? But it's all screwed up—"

"Hey, it's not your fault." Anne stood and loped over to Cassie, throwing her arm over her shoulders. "But times change and you've been gone a long time. And no one planned this murder to coincide with your visit."

"That's not what I mean, that is, it is, in a way. But it's not only that. Uncle Frank looks so *old*. And I'm afraid Aunt Sylvia may have left him. Not to mention that your asshole brother is going to arrest him for getting whacked on weed and killing this Nick guy. Not that he did, but you know what I mean. It's all a huge mess!" Cassie's voice rose until it broke off with a stifled wail. Clutching her friend's slender shoulders, she cried, angry at herself and yet unable to stop the convulsive tears. "I'm so afraid."

"It'll be all right."

"No, it won't! It's all different. I avoided Peyton because I couldn't bear to see my aunt and uncle argue, or worse, see Uncle Frank go to jail for drugs. If he's arrested, it's going to kill him."

"Jim isn't going to arrest your uncle! Listen, do you want me to call him?"

"No!" Cassie pushed her away. Sniffing, she grabbed a paper towel to blow her nose and wipe her burning eyes. "No. I'm sure he thinks Frank killed Nick."

Anne laughed. "Why would he believe that? He grew up here. He *knows* Frank. He's not going to arrest him. I mean, Frank's what? He's got to be pushing seventy, now."

"He was seventy-three last September. He looks so frail, Anne. There's no way he could have killed a young man. But I'm worried about him. And then there's my aunt. Do you think Sylvia really left him? Why would she do that, now, when he needs her the most?"

"You know Frank. He probably forgot when she told him she'd be back."

"I don't know, Anne. They were supposed to go on vacation together. Something is bothering him. I mean, I know I haven't been here, but he had stopped doing weed ages ago because Sylvia asked him to. Why would he start again unless he knew she wasn't coming back?"

"You don't know when he started or even if he's using. Don't borrow trouble."

"I'm not. I know he's using. I saw him. And you can smell it a mile away."

"What if it was one of those placebo thingies? Like, oh, I don't know, those clove cigarettes? Maybe that's all it was?"

"And he was down there at the stream with the body! Just sitting there and smoking."

"Sit down and drink your chocolate. You're way overreacting."

"I know I'm overreacting! That's why I called you! I can't seem to stop thinking and worrying about it all, even though I'm sure I've taken more meds today than I'm supposed to. Everything is totally out of control. Nothing is like it should be. I want to sit here and cry, and that's so not like me!"

"I know, Cassie." Anne gave a half-hearted laugh. "In fact, I'm not sure what to say because I've never actually seen you like this before. I'm usually the hysterical one. You're the rock telling everyone what to do in an emergency."

"Maybe I've been a rock too long and I've finally cracked," she said with a bitter edge ripping her voice. "I'm tired. Really tired, Anne. That's why I came home." She swallowed, hating the admission of weakness and the fact that the pressures of her job were becoming too much for her to handle. She hadn't had a break in years and there was no one she could rely on in Raleigh. And the stress battened upon her deeper fear that there was no one she could depend upon for anything. No one but herself. Then she glanced into Anne's sympathetic eyes and shook herself. "I'm sorry. I'm worried sick about Frank. Something is terribly wrong. He's given up. I'm scared."

Anne studied her for a moment before giving her another hug. "I can see that. I wish you'd let me call Jim."

"No! I mean it—no. He's giving me freakin' nightmares already. Do *not* call your brother. I'm trying to avoid him, and all police, until I can go back to Raleigh. That's all I want to do. Keep Frank away from the cops until my two weeks are over. Then I can go back to civilization."

"How do you propose to do that? There's a murder investigation—"

"And they're going to be all over Uncle Frank. You know they are. It doesn't matter that he's never done anything worse than marijuana. And he's the sweetest person you'd ever want to meet. They're going to railroad him because he was there at the scene of the crime."

"Doing drugs!"

"Smoking, just smoking, and it may not have even been marijuana! It may have been oregano for all I know!" Her voice rose as hysteria gripped her. "He was sitting there, not hurting a fly, until the cops came along."

"You mean, until you discovered a body."

"I mean, until the cops came along, accusing everyone and making threats."

"Did Jim threaten you?"

"His mere presence is a threat! You know what cops are like!"

"What cops are like? They help people."

"Help people? Since when? The only time a cop ever stops to help is to give you a ticket or to help arrest you. Do you ever see one stopping for any other reason except to give you a ticket or arrest your ass?"

Anne's eyes flickered toward the door, "Cassie—"

"Oh, wait! Of course! There's always the cop who stops by the side of the road to help you when you have a flat tire. And who then turns out to be a psycho-nut-job killer who stole a police cruiser and put on a fake uniform he bought at Uniforms-R-Us. Then while you're wrestling with the spare tire, he knocks you over the head with the tire iron, cuffs you, throws you into the trunk, and drives to a secluded spot where he rapes and murders you before cutting up your body and feeding it to a nearby family of rabid raccoons."

The sound of the kitchen door creaking made Cassie break off, but only for a second. The fierce momentum of her fears drove her to continue despite part of her mind shrieking for her to stop. "You mean those kinds of helpful cops? Because I really can't think of any other kinds at the moment."

"Hi, Jim," Anne said, raising her hand in a half-wave. Her gaze flicked from Cassie to her brother. "What are you doing here?"

"Apparently getting ready to hit some unsuspecting female over the head. Except I forgot my tire iron in the trunk. You want me to go get it?"

Cassie whirled around and covered up her burning, toe-curling embarrassment with sarcasm. "Yes. That would be nice. And this time, knock when you come back. And bring a warrant."

"Jim, Cassie's upset."

"Really? I hadn't noticed." Jim leaned against the door frame, his face a portrait in stone.

Cassie eyed him and briefly considered an apology. But she couldn't bring herself to utter the words. He had come in without knocking, prepared to defend his sister against the drug-crazed, murderous descendants of Blackbeard.

And as such, he deserved to hear the worst. It might teach him better manners in the future.

"What brings you here?" Anne asked, breaking the awkward silence.

"Saw your car out front. It seemed a little late. I wanted to make sure everything was all right."

"We're just peachy-keen here. How are you?" Cassie asked, aggravated that she had been right about his reasons for his casual decision to "stop by" in the middle of the night.

Anne squeezed Cassie's arm, trying to calm her. "I'm fine, Jim. I came over for some hot chocolate and girl talk."

"Are you sure you don't want to arrest anyone? I can drag Uncle Frank out of bed if you want. He's only seventy-three, so it's not like he needs that much sleep or anything." Face flushed, Cassie's renewed sense of danger overrode her common sense. She was terrified that Jim Fletcher really had come to arrest Frank. Or drag the old man out of bed to question him, hoping that a sleep-deprived Frank would be dazed, confused, and more likely to tell the truth.

Although if he knew Frank at all, he'd know that Frank was always so dazed and confused that he usually couldn't pull a lie together under the best of circumstances.

"If you're worried about Frank, that is." Cassie crossed her arms.

"Not exactly," Jim replied in perfect deadpan.

"Well, I'm sorry," Cassie replied, "but I didn't kill Nick, either."

Anne laughed. "If you knew Nick, you wouldn't be sorry. I'd like to have killed him a few times myself."

"What?" Cassie stared at her, startled out of her indignation.

"He thought he was God's gift to women." Anne rubbed her rear end. "I still have bruises. I don't think he ever learned that women don't like to be pinched and it's not done anymore."

"It's not politically correct?"

Anne rolled her eyes at Cassie. "I don't care about P.C. But I do get annoyed when customers grope me."

"He sounds like he was a jerk, but I still didn't kill him." Cassie glanced at Jim. He leaned against the door jamb as if he thought the house would fall down without his muscular support.

He gave her a half-smile. "I never thought you killed Nick. However, accessory after the fact, conspiracy—"

"You can't seriously believe Uncle Frank would kill someone?" Cassie's shoulders slumped as a sense of defeat rolled over her.

"Perhaps not deliberately."

"Not deliberately and not by accident, either." She tried to make her voice firm, but it wobbled with wretched exhaustion. "Uncle Frank may be, uh, eccentric, but there's no way he'd kill someone and then just sit there next to the body."

"I've known your uncle a long time, Ms. Edwards. He doesn't always choose to handle his problems head-on. In fact, for the most part, he lives in a world of his own. He may not have realized Nick was dead, not knocked unconscious."

Unfortunately, it was one of the few reasonable explanations for her uncle's weird behavior. The perceptive assessment made Cassie hesitate. His evaluation of her uncle's behavior echoed hers almost exactly. She studied the sheriff.

How did Jim Fletcher know so much about Uncle Frank? And if he knew him so well, why couldn't he see that Frank was innocent?

If Frank was. An icy trickle of doubt made her shiver.

Of course he was innocent.

"Leave her alone, Jim." Anne walked over and punched her brother affectionately on the bicep. "She's already on drugs for stress. Quit harassing her."

"Anne!" Cassie gripped the counter. "I'm not 'on drugs.' I have a prescription, but I'm fine. Really. I was upset earlier. And I'm sorry about the tirade. I don't know what possessed me."

"Your unnatural dislike of authority?" Jim offered. A light deep in his gray eyes glimmered with unsuspected humor. "Or maybe Blackbeard's ghost temporarily possessed you?"

An odd electricity sizzled down Cassie's back as her gaze roved over his face. "I don't dislike authority."

"Then you dislike me?"

Almost as if the tranquilizer had finally kicked in, she managed to avoid picking up the casually offered bait.

In a guarded reply to his question, Cassie offered one of her own. "Why did you really come here? You can't seriously believe Anne was in danger. She's my best friend."

"It's late. I saw her car—I wanted to make sure nothing was wrong."

"Oh, so you were worried about us? That Anne might be here because of some kind of emergency?" Cassie suggested an alternative, a better motive, and waited. The back of her neck tightened as she stood there, wanting him to take the olive branch from her hand.

"Something like that," he replied in a neutral tone.

Her throat closed. Not an obvious rejection and not unkind, but a definite, gentle push away. Almost as if he were saying, I'm the good guy, you're the bad guy, and never the twain shall meet.

Well, if that's the way he wanted to handle it, fine.

She could be tough, too.

She wished she didn't have a desperate urge to bury her face against his broad chest and break into helpless tears.

CHAPTER SEVEN

Jim's body tightened with irritation as he watched his sister give Cassie's arm a squeeze, offering reassurance after his cautious remark.

What did they expect? A dead man had been found that afternoon on the Edwards property and an investigation was underway. Under the circumstances, he needed to keep his distance and objectivity.

Cassie turned away from him, shrugged, and shook her head at Anne, as if she had expected nothing but grief from him. Her hostility toward authority figures appeared to have grown over the years.

In the brief silence that followed, a chill dampness settled around them. Night deepened toward midnight and even the air tasted colder.

Examining Cassie's face, he saw a fragile quality accentuated by the heavy circles under her eyes and sharp cheekbones. She was too thin, too tense, and yet she still looked like a happy-go-lucky hippy chick with her long, straight dark hair and a strangely sensual way of moving. As if each gesture contained a hidden caress.

"It's late," Anne said. "I probably should go. Are you going to be okay, Cass?"

"Sure." Cassie flicked a quick glance at him. "I'm fine. Are you leaving, too?"

He raised his brows. "Do you want me to stay?"

"I thought you might want to search the place. Or beat a confession out of me."

"That can wait until tomorrow," he replied dryly.

"Are you sure?" She stuck out her thin wrists, hands fisted as if waiting for him to snap handcuffs on her.

Her hands shook, and his gut clenched with guilt. She was afraid of him. With an effort, he pushed away an intense desire to enfold her in his arms and reassure her.

"This may be your last chance," she continued. "I mean, since Uncle Frank is such a savage killer, I may not even be alive tomorrow."

"I'll risk it. Who do you believe killed Nick Gracie?"

Her blue eyes grew cold, bleak. "How should I know? All I can tell you is my uncle is innocent." She sighed and ran a hand behind her neck, lifting the heavy hair and rubbing her nape. "And I'll prove it to you."

"No, you won't. If your uncle is innocent, he'll be fine."

"Oh, like you've never arrested an innocent man?"

He hummed slightly for a few seconds, letting the hot buttons she was so busy pressing pop back to normal. "No, I haven't."

She snorted.

Anne stepped between them, glancing uneasily from one to the other. "It's late, and you're both tired."

"And sick," Cassie said.

"Sick and tired," Jim said, picking up the line his sister threw out.

To his surprise, both women rewarded him with brief smiles. Catching Cassie's gaze, he saw a glimmer of humor.

"Yeah," Cassie said. "We're all sick and tired. But mostly tired."

"Come on, Jim." Anne grabbed his arm and shoved him outside. "Quit harassing people."

"See you tomorrow," Cassie called from the doorway. "Anne, that is," she added when she caught his glance.

He held her gaze before nodding in her direction. "See you."

She shut the door and he heard the metallic sound of the lock snapping into place.

"She's innocent, bro—you know it. And Frank Edwards wouldn't hurt a fly." Anne said as she climbed into her toy-sized car. "Quit messing with them. Cassie has enough problems."

He leaned his arm against the car's roof and stared down at his baby sister. She tended to believe the best of everyone. To her, murders were always committed by person or persons unknown who were passing through and would never be seen or heard from again. It couldn't possibly be anyone she, personally, knew, and certainly not her anti-establishment best friend's uncle.

Of course the fact that he shared a good many of her wistful views didn't make them correct.

"What kinds of problems?" he asked.

She clutched the steering wheel as if she could break it in half. "Work, you know, the usual. She works for a real jerk."

"Then maybe she snapped." He grinned as his sister scowled up at him.

"She didn't snap. Even you—you dumb-ass—know she didn't kill anyone. She wasn't even here until around three-something today."

"So she wasn't here today. That doesn't mean she wasn't here yesterday. Or the day before."

"Then maybe she's right! Maybe you're too stupid to find who really killed Nick."

"Oh, I'll find him—or her." He straightened. "But for now, I'm following you home."

"No way. You live in the opposite direction. Go home and get some sleep. They say it improves your reasoning ability."

"Then you ought to be a genius by now." He slammed the door shut with a grin.

When she started her car and began puttering in reverse down the driveway, he jumped back in mock alarm. She swung out on the street with a squeal and thrust her arm out the window. As he watched, she flashed him the bird above the roof.

CHAPTER EIGHT

The next morning, Jim got to the coroner's office early for the autopsy, feeling irritable and impatient. Tamping down his revulsion at the gruesome procedure, he watched impassively.

"Can you pinpoint the time of death more accurately?" Jim asked.

Bolander didn't look up. He distractedly flipped past the generic outline of a humanoid to write notes on the lined paper beneath it on his clipboard. "There are difficulties. The body was left in the stream. But only the lower half was immersed. It's not as simple as television makes it out to be."

"It never is. What about insect life?" Jim asked, thinking about the fancy labs and hordes of experts in popular crime shows. He sighed. Any specialized analysis would have to come from the state's overburdened crime laboratory division in Raleigh, or the smaller lab in Asheville. In either case, the analysis would take months, and the cities would give priority to high-profile and local cases.

Bolander chuckled. "I've taken temperatures at several locates. And Milt provided me with the temperature of the water as well as the weather for the last few days. That and the condition of the body provided a rough guesstimate. Thirty-six hours or so, give or take four hours either way. I'd guess he was killed sometime Saturday afternoon."

"Sometime?"

"Between noon and five. Or so."

"What killed him?"

"Your classic blunt force trauma. Depressed, right temporo-parietal fracture extending across the base of the skull. In other words, something crushed the back of his head, behind the right ear." Bolander held out the clipboard, pointing to the carefully drawn injuries on the generic human form.

"Can you tell what the weapon might have been? Hammer, maybe?"

"No, not metal. Glass." Bolander picked up a small, kidney-shaped container and held it up for Jim's inspection. A few shards of glass lay on the bottom. "It's not safety glass—sharp edges—but thick. Heavy. A crystal vase, I'd say."

"Vase?" Jim raised his head, senses suddenly alert. "Like a flower vase?"

"Something like that. Perhaps."

"And it's on the right side. Right-handed assailant?"

"Perhaps. Could be ambidextrous. Or even left-handed. Although the blow was pretty forceful, which makes me agree, tentatively, with you that it was probably a right-handed person using both hands to hit him from behind."

Jim hummed with thought. "Starting the swing at the right shoulder and using both hands. Not an accident, then."

"I wouldn't think so. However, it's possible he was pushed and hit his head against a glass object. Or it fell on him. Or he fell on it."

"Possible, but how likely? How deeply was the glass embedded in the wound?"

"Nearly seven millimeters. Too deep to be the result of a fall, but stranger things have happened. Hell, if it's possible for a piece of straw to pierce a palm tree during a hurricane, it's possible Nick Gracie died as a result of an accident. However, I'd have to say it is a very remote possibility."

"Anything else?"

Bolander smiled, his brown eyes lighting with sardonic humor. "As a matter of fact, yes. Did you take a good look at his clothing?"

"I noticed his shirt looked too tight."

"And no socks—"

"With running shoes." That had struck Jim as strange at the time, but not everyone wore socks. However, all the pieces taken together formed an odd picture.

"He had on boxers." The coroner glanced up as Bill Meyers walked into the room. "Very large boxers."

"How's it going?" Bill asked, slipping a mask over his nose and mouth. "Find anything interesting?"

Jim suppressed the surge of irritation Bill's condescending and artificially happy tone always generated in him. He had to work with him, even if the man sounded like a demented kindergarten teacher.

Bolander held up a plastic evidence bag. "An extra surprise caught between the scrotum and his thigh."

A used condom lay in the bottom of the bag. A ribbed, black condom.

"He didn't dress himself," Jim commented in a heavy voice.

Bill's eyes glittered with all the excitement of a wino discovering his bottle isn't empty after all. "Maybe he was raping a woman. And she hit him, thereby killing him."

Jim stared at the body on the table. Bill's suggestion had a certain merit. "Is there anything else?" Jim asked the coroner.

"Nothing unusual, unless you consider being physically fit, odd. I'll send off the condom for DNA testing. Don't expect results back anytime soon, though."

"Thanks." Jim moved toward the door. "Can I get your preliminary report today?"

"Tomorrow morning. But it'll be incomplete until I get the tox screen back. I want to make sure there weren't any drugs in his system." He flicked a sardonic glance at Bill. "I'm not a fan of the rape scenario for this one, but I can't rule it out completely. Keep in mind it couldn't have been the woman—or man—who hit him. Whoever killed him was standing behind him. Jealous husband, maybe."

Another possibility, Jim thought. Howie-the-butt could have walked in on his bodyguard overzealously—and nakedly— guarding the body of his wife.

That scenario might have had some merit, except for last night's visit. Mrs. Butler had looked and acted uneasy, but Mr. Butler hadn't.

Jim thanked the coroner again and left. It was a relief to escape the chilled room and the stomach-churning odors. Unfortunately, the rest of the building smelled so strongly of ammonia that it wasn't much better. His eyes stung and he rubbed them tiredly.

Outside the outer offices used by his staff, Jim bumped into Milt. The deputy looked rumpled and exhausted. Heavy pouches drooped under his eyes.

"You look like hell," Jim commented, holding the door open.

"You smell like hell," Milt replied, rubbing his face. "Autopsy?"

"Yeah."

"So?" Milt plodded forward, slightly behind him.

Jim glanced down the corridor. "Where's Bill?"

"The eager-beaver? Already here—least his car's in the lot."

"I know he's here. He was at the autopsy. I thought he followed me."

"Nope. Guess you escaped the corpse room without a tail. By the way, Frank and Cassie Edwards were here. I took their statements and left the paperwork on your desk. Nothing new. Frank is sticking to the fishing story. And Cassie still claims she didn't arrive in Peyton until sometime after three, yesterday."

"Thanks." Jim felt the edge of disappointment wedge itself like a sliver under his skin. He had hoped to question the pair himself.

The men filed through the narrow space between the two desks in the room and headed for Jim's office. Rounding the corner of his desk, Jim glanced up to see Bill entering the outer office. He stopped to pick up a brown envelope from his desk before joining them.

"I've got the photos," Bill said. Without waiting for acknowledgment, he sat down in one of the chairs opposite Jim's desk. Then he began methodically flipping through the crime scene photos.

Jim watched him for a moment before taking his seat. His knees creaked. He felt older than dirt.

"We'll have the autopsy report tomorrow morning," Jim said. "However, it looks like Mr. Gracie was a busy man right around the time he died. The coroner found a used condom on the body."

Milt straightened. His reaction reminded Jim of a pointer suddenly catching a scent. "DNA?"

"Yeah. We'll send it off and see what we get. Unfortunately, that also means we'll have to have DNA to compare against, unless he was having sex with someone already in the system," Jim said.

"Miss Edwards?" Bill suggested.

"He had a girlfriend." Milt leaned back and stared thoughtfully at the window behind Jim's shoulder. "Most likely it'll be hers."

Jim nodded. "Although that makes it a little tough to figure out why anyone would kill him while he was having sex with his girlfriend."

"Old boyfriend?" Bill was clearly determined to develop that theory.

"It's a vulnerable position," Milt commented. "He'd be an easier target while doing it. Could even have been planned. The killer gets his girlfriend to seduce him and then—" he hit a fist into a meaty palm "—wham! The guy kills him."

"It seems a little elaborate, doesn't it? Why wouldn't the murderer just shoot him? Why involve a woman?" Jim asked.

Milt nodded. "So maybe he was messing around with his girlfriend, and the killer took advantage of the opportunity."

"Wouldn't his girlfriend report it, if that was the case?" Jim pointed out the obvious.

"Unless she was afraid to. Maybe they were doing something illegal. And she was afraid to get us involved," Bill said in a smug tone that suggested that was exactly what he would expect from a woman involved with Nick Gracie.

"Fornication may still be on the books, but no one has prosecuted in years, boy," Milt said. He shifted his bulk and scratched his hip. While Bill flushed with anger, Milt gave him a considering stare. "And it may be a mite embarrassing to be caught in the arms of your lover, but that's hardly motivation to be an accessory to murder."

"Unless you're married," Bill said through tight lips.

Jim held up a hand. "Speculation. We won't know anything until we get the results back from the lab. So, Bill, what have you got?" Jim held out his hand for the photographs.

Bill slipped the photos back into the envelope and handed it to him. "Not much new that I could see."

As Jim examined each photo, he handed it on to Milt. After a few minutes, he sighed. "You know, if this was TV, we'd look at these pictures and find the killer staring at us through the trees. Or one of his credit cards."

"Or his name, written by the dead man in the mud in the seconds before he expired," Milt said, passing the pictures back to Bill.

Bill picked up the brown envelope and carefully slipped the photos inside. "But we do know that Frank Edwards was there?"

"That's his property," Jim said.

"Exactly." Bill smiled. "It keeps coming back to Edwards, doesn't it?"

Grinding his teeth, Jim had to agree. No matter how hard he tried to think of another scenario with other players, he couldn't get away from Frank Edwards sitting in a lawn chair next to the corpse.

Or the condom caught in the victim's shorts.

CHAPTER NINE

After a long, restless night, Cassie got up, determined not to worry. She told herself that Jim Fletcher was not a complete idiot. Eventually, he'd realize neither she nor her uncle were responsible for the death of Nick whatever-his-last-name-was.

When Frank seemed too distracted to fix breakfast, Cassie made two Spanish omelets. Despite his protest that he wasn't hungry, she insisted he remove the horticultural journals off the kitchen table and sit down to eat. He dutifully did as he was told and when his plate was clean, he wandered off to the greenhouse. As Cassie watched him shamble away, her hand strayed toward her cell phone. Had she gotten any e-mail? Any good e-mail? Okay, that wasn't going to happen. There was no such thing as good e-mail. There was junk mail and work mail.

Her chest tightened. What if there were problems at work?

No. She wasn't going to check. That was the point of this two-week vacation—to rest and relax. If she started to read her e-mail, she might as well have stayed in Raleigh. She turned to the sink and did the dishes, instead, which took all of ten minutes.

Now what? How was she supposed to relax? Maybe she could read a book. Go for a walk. Go fishing.

Well, maybe not go fishing. She didn't exactly want to go back to the stream, ever. Or eat anything she caught from it. Shivering, she tried to forget the bloated appearance of the body and the sporadic ripples under the gray-white skin.

Finally, she grabbed a book at random from the shelves in the living room and tried to concentrate on *Huckleberry Finn*. She crossed her legs, then re-crossed them, squirming on the sofa. It was no use. She couldn't concentrate. Looking at the thin layer of dust on the coffee table and scattered piles of papers, magazines, and books, she decided to clean house, which kept her occupied until ten A.M., when she really got the shakes.

Had anyone sent her an e-mail? Something urgent? Would it hurt to check?

Yes. She wasn't going to give in to the electronic seduction of e-mail. If worse came to worst, she'd check tomorrow. For today, she was going to relax.

Only she couldn't. All she could think about was Jim Fletcher. She had to admit he had grown into a damn fine man with broad shoulders she longed to lean against. Unfortunately, he didn't appear to have a particle of sense between his ears, even if Anne had said he had gotten a partial scholarship because he was so smart.

Cassie knew book-learning only coincidentally applied to reality. Even the computer documentation she relied on, which should theoretically be fairly accurate, seemed only accidentally, and infrequently, correct.

She gazed unseeingly at the duster in her hand and thought back wistfully to the reedy, intense bookworm Jim used to be. He had had such a nice, shy smile when he bothered to notice her hanging around with Anne. She flicked the duster through a cobweb in the corner of the bathroom door.

However, Jim Fletcher was not the sweet young novelist-to-be anymore. He was the law around here, and far be it from her to interfere with him, or his stupid ideas. He would find out soon enough that Uncle Frank was innocent.

That is, as soon as he got his head out of his ass.

After scrubbing down her bathroom for the fourth time, she

finally quit, afraid the cleaning fumes were affecting her thinking. She'd never been so indecisive and confused in her life. She wanted to trust Jim, but she was afraid he had already leapt to the wrong conclusion and might be reluctant to change his mind. And the urge to prove her uncle's innocence was all but overwhelming. However, for the life of her, she couldn't figure out how she was going to get that proof without looking like she was tampering—again—with evidence.

"Phew!" her uncle exclaimed from the bathroom doorway. "You drop a bottle of bleach in here?"

"No," Cassie said, trying not to breathe too deeply. The scent of chlorine was so strong her eyes burned. Belatedly, she threw open the tiny window. "I was cleaning."

"You can smell it all the way downstairs." He sneezed and backed away a few feet. "How about we go, make our statements to the police, and then go out for lunch?"

"Sure. You want to go to Anne's?"

"I was thinking about that new Italian place. I hear they've got a good lunch. But maybe you ought to change, first."

She looked down at her ragged shorts and pink T-shirt, now blotched with huge white spots. "Sounds great. Give me a sec."

After changing into a more respectable blue blouse and jeans, Cassie drove her uncle to the sheriff's office. To her relief, the sheriff was busy. Milt Singleton took their statements in a bored, "Let's get this over with," kind of way. After watching his fat fingers fumbling over the computer's keyboard, she even relented enough to type and print out the statements for them to sign.

When she and Uncle Frank left the office, Cassie sighed with relief. Perhaps her vacation might work out, after all. She took another deep breath of the fresh air and was pleased to feel her stomach rumble with normal, healthy hunger. Leaving the car parked on the street across from the courthouse complex, they walked the two blocks to the recently revitalized center of town.

The restaurant was part of a new block of small stores adorned with charming green awnings and huge pots of trimmed rosemary decorating the doorways. Cassie felt an immediate liking for the area, despite the calculated quaintness. She felt safe and comfortable walking along the street. A few vaguely familiar folks even waved to her. The Italian place, Giordo's, was a narrow, red-brick building, across the street from Anne's diner, Peyton Place.

"Hey," Cassie said as her uncle opened the door to Giordo's. "After we eat, let's go over to Anne's for dessert." Despite her relief at their quick exit from the sheriff's office, she was consumed with curiosity about what Jim Fletcher might be thinking. It was possible that he had talked to his sister. If so, Cassie could extract the latest information from Anne.

With luck, they might even have arrested someone.

"Sure," Frank said, absentmindedly. "Unless you'd rather have tiramisu."

"Apple pie, à la mode. From Anne's." She slid into a booth along the wall and looked around.

The restaurateur had left the walls as unfinished brick and used distressed pine for the floors. Huge planters of green ferns and ivy filled the corners, giving the long, narrow room a great deal of rustic charm. Cassie glanced around happily and picked up the laminated, single-sheet menu. They both ordered lasagna and a small salad, and sat back to enjoy an unhurried meal.

The food was excellent, and the service was great despite the fact that almost every table was occupied. To Cassie's surprise, the crowd was mostly older folks. More often than not, newcomers ended up dragging tables together as they recognized friends already there, until Cassie and Frank were surrounded by three huge amoebas that threatened to absorb them, too.

However, Frank was too distracted to do more than acknowledge a few hearty greetings in a distracted way. He ate his huge plate of lasagna as if he hadn't had a decent meal in days.

"Are you worried, Uncle Frank?" Cassie asked after the waitress had refilled their glasses with sweet tea. "I'm sure they've realized by now that you didn't have anything to do with that man's death."

"Oh, sure." He nodded. Then he glanced up at her, his fork halfway to his mouth. "With what?"

After placing her napkin over the worst of the tomato sauce stains she'd dripped onto the table, Cassie leaned forward with her elbows braced on either side of her plate. "With that man's death."

"What man's death?"

"Nick. The man at the stream. Uncle Frank, you don't have to pretend. It's okay. I understand."

"Are you sure Nick's dead?"

"Yes, I'm afraid so."

A weird look passed over his droopy face, almost like relief. He shook his head before draining his glass.

"You do remember, don't you?" she asked, trying to hide her exasperation.

"Sure. It seems so unreal."

"I know." She patted his hand before picking up the check. "Shoot, I think they forgot to add in my lunch."

Her uncle smiled. "How much is it?"

"All told, less than ten dollars."

"That's cool. They have a great lunch here. And it's cheap. That sounds about right to me."

Still shocked by the low price, Cassie paid the bill and followed her uncle out, thinking it might be less expensive to eat out all the time than buy groceries. Less work, too.

"So, did you save room for dessert? Do you still want to go across the street for some ice cream at Anne's?"

"Cool," he agreed, blinking in the bright sunshine and glancing around.

Stepping down off the curb between two parked cars, Cassie started across the street before she realized her uncle was lagging behind. His attention had been caught by a rope dangling down the wall of the restaurant.

"Uncle Frank!" she called.

Acknowledging her with a flap of the hand, he glanced up. He stared, apparently fascinated by the sight of a window washer. The workman knelt on a platform suspended over the door, scrubbing a row of dark windows that ran around what appeared to be a false second story. Not watching where he was going, Frank tripped over the curb.

"Uncle Frank!" Cassie took a step forward, only to slam her hip into the bumper of one of the cars parked in front of the restaurant. Doubling over, she swore.

Then a strange noise, like a "pop" made her jerk her head around. There was nothing unusual in the street, and she looked back to her uncle. He stumbled and reached for the rope dangling down the wall next to Giordo's front door. The end of the rope was fastened to a small wrought iron peg near the doorframe.

He grabbed the rope. A short length of it came loose in his hand.

"Hey!" he exclaimed as he fell to the pavement.

"Uncle Frank!" she screamed.

Belatedly, she realized that the weird pop sounded a lot like a gunshot on TV. She glanced around, but no one else caught her gaze because the air was suddenly filled with the horrendous sounds of metal clanging, glass breaking, and people screaming. She flinched and huddled between the parked cars, shaking with shock.

She peeked around the bumper of the car in front of her,

almost afraid to look. In front of her, a breathtaking scene of destruction unfurled.

The rope Frank had grabbed to break his fall had untied, or it had broken at a critical juncture. Unfortunately, it was part of the system of ropes and pulleys holding up the precarious platform on which the window cleaner perched. The supporting web unraveled as Cassie watched in open-mouthed horror.

Uncle Frank struggled to his feet. Cassie heard another "pop."

Part of her mind leapt to a terrible conclusion. Someone was shooting at Uncle Frank!

Thankfully, the bullet had missed him. Instead, it had made a small round hole in the plate-glass door of the restaurant. The hole only existed for a fraction of a second—she may have even imagined seeing it—before the glass shivered and cracked, hiding the hole in a network of jagged white lines.

The window washer's platform, suddenly suspended by only one rope, swung down sharply. The bucket of water tied to the platform swung in a brief arc. The pail hit the plate-glass door in approximately the same location where the bullet had left its web of cracks. The door dissolved into a shower of fragments, which fortunately hurt no one but the pavement.

The quick-thinking window washer pushed his feet against the wall and threw himself with surprising grace over to the right. He landed on the lovely green awning shading the restaurant's huge front window. Fortunately for him, the awning served to break his initial fall.

Unfortunately, it did not completely negate his forward momentum. He rolled over the awning to the edge and tried to catch it to stop.

And for one golden moment he hung there, safe and secure.

Two seconds later, the metal rails holding the awning snapped. The entire structure slowly came down over the restaurant's front window. With a brief yell of surprise, the man swung away from the collapsing canopy. Miraculously, he landed on his feet a mere six inches from where Frank stood, rubbing his knees.

Inside Giordo's, the customers sitting at the front window screamed as the sunlight streaming in from the front window was slowly extinguished by the awning settling over the glass like a curtain.

Through the tumult, Cassie heard a few shouts in Italian. It sounded like the owner trying to calm his patrons.

Everyone ignored him.

Cassie ran over to her uncle. "Uncle Frank, are you okay?"

"Cool, it's cool," he replied. He glanced down at the piece of rope in his hand and then looked around.

"You're sure you're not hurt?"

"Sure, no problem. I'm cool."

The window washer, dusting himself off, caught Cassie's attention as she checked the holes in her uncle's pants. "What about you?" she asked. "Are you okay?"

"Yeah, I'm fine. What about you and your dad?"

"He's my uncle, and we're fine."

Uncle Frank solemnly handed the bit of rope to the window washer.

Cassie flicked a nervous look over her shoulder. The skin between her shoulder blades crawled. "Perhaps we should leave."

"Leave?" The workman stared at her before glancing thoughtfully at his platform, swaying gently from the end of one rope. Then he noticed the short length of rope still clutched in Frank's hand.

He'd think she was nuts if she told him she thought people were shooting at them—or at least her uncle. So she gestured toward the restaurant. "We should go. Before they come out. The owner may be a little angry."

"Oh, yeah." He studied the ropes. "I thought I tied that off."

He took the piece of rope from Frank. "Must have broke."

"Well, accidents happen," she replied evasively. "Hope you don't get fired."

"Me, too. This was my second job this week." His gaze slid over her uncle. "Are you sure your uncle is okay? He looks a little shaken up."

"He always looks like that."

"I'm cool," Uncle Frank repeated, brushing off his knees. His jeans looked a little worse for wear. As she examined them again, she saw a dark stain spread around one of the holes over his knee.

"Come on, Uncle Frank," she said, leading him firmly by the arm. "Let's go over to Anne's and get some ice cream." And first aid.

When Cassie and Frank slipped into Peyton Place, she stopped short in the doorway. Most of the tables were full. To her horror, Jim Fletcher was sitting at the counter with a cup of coffee and a thick slice of black forest cake decorated by enough maraschino cherries to make a pie. She grabbed Frank's arm to drag him back out when she caught Jim's eye. His glance flicked over her, then to Frank, and back.

She couldn't back out of the diner now.

Uncle Frank took her hand and ambled forward, dragging her along. With a smile, he took a stool and patted the empty, red vinyl seat between him and Jim Fletcher. It looked as appealing as the electric chair.

"Hey-ya, Fletch-man," Uncle Frank said, completely oblivious to the tension. He smiled and nodded to Jim. "Have a seat, Cass."

In that moment, Cassie realized without a doubt that her uncle was innocent. It was so obvious even a moron could see it. A guilty man wouldn't be so happy to sit next to the law.

Besides, someone tried to kill him. Maybe. She was pretty sure.

"Cass!" Anne called, coming through the doors from the kitchen with steaming plates balanced along both arms. Gracefully, she shimmied between the tables and dropped off the food with a smile and a hug for anyone within reach. Cassie watched, envying her. Not a single awkward moment. If Cassie got closer than three feet to anyone, she was immediately stricken with mind-numbing shyness. Fears ranging from simple anxiety about the effectiveness of her deodorant to more complex human relationship terrors tensed her muscles into rigidity.

No wonder she preferred computers.

"Are you all right?" Jim asked, cradling a heavy white mug of coffee in his hands.

"Yes. Why?" Cassie asked, sitting tentatively on the edge of the stool. The seats were very close together, and Jim Fletcher took up more than his fair share of the room. His muscular thigh almost brushed hers, even when she kept her legs pressed tightly together.

"You look pale," he said.

Anxiety made her voice sharp. "You'd be pale, too, if someone took a shot at your uncle."

The coffee cup stopped midway to his mouth. "Someone tried to shoot Frank?" He leaned back and glanced around her to Frank.

Oblivious, her uncle was leaning forward over the marble counter to get a closer look at the pastries Anne kept in a glass case.

"Take a look across the street. Not that you'll find anything. I doubt anyone realized what happened."

"Why would you think someone shot at you?" Jim asked, disbelief staining his voice.

"Uncle Frank, not me." She paused. What the heck? He already thought she was a nut and a liar. She plunged on recklessly. "I thought I heard a shot. Then the window cracked, right before the window washer's platform came down. Uncle Frank tripped, and that's the only reason he wasn't hit."

To her surprise, Jim got up, flicked a twenty dollar bill onto the counter, and walked toward the door. "Stay here."

She saluted his back. "Yes, sir." Her stomach burned. She pressed her palm against her belly as her skin grew damp and chill with delayed reaction.

She touched Frank's arm to reassure herself. He was all right.

He rubbed his knee absently and smiled at her.

Her stomach and esophagus felt like she had swallowed a pint of battery acid. She should never have eaten lasagna. Tomato sauce was deadly.

"So," Anne said, coming around the counter. "What'll you have?"

"Banana split," Frank said.

"I've got to use your restroom," Cassie fled, her hand covering her mouth.

When she came back, she felt flushed and weak from being ill. This had to stop. Despite her doctor's assurances, the medicine he prescribed was not controlling her ulcers, and he appeared to be wrong about stress not being a contributing factor.

If this continued, she was going to get carved up by some maniacal surgeon because a stupid, unstoppable bacteria rampaged through her stomach. What she needed was some real time off with no pressure and much more effective antibiotics. It shouldn't be so difficult. Millions of people took vacations every year, relaxing under the sun, drinking gin and tonics without a care in the world.

What was wrong with her?

"Do you, uh, want anything?" Anne asked when Cassie gingerly sat down next to her uncle.

"Vanilla milkshake?" Her stomach didn't immediately clench at the thought, so she nodded for emphasis. She sighed, hungry again. "And a salad with broiled chicken."

Anne passed the order through the window to the kitchen and then began working on the shake. "Jim sure left in a hurry. What happened?"

"There was an accident at the Italian place across the street."

"No one was hurt, were they?"

"No, I don't think so. Although Frank scraped his knee. You don't have any bandages, do you?"

"Sure! No problem." Anne hurried off to get her supplies.

Cassie glanced at the big plate-glass window covering the front of Anne's diner. She felt an uncomfortable tickle running down the back of her neck. When her stomach grumbled a warning, she took a long swallow of soothing vanilla, surreptitiously taking two pills.

She had to calm down and think. Looking again at the window, she winced at the sound of sirens as the town's fire truck, ambulance, and an unmarked police car pulled up.

A huge crowd of maybe twenty people clustered outside. They pointed excitedly toward the window washer's dangling platform and the limp, broken green awning. At least the clay pots of rosemary on either side of the missing window were still there and undamaged.

The sheriff stood outside, studying the situation. Then with a flashing glance at the diner's window, he strolled into the restaurant.

Cassie drank the rest of the milkshake, ignoring the sinking feeling that like that ancient mystic, Cassandra, she was destined to be the victim of disbelief, if not downright contempt.

Chapter Ten

Jim examined the window washer's platform and shredded awning in silence, blocking out the hysterical chatter around him.

When the restaurateur walked outside, Jim stepped in front of him. "What happened?"

Hector, the owner of Giordo's, shook his head. "Damn window washer didn't tie off his platform. Now look! Look at this front door—glass everywhere! And my awning—ruined!"

"Hector, did you hear or see anything unusual before the window washer fell?"

"Unusual? Like what? What would you call unusual in a restaurant? No. We had the usual lunch crowd. We were busy. And then this had to happen."

Jim nudged a fragment of the broken glass with the toe of his boot. There was no way to know what had broken it. Glancing through the open door, he saw it was a straight line from the front door to the back of the restaurant, with the public dining areas branching off the hall to the right. The kitchens occupied the space to his left.

In an alcove on his immediate left, one of the customers stood in front of a payphone, receiver pressed to his ear. He gestured and spoke agitatedly, ignoring Jim.

Jim turned back to Hector. "Did you notice exactly when the door glass broke?"

"I was in the kitchen. The first I knew of it—everyone was

screaming. The damn idiot jumped onto the awning and broke that, too. Scared everyone shitless."

"I wouldn't worry about it. The excitement might bring you more customers." Jim walked further down the hallway and turned, noting the pattern of glass. Then his gaze drifted to the back door. "No one was in the hall when it happened?"

"The wait staff—in and out. Customers come in and out. How should I know?"

Jim strolled to the back door. He opened it, gazing out into a back alley. The confined space smelled of garlic and sour milk. A round tinfoil pan rested on the top step with a few bits of what looked like meatballs clinging to the bottom.

Glancing around, he saw a large cat watching him. After a silent hiss, it turned away, slinking behind the green garbage container against the far wall.

"What is it?" Hector asked, coming to the door. "Is that cat back?"

"Looks like someone was feeding it here." Jim nudged the foil pan with the toe of his boot.

"That Benny is always feeding the damn animal. I say let it earn its keep and catch a few rats." Hector picked up the pan and flung it into the dumpster like a Frisbee. Then he wiped his fingers on his apron and frowned at Jim.

Noting that the back door stuck in the open position as they stood outside, he looked toward the front of the restaurant again, struck by the tunnel effect. It was a straight line, front to back.

"When did he put the food out here?" Jim asked.

"Not too long ago. I took out the garbage myself at eleven this morning. There was no pan then."

"Can I talk to Benny? Send him out here, will you?"

"Sure, sure." He eyed Jim. "It's not illegal—feeding a cat with scraps from the kitchen."

"No. He didn't do anything wrong. I only want to talk to him for a minute."

After Hector disappeared inside, Jim walked across the narrow alley in a direct line with the door. The dumpster was in the path. He examined it briefly, but not too closely. The weather had been warm and a nauseating stench filled the small, dead area behind the restaurant. There were plenty of dents and scrapes on the front of the metal container, but nothing helpful. Nothing that proved Cassie's startling claim.

However, something told him that her improbable story was possible. A shot fired at Frank or Cassie could have gone through the front door, straight down the shotgun hallway, and out the rusty back door, stuck open as Benny fed the cat.

Ideally, he should find the bullet. That would be perfect evidence. However, if it hit the dumpster, it had not fallen anywhere in the alley that he could see.

Standing directly in line with the doors, he could look straight out the front. Since the glass was missing, his line of sight ran across the street and directly into the gap between Peyton Place and the pottery store next door. The shooter could have stood in the shadows between the two businesses.

If there was a shooter.

Slowly rotating, he stared at the brick wall above the dumpster. Then he stared harder. One of the bricks had a fresh, shallow depression with a flake the size of his thumbnail missing. A sense of alertness quivered through him. What were the odds?

"You waitin' for me?" Benny asked, his tone belligerent. He stood on the top step, arms crossed.

"I wanted to know when you fed the cat."

"Last I heard, it wasn't illegal."

"Settle down. I thought the back door might have been stuck open, like it is now, while you fed the cat. And I need to know if it was before the window washer fell?"

" 'Bout the same time, I guess. Why?"

"Where were you standing?"

"Here. I took a plate of meatballs out here, put it on the steps, and then all hell broke loose."

"You were bending over to put the plate down when the window washer fell?"

"Yeah."

"Thanks."

Benny shrugged and left while Jim turned to stare distastefully at the dumpster.

Unhooking his flashlight, he knelt and examined the concrete under the dumpster, aiming the light at the base of the brick wall. Stinking puddles of greasy liquid pooled beneath the metal container, but no sign of a bullet. If there was a bullet.

Maybe he was crazy to believe Cassie.

And maybe this last incident was proof that Frank was in the middle of the local equivalent of a drug war.

Dusting his knees off, Jim stood and glared at the dumpster. With a sense of fatality, he realized he'd have to look inside if he was going to be convinced, one way or the other.

With a sigh, he wished they issued the sheriff's office hazmat suits along with handcuffs.

After getting a few plastic garbage bags, rubber gloves, and a roll of duct tape from Hector, Jim suited up, taping the plastic bags over his boots to protect them. Then he climbed gingerly over the edge of the dumpster. Each step released another cloud of noxious fumes. He gagged and swallowed convulsively. Breathing through his mouth, he positioned himself directly in line with the chipped brick. Then he picked through the trash, carefully shaking each item. It was miserable, filthy, and thoroughly unrewarding work.

Until he heard a clink. Something metallic had fallen into the muck at the bottom.

Pushing aside a putrefying cabbage, he heard the scrape of metal against metal.

Less than a minute later, he climbed out of the dumpster. Trying not to breathe, he dropped his find into a plastic bag. Then, still breathing through his mouth, he slit the duct tape around his calves and pulled off the plastic, throwing it into the dumpster. Even after he walked back through the restaurant and out the front door, he could still smell rotten milk and cabbage on his clothes.

But he had found what he was looking for.

To his surprise, Cassie and Frank were still seated at the counter in Peyton Place, and the stool he had vacated remained empty.

Jim edged around the crowded tables to the counter. Several patrons wrinkled their noses as he passed them. One older woman sneezed and gave him a furious look.

"Sheriff?" Cassie said before turning green. She tilted her head away and started breathing through her mouth.

"Sorry," he said. "Investigations can get dirty."

"And smelly."

Anne appeared, sniffed, and disappeared again. When she returned, she carried a spray bottle of fabric freshener. "Over here, bro," she said. "Now."

Slipping off the stool, Jim stood, arms outspread while his sister doused him. It didn't cut the odor which had sunk into his skin and lungs, but everyone else seemed relieved. Taking his seat again, he smiled at Cassie, who looked a little less green but still pale.

He threw the baggie containing the bullet on the counter. When Cassie reached out for it, he stopped her, gripping her wrist.

"Evidence," he said.

She searched his face with anxious eyes. "You found it? In

the restaurant?"

"Behind the restaurant. It went straight through. Ended up in the dumpster."

"Why are you showing me this?"

"Still paranoid about authority?"

"I guess that depends upon what happens next. I mean, you could say I took a pot shot at my uncle to try to convince you of his innocence or something."

The left side of his mouth quirked. "Did you?"

"Don't be an ass."

"I'm not a totally mindless, state-built android. As long as you tell me the truth, we're fine."

"I've been telling you the truth." Her fingers threaded through her hair as if she were going to pull it. But after a spasmodic, clutching gesture, she only pushed a heavy lock away from her face.

"You tampered with my crime scene, then lied."

Face paling, she clutched her stomach. "Look, can we talk later? I just ate and I'd like to, um, let it settle. Can you come over to the house? Later? Like after you have a shower or something?" She stood up, pushing some money across the counter to Anne. "I'm sorry, but we've got to go." Grabbing her uncle by the arm, she dragged him out of Peyton Place.

"Way to go, bro," Anne said when she came back out of the kitchen. "Scaring all my customers away. And you're probably a health hazard. Will you please get out of here before anyone else leaves?"

He sighed. "My popularity in Peyton is truly heartwarming."

"Yeah, well, go warm someone else's heart, will you? But take a shower first. You really do stink."

CHAPTER ELEVEN

When Cassie returned home, she stopped her uncle before he could escape.

"Uncle Frank, we need to talk."

"We've been talking all day, Cass. And I've got to get back to work."

"Why are you acting like this? You're not fooling anyone with this spaced-out, hippy act. I know you, and you're one of the most intelligent people around."

"You don't know anything," he said, his voice suddenly deep and dark with suppressed emotion. "You've been gone a long time. You don't know what's been going on here. Not anymore."

Taken aback, she stared at him, a thread of fear tightening around her. "But—"

"No one needs your interference. You're supposed to be on vacation. Cook something. Sleep. Read. Do anything you want except interfere."

"You don't mean that! And I'm not interfering. I'm trying to help you."

"Did I ask for help?" When he looked at her, his face was cold, almost hostile. "You haven't been back for six years and yet we've managed to survive. So enjoy your vacation."

She felt sick at heart. How had all that time slipped away? What had she been thinking? "I'm sorry. There's no excuse for staying away, but I'm here now. Please let me help you. I know you didn't have anything to do with whatever happened."

"You don't know anything about me. Kids see what they want to see." His tone softened slightly. "I know about careers—I'm married to Sylvia, aren't I? Or at least I used to be—"

"You still are! She'll be back. Everything will be all right."

He shook his head.

"It will! And I'm going to make sure those idiots at the sheriff's office know you're innocent."

To her surprise, his lips thinned and his face grew cold again. "That's none of your business. Leave it alone, Cassiopeia."

"Uncle Frank—"

"I said to leave it!" Frank turned his back on her.

After collecting his cloth-covered journal, he disappeared into the greenhouse with an obvious desire for solitude. Cassie watched him close the door, thinking he would have locked it if there was a lock. She felt confused and guilty. Due to the pressures of her career and her sheer cowardice at dealing with complex emotions, she had neglected her family—the two people who had offered her a home and love when her parents died.

And now they felt they could not rely on her, or ask for her help.

When she looked back, she had to admit they might have a very good reason for their mistrust. She had always disliked arguments and fled, rather than face a confrontation. Her aunt and uncle must have recognized that work wasn't the only reason she'd avoided coming home. Sylvia and Frank's arguments, even when conducted in hushed voices, made Cassie feel ill.

A clever psychologist might conclude that Cassie feared the fights might end in a final breakup that would result in her losing her home—and security—again. However, understanding that didn't change her feelings.

And she couldn't process her uncle's chilly response to her

questions. Maybe because this time she wasn't ready to run away, or stick her head in the sand.

She rubbed her arms, feeling cold. For the first time she had to consider the possibility that she was wrong about Frank's involvement with Nick Gracie. Her uncle might be caught up in events that had led to murder.

Clutching her arms more tightly against her body, she paced.

A fan of Dostoevsky might point a thin, quivering finger at Frank's poor appearance as additional proof, should she need it, that he was suffering from a guilty conscience. His skin was an unhealthy gray, and he looked like he had spent the entire night awake.

And then there was the attempt on his life, today. Obviously, Uncle Frank was involved in the sort of criminal activity that led to gunshots in front of Italian restaurants.

Then, like the moron she was, she had pointed this out to the sheriff.

No wonder Uncle Frank didn't want her help. If she continued, she might as well give him a lethal injection, since she seemed to be doing everything she could to prove he had killed Nick Gracie.

But she couldn't believe it, and she was determined to help him. Even if, despite her efforts to reassure him and prove his innocence, he refused her help because she couldn't be trusted and only made things worse. His refusal to discuss anything frustrated and worried her.

Paradoxically, it also made her think he might be innocent. Maybe he was trying to protect her.

Cassie sighed. She had never been a "people person," who got energized by social contact. Her efforts to prevent her uncle from diving over a legal cliff like a suicidal lemming were taking every bit of energy she had. She was exhausted, but too restless to sit down. Nonetheless, knowing that the sheriff would show up at the worst possible time and under the worst possible circumstances, she made a slow sweep through the house. As she moved from room to room, she randomly straightened the piles of books and magazines and tried not to worry. It might not be too bad. At times, Jim Fletcher actually seemed human. Maybe even sympathetic.

Some solid, warm quality in him made her want to trust him.

Deep in thought, she came back to the kitchen and immediately knocked a glass off the counter. She stared at the mess on the floor and sighed. *What can go wrong, will go wrong.*

She crouched to pick up the larger fragments. As she kneeled, she leaned too far forward and lost her balance as her fingers touched the jagged-edged bottom. Flailing to stop from falling into the shards, she teetered unsteadily. A piece of glass sliced into her palm as her hand convulsively gripped it. But at the last minute, she managed to lean back and land on her rump instead of on her knees.

"Damn," she swore, her heart fluttering. She cradled her bleeding hand, trying to keep it from dripping all over her.

Standing up abruptly, she pressed the wound shut to control the bleeding. Then she ran to the sink and washed her hand under the water. As she watched the blood swirl down the drain, her now resentful thoughts turned back to her nemesis, Jim Fletcher.

Why couldn't he have turned into a professor somewhere? He'd be gorgeous if he would relax and smile once in a while. And not chase after the female students.

Not that he showed any sign of chasing after anyone. Although he could very well have dozens of girlfriends, for all she knew. She realized that while he was poking his nose into her family's private life, she knew absolutely nothing about his.

She pulled out the first-aid kit from under the sink and bandaged her hand, determined to regain control. Then she swept up the rest of the glass and dumped everything into the trashcan in the corner.

"Uncle Frank!" she called, thinking the sheriff was going to show up soon, ready or not. "Frank?"

Nothing. She wiped up a few stray droplets of blood from the edge of the sink. When there was still no sign of her uncle, she walked into the greenhouse. The warm humid air hit her like damp, cotton batting.

Sharp scents of potting soil, enriched with humus, tickled her nose. She sniffed, smelling the delicate cherry-vanilla scent of heliotrope, laced by the perfume of other flowering plants and herbs like mignonette. Several fragrant Datura bushes blossomed near the door, thick with trumpet-like flowers in lavender, pale yellow, and apricot. In the far corner, a Meyer lemon grew in a huge pot standing on a narrow rectangle of bricks where it could get plenty of sun.

Cassie looked around and took a deeper breath. She had always loved the huge glass room. It was like visiting a tropical rain forest without the bugs and snakes.

"Uncle Frank?" She walked through the main aisle, touching the thick leaves of a few Dendrobium orchids. As warm droplets sprinkled over her fingers, she smiled, relaxing.

When she neared the far end of the greenhouse, she heard the creak of a metal hinge that needed oiling. She looked over at the large wooden storage cabinet that covered most of the back wall of the greenhouse. The door was partially open.

She stared.

Her uncle stepped *out* of the cabinet.

"Uncle Frank! What are you doing?"

A horrified expression passed over his long face. He stood there, one foot on the dirt floor, the other still in the cabinet. One hand gripped the edge of the door, and he gave the distinct impression that he was one millisecond away from going back inside.

"Were you in there?" Her gaze skimmed the greenhouse and cabinet.

Had Frank been sitting inside? The cabinet was only about sixteen inches deep, so it would be a pretty tight fit, although it was tall and wide enough. She couldn't imagine anything else, though. To her, it looked like the greenhouse ended at the opaque glass wall behind the storage cupboard.

As she watched, he stepped out. Hunching his thin shoulders, he shut the door.

"What were you doing?" She pulled the door open.

The cabinet looked empty. A few shovels leaned against the right side and a half a dozen clay pots rested on the bottom. Frustrated, she was about to shut the door when she noticed a line of light running along the left side of the back panel. She pushed her fingers gingerly into the gap and felt the wood move. She slid the panel to the right.

A jungle exploded in front of her through the opening.

"Cassie—no!" Uncle Frank reached inside the storage unit and tried to pull her out. "Aw, jeeze, don't go in there." He yanked harder on her arm.

"Ouch, you're hurting me." She shook him off. Twisting sideways, she stepped through the gap in the back panel.

The greenhouse-behind-the-greenhouse was tiny, no more than four feet deep. However, it was as wide as the regular greenhouse, nearly sixteen feet. And instead of the clear glass panes used for the main structure, this secret enclosure had the milky opaque ones used for the back wall—the false back wall.

"What is all this?" She ran her hand through the thick growth. Long, thin, saw-toothed, deeply lobed leaves tickled her fingers. "This is marijuana!"

"Aw, Cassie," her uncle said, staring at her through the

cabinet. "Why'd you go in there?"

"Are you crazy? What are you doing growing this stuff? You promised!"

"I know." His lower lip trembled, making him look like a wrinkled, horse-faced baby.

"This is why Aunt Sylvia left you, isn't it?" Cassie climbed back out. She slid the panel closed and faced her uncle.

Tears drowned his faded brown eyes, and he kept blinking and wiping his nose on his arm.

"Don't cry." She patted him awkwardly on the shoulder. "We'll work something out. Why'd you do this again? After you almost got caught that last time?"

He sniffed and stared at a nearby orchid, absently twisting off a paper-thin, dead blossom.

"Say something! You know Milt warned you that if he ever caught you growing again, he'd have to bring you in. This is serious. You could wind up in jail—at your age!"

"I know!" he said in a low, grudging voice. "I know."

"Aunt Sylvia—"

"Is never coming back. I screwed up."

Cassie let out a long breath, feeling unutterably sad. "You don't know that—"

A sharp rap interrupted her. She glanced over at the glass door that opened out to the garden.

The glass trembled under another burst of raps.

"Hey! Oh, here you are," the sheriff said, walking inside. "I thought I heard your voice."

Stepping away from the cabinet, Cassie smiled brightly. She pushed her uncle firmly ahead of her.

"Why don't you go on into the house, Uncle Frank, and get cleaned up?" When her uncle turned to obey, she covered his exit by moving closer to Jim. A determined smile strained her facial muscles. "Pretty amazing, isn't it?" She touched a long spray of yellow orchids flecked with deep mahogany spots. An Odontocidium orchid. "Most people don't realize that Uncle Frank is one of the country's leading experts in orchid hybridization. He's hybridized and patented over forty varieties—and discovered new ways to reproduce them from only a few cells."

Gesturing exuberantly, she showed off the small lab in the corner of the greenhouse, well away from the storage cabinet in the back. She kept a wide smile on her face like a brainless game show hostess as she waved her hand over the microscope and trays of sterile growing medium. Several trays had small plants far enough along to see tiny green stems, minute leaves, and thin, threadlike rootlets.

"I had no idea," Jim said.

"No one does. Everyone thinks Frank is some brain-dead hippy. They don't think he could possibly be one of the foremost experts in the world. I mean, he's made a fortune on his patents. And not only for his plants, either, but for his, uh, *stuff.*" She blushed, knowing she sounded like a complete idiot.

He studied her, amusement lightening his eyes before a slow smile creased his face. "I always thought your uncle was a lot sharper than any of us realized."

"Sharper? He's a freakin' genius!"

Oh, shit! She shifted from one foot to the other. Now he's going to think Frank is smart enough to kill Gracie and hide it by acting like a whacked-out hippy.

His grin grew. He ran his large hand under a spray of a pure white, moth-shaped Phalaenopsis orchid. His touch was surprisingly gentle. Cassie glanced away, touching a dark purple, corsage-type, Cattleya orchid. She was too aware of him in the narrow, humid walkway. The huge, open wooden shelves of plants growing lushly out of every kind of container seemed designed to push them together.

Jim crossed his arms, relaxed, and glanced around. He had on a short-sleeved shirt and his muscular forearms caught Cassie's gaze. His arms were lightly dusted with soft, dark hair and he looked intensely masculine, standing there with his hip resting against the corner of a plant table.

Jim said, "Can we go inside? You were going to tell me what happened. At the stream."

"Didn't I already do that?"

"I'd like to hear it once more. In case you've remembered anything new."

She smiled at him, turning toward the door to the house. "Sure." She'd run through her story again and get rid of him. Then she needed to burn her uncle's secret stash of plants.

He examined the greenhouse again, his gaze lingering on the cloudy glass of the back wall. A frown scored his forehead. "You know, from the outside, this place looks larger."

"I know." She opened the door to the kitchen and stepped aside, holding it for him. Her free hand rubbed her hip with nervous impatience. She had to get him out of the greenhouse. "It's all the plants. They are so packed in, they make it seem much smaller when you're inside than it looks from the outside."

He focused on the back wall. Then, to her relief, he shrugged.

"Do you want anything to drink? Eat? We still have some brownies left," she said, entering the living room.

"No." He eyed her. "Are you going to sit down?"

She hastily sat in the squat armchair across from him and leaned forward with her palms on her thighs. "Are you sure you don't want anything?"

"The truth would be nice."

Crossing her legs, her hands gripped the armrests.

His gaze focused on her white-knuckled fingers. "What happened to your hand, Cassie?"

"I cut it on a piece of broken glass. Right before you got

here." She waved away the concerned look in his eyes. "So, what do you want to know?"

"Exactly what happened?"

"We already gave our statements."

He pulled out both a small notebook and a digital recorder. "You mind?"

"No, go ahead." She stared at the recorder with aggravation. "I don't even know where to begin."

"Your arrival here. You didn't seem to cover that part in your statement."

"Oh, okay. I got here on Sunday afternoon. After I stopped at Anne's diner, I brought my stuff into the house from the car. Then I went for a walk. I ended up at the stream and ran into my uncle. I don't really know how much more I can add."

"You can explain why you tampered with the evidence."

She stared at him. "What evidence?"

"The marks your uncle's chair left in the mud."

"Evidence is junk left behind after the commission of a crime," she replied, lacing her fingers over one knee. "I didn't touch any of that stuff."

"What stuff would that be?"

"I don't know. Whatever is related to that man's murder!" She took a deep breath and clutched her knees. She was such a terrible liar. All she wanted to do was to tell him everything exactly as she remembered it so that she wouldn't have to edit what she had said, or should say.

He eyed her, his face idling in neutral. "Why did you try to rub out the marks left by Frank's chair?"

"Because he wasn't the killer. And the whole situation looked so bizarre, I knew the authorities would get the wrong idea."

"Which wrong idea would that be?"

She frowned and leapt to her feet. She paced around the chair and then caught herself in mid-stride when she looked up to find Jim studying her. Shoulders hunched, she eased back around the side of the chair. She slumped and sat down.

"You know about Frank, don't you?"

"Why don't you tell me, Miss Edwards?" The formal use of her name made her glance at the tape recorder, ice sliding over her muscles. She shivered.

"You know about Frank," she said in a tired voice. "He uses. You know. Marijuana." She closed her eyes, praying this interview wouldn't end in Frank's arrest. It would kill him. "He hasn't for years. But I think he's been under some pressure lately. His wife is gone. That is, she went on vacation without him." She moved her hand in a listless gesture and closed her eyes, wishing it would all go away. "Uncle Frank wasn't all here—if you know what I mean—when I found him by the— uh—body. He, that is Frank, was really *mellow.* For God's sake, he was trying to share a joint with a dead man! There's no way you can tell me that a killer would be sitting there, sharing a joint with his victim!"

The ghost of a chuckle escaped Jim before he covered it with a cough and a frown. "So he was using marijuana?"

"Yes! I didn't want him arrested for it. At his age, it's almost medicinal. He's under stress! But I couldn't figure out how to explain it. Or how he could have been sitting there in a freakin' lawn chair getting whacked with a dead man! Of course I smudged the chair prints! Any sane person would have done the same."

"Any sane person would have realized that the investigators would recognize the truth. And an honest, sane person would not have tampered with the evidence. Do you understand that there could have been other trace evidence you destroyed by compacting the mud?"

"Jesus, I'm sorry," she whispered, getting that light-headed, sick, I'm-in-big-trouble-now feeling she hadn't felt since her last trip to the high school principal's office. "I don't know what to say except I'm sorry."

"Fine," he said, although he didn't sound like he meant it. "So go through it one more time. And this time, include all those details you keep leaving out. Even if they sound completely insane."

"Are you going to keep that recorder on?"

"Yes."

She eyed him. "I can't talk knowing that. It's too weird."

He sighed and turned off the device. "Now, one more time. Everything you remember."

"That should be easy. I have a terrible memory."

For some reason, he didn't find her comment funny.

CHAPTER TWELVE

After a painful hour, Cassie showed the sheriff to the door. With relief, she watched him ease his car out of the driveway and head down the rutted road toward town. When he had completely disappeared from view, she did the only reasonable thing she could do. She went back to the secret greenhouse.

She wanted to be honest with Jim. But using a little marijuana once in a while was one thing. Growing it was another. Particularly in the quantity Uncle Frank grew it. Oh sure, it wasn't like acres. It wasn't enough for him to ship tons of the stuff out of state. However, it was certainly enough to form the foundations of a lucrative and thriving criminal enterprise in a town as small as Peyton.

Hands on hips, she surveyed the jungle. The plants were so packed in the confined space that the slightest movement made the ferny branches slap her in the face. She pushed them aside and held them back to assess the magnitude of her uncle's lapse into criminality. Big plastic tubs, clay pots, and smaller containers right down to yogurt cups with drainage holes cut into the bottoms sat on wooden planks held up by bricks.

A blue plastic tarp was tucked beneath a plant stand. She pulled it out and started dumping the pots out onto it. When she got a load, she grabbed two ends and pulled it out through the greenhouse to the side door. She stumbled through the yard and jerked to a stop in the center of the lawn, behind the house. Looking around, she figured she was alone and far enough from the trees to pose no threat, so she dumped her load. After yanking the blue tarp free, she made another trip back to the secret room. Then another trip and another. It took nearly ten exhausting, and surprisingly dirty, trips to clean out the secret greenhouse.

When she was done, she had a healthy pile of greenery and potting soil.

The amount of plant material filled her with dismay. With a tired sigh, she grabbed a shovel and dug out most of the dirt. She piled it up, thinking it might be reusable if they sterilized it.

However, the cost of high-quality potting soil was the least of her worries. What she did need was a good accelerant because green plants did not burn very well.

Glancing around, she spied the gas can for the lawn mower. *Excellent.*

Now she could burn all of it and at least a few of their problems would go up in smoke. Once that job was done, she'd work on Uncle Frank to give up his habit once and for all. If he would at least agree to try, Cassie would see if she could find her aunt and convince her to return. Because looking at the pile of weed, Cassie realized that this had to be the underlying reason for the rift between her uncle and aunt.

They had had difficulties before over Uncle Frank's indulgences. Aunt Sylvia frequently reminded him that their work would be considered tainted, or discounted completely, if anyone found out that Frank Edwards was a pothead.

Regardless, this drug business was over. At least for the next week and a half. Unfortunately, after pouring gasoline over the broken, wispy mound of weed, she realized she didn't have any matches.

The kitchen was surprisingly free of matches, as well. Her nervousness increased. The pile of marijuana was right out in the open if anyone happened to walk behind the house, and she would not put it past the sheriff, or his deputies, to suddenly feel the urge to take another look at the corpse's dump location. She rifled through a few junk drawers in the living room where she had found the Mason jar and burning incense.

Nothing.

Her uncle walked into the room. He paused when he saw her. "You seen the latest copy of *American Horticulture Today*?"

"No," she replied brightly, straightening.

"Looking for something?"

"Uh, no."

His gaze dropped to her hands. Her injured hand was shoved under a pile of seed packets in an open drawer. She withdrew her hand and gently closed the drawer while maintaining a strained, but sincere, smile. "Well, that is, yes. I was looking for a . . . photo. I'm collecting photos to, uh, scrapbook. I'm going to scan them and make a scrapbook."

He stared at her as if she had lost her mind.

She widened her smile and nodded. And as her head bobbed up and down, she experienced a sudden, sure vision of the sheriff walking around the house and spying the pile of weed.

She had to destroy the evidence.

"What happened to your hand?" Uncle Frank asked.

"Cut it. I think I know where Aunt Sylvia kept some pictures. Gotta go," she said gaily. "Oh, I picked up a pile of magazines and put them on the end table on the other side of the sofa. Maybe your journal is there."

Cassie didn't wait to see if he found what he was looking for. She escaped through the kitchen to the garage, where she found a grill lighter lying on the wire shelf of an old, dusty grill. But when she tested it, nothing happened.

"Damn!" She dashed back into the kitchen, grabbed several paper towels, and twisted them together. Holding them with a pair of tongs, she turned on one of the stove's gas burners.

Gripping the flaming twist of paper, she skittered out the back door.

She almost set her uncle's shirt alight when she bumped into him. He stood in the backyard, staring morosely at the pile of marijuana.

One look at the burning paper towels in her hand turned his face the color of damp, gray newspaper.

"What's going on?" he asked.

She shouldered him aside and bent over, sticking the last, flaming fragments of twisted paper into the middle of the heap. "I'm sorry, but it's got to be done."

"I smell gas."

A small flame nibbled one leaf, sending up a plume of smoke. She coughed and used the tongs to push the embers deeper into the tangle. This time there was a satisfying crackle of fire. The gas and evaporated fumes whooshed and exploded into flames. Smoke, acrid and tainted with an underlying sweetness, filled the air.

Cassie stepped back, wiping her hands on her hips. "You can't grow that stuff, Uncle Frank. You know that."

"But I—"

"No buts about it. It was bad enough when I had to tell the sheriff that you were smoking it the other day next to a dead body. Growing it is an entirely different matter. You could go to jail for a long time."

"It doesn't matter. Not anymore." His shoulders slumped. He sighed, glancing off with unfocused eyes toward the trees. "And I never meant to get anyone in trouble."

"Then why did you start growing it?"

"I didn't want to. But Nick—"

"Nick made you? The *dead* guy? How could he make you?"

"He threatened to tell Sylvia I was using again. You know how she feels about it. She said she'd leave me the last time."

"But she found out anyway. Isn't that why she left?" She waved toward the burning plants. "Or is this the reason she left?"

"She didn't find out until later. A long time later, after it was way too late. There's a point of no return, Cassie. There always is."

Cassie felt her knees wobble with sick despair. "How long have you been doing this?"

"Almost a year." He rubbed his face tiredly, his whiskers whispering against his palm. "You've got to understand. I started having trouble with my eyes."

"Your eyes?"

"You know what that means. I depend upon my eyes. And I . . . needed something. When I started, you know how I am. I can't help experimenting." He gave her a sad smile. "Got to build a better plant."

Her heart twisted. "Oh, Uncle Frank."

"Anyway, I thought I could grow a stronger strain of marijuana for my own use."

"But that doesn't help. You *know* that. It's never helped anyone."

"But it helped me *not* think about getting old and going blind, Cassie. It helped *me.*"

Torn with conflicting emotions and overcome with sudden sympathy for what her uncle suffered, Cassie hugged him. As she wrapped her arms around his thin chest, she was painfully aware of the passage of time.

"I'm so sorry," she whispered.

"Everyone's sorry."

He had given up. She could hear it in his voice. Getting older was no joy. And to be terrified of going blind and then to have his wife leave him—no wonder he smoked. Cassie thought about her own stack of prescription pills and out-of-control life. They both had to make changes. They were both heading the wrong way down a one-way street. Regardless of the difficulties, they had to turn around and face the road ahead, even if it scared the piss out of both of them.

Unfortunately, she wasn't exactly sure what changes she ought to make. It wasn't like she could quit working. She had to make a living, and all jobs had a certain amount of stress.

"I'm so sorry about your vision, Uncle Frank. What did the doctor say?"

"Glaucoma." He gently pushed her away. Turning, he stared fixedly at the flames, which were starting to die down after their initial burst of fervor.

Cassie idly pushed a few half-burnt stalks deeper into the remaining flames. "Don't they give you eye drops or something for it?"

"Sure. Don't worry about it."

"But I am worried, Uncle Frank. I love you and Aunt Sylvia. Let me help you. Are you sure you're going to a good eye doctor? Are you getting the care you need?"

"Yes." He patted her on the shoulder, although his gaze remained on the fire. "Don't worry."

"What if I contact Sylvia? She'll come back, won't she? Now that this is gone? Now that you're going to clean up, too. You are going to clean up, aren't you?"

"Oh, yeah. Sure."

"I mean it, Uncle Frank."

She heard someone driving down their dirt road. With a frantic glance at the embers of the burning plants, she ran around to the front of the house.

In a near panic, she watched Jim Fletcher ease out of his car. He shoved his hat onto his head and started toward her with a determined stride.

"What's burning?" he asked as she hurried to meet him.

"Some garden waste. Leaves and all. Why?"

"You can see the smoke clear to town." Face grim, he strode around the side of the house. By the time they reached the burn pile, Frank had disappeared.

"See?" Cassie said. "Garden trash."

The sheriff kicked a few branches with the toe of his boot. The glowing twigs broke apart in a shower of sparks. Against the remaining, smoldering embers, a charred leaf stood out for an instant, the perfect black silhouette of a marijuana leaf.

"Garden refuse, huh? What's going on, Miss Edwards?"

"Cassie, please. Or Cass. I was only burning—"

"A lot of marijuana. You can smell it all the way down Oak Street. I'd be surprised if everyone on this side of town isn't high by now. The air reeks of it."

"I found some plants. I burned them. End of story."

"I appreciate that. However, this is an illegal substance. We have a murder investigation going on. You gave me your word that you were going to cooperate."

"I *am* cooperating. This was a private matter. It doesn't have anything to do with the murder investigation."

"Are you sure about that?"

"Of course I'm sure."

He kicked another ember back into the smoldering pile. "That's a lot of marijuana. Looks to me like someone was growing it for sale."

"Uncle Frank is going blind from glaucoma!"

"So he was growing this for medicinal purposes?"

"Yes."

"Marijuana has not been proven efficacious for glaucoma. In fact, it has no effect at all. Your uncle is a scientist, or was. He ought to know that."

"I know," she said, her voice wavering. She wanted to cry with frustration, anger, and worry. Why couldn't the police go away and leave them alone?

He stared at her for a long time, studying her face until she looked away. She eyed the path to the creek and then looked back at him, desperate for a break of some kind.

His hard eyes seemed to soften with a glimmer of sympathy. With a twisted grin he said, "Why did you have to burn it?"

"What do you mean? He shouldn't have been growing this. It's illegal. I *had* to burn it."

"Why didn't you bury it? Everyone in town knows by now that you burned a boatload of marijuana."

"Bury it?" She shoved her hands in her back pockets and kicked a clot of potting soil. She couldn't believe her own stupidity. "I never thought of that. Guess I'm not a very good criminal."

"Apparently not." He grew silent as he studied the bonfire.

She had the distinct impression he was letting the idiocy and seriousness of her actions sink in as fully as possible. Finally, he asked, "Do you think your aunt knew he was growing marijuana?"

"I don't know. She's not here—we didn't lie about that. I think she may have gone on the trip they were planning to West Virginia, and Frank decided to stay behind. Maybe they argued a little. You know how it is. Anyway, that's why I'm here. I was going to housesit for them. Uncle Frank probably forgot I was coming. Or maybe she didn't tell him." Cassie couldn't bring herself to admit her real fear, that her aunt may have left Frank for good, despite knowing that he might be going blind.

"Don't you think it raises interesting questions about Frank?"

"What questions? There are no questions about Uncle Frank."

"What made him start growing that stuff?"

"He has glaucoma. It was freaking him out."

"This is more than one man would need for his own use. A single plant I might understand. What are your thoughts?"

"I don't have any thoughts," she replied brutally. "I take prescription drugs to avoid having any thoughts."

Taking her by the elbow, he guided her back toward the house. "Why don't we talk about it?"

"Haven't we talked enough?" She pushed open the kitchen door.

"No." He pulled out a chair and sat down at the table.

"You want something to eat?" The aluminum pan of brownies, only half empty, rested on the counter. She pulled the metal cover off the pan, releasing the intense scent of dark, rich chocolate.

When she caught Jim's eyes on her, she lifted the pan and waved it slightly to let the tantalizing aroma reach him. He sniffed and sat back, looping his arm over the back of the chair.

With a chuckle, he said, "You win. I'll have a piece."

"À la mode?" She flicked a flirtatious smile at him. "Come on. You know you want it. And with those muscles, you'll work it off on the walk back to your car."

"Right. You know, flirting with an officer off the law could be considered obstruction of justice."

"Only if it works. Besides, who's flirting? I'm just fixing a snack. Southern hospitality demands that I offer some to you, too." After melting a half cup of semi-sweet morsels with a few drops of water in the microwave, she stirred it into a syrup and drizzled that over the brownie in each bowl. To that, she added a large dollop of real ice cream and as a final touch, a maraschino cherry.

She placed the bowl with a spoon in front of him and sat down in the chair opposite. At least the food kept the questions at bay while they ate. Unfortunately, the respite did not last forever, and Cassie found herself wishing her uncle had added an extra, special ingredient to the brownies that might have made Jim Fletcher forget to ask any more questions.

"You done?" she asked, picking up the bowls and taking them to the sink. "Wow, look at the time! I didn't realize it was so late."

"Only a few more questions," Jim said, undeterred by the thought of the dwindling daylight.

"What more can I *possibly* tell you? About the only thing you don't know about my family, or me, at this point is my bra size." She rested her fisted hands on her hips. "What is it with you? Is this what they call police harassment?"

"Even you must admit you seem to be doing everything you can to provoke the interest of the law. The truth is, I've been trying to keep your uncle out of jail. You're not making it easy."

She ran a hand through her hair, which smelled of smoke and weed. "I don't see what more I can tell you. We keep going over the same questions."

"And your answers keep changing."

"They do not!"

He stared at her until her gaze dropped to the floor. She blushed and awkwardly sat down again at the table. A few dark crumbs and a drop of ice cream smudged her plastic, sunflower-bedecked placemat. The smear caught her attention. She couldn't stand it. Starting to rise to get the sponge from the sink, she stopped when Jim reached out and grabbed her wrist.

"Sit," he said.

"Yes, sir." After sitting, she clasped her hands together on top of the table like a good little girl and gazed expectantly at him. *I'm going to be good. I'm going to answer his questions, and then he's going to go away, and this is all going to be over.*

"Let's start again. At the beginning."

She groaned and dropped her forehead to her hands. "I told you. I drove up from Raleigh on Sunday. I stopped at Peyton Place. I came here. I went for a walk. I found a dead guy. I called the police."

"You called Anne."

"To call the police. Whatever."

He frowned. "Why not on Saturday?"

"Why not what on Saturday?"

"Why didn't you drive here on Saturday, or Friday night for that matter? If you were going to housesit for your aunt and uncle, why didn't you come down after work on Friday? So you could spend some time with them before they left."

"Because I planned to spend time with them when they got back from West Virginia."

"So you didn't want to see them before they left?"

"No. That's not what I meant at all," she replied, exasperated by his deliberate obtuseness. "It's hard for me to get away from work."

"You worked on Saturday?"

"I work a lot of weekends. You must be familiar with working long hours and weekends. And I had a lot to do. I'm not lying." She unclipped the smartphone from her belt and slid it over the table to him. "Look for yourself if you don't believe me."

He studied it before glancing up, his eyes lit with amusement. "It's off."

"I know it's off. Turn it on." *If he thinks he's under pressure, he has no idea. No one has any idea.* She leaned back and crossed her arms. "And the password is *Gymnadenia conopsea.*" When she caught the look on his face, she spelled it slowly and added, "It's the scientific name for the Fragrant orchid. It's my favorite. It smells a little like cloves. I like it. So sue me."

"You're into orchids, too?"

"Well, you can't really escape it around here."

"I guess not." The minute he turned on the device's power, it vibrated and beeped like an alarm clock on speed. When he tried to hand it back, she shook her head.

"Go ahead, type in the password." She repeated it for him.

"Now, take a look at the e-mails. That's why I can't get away from work. That's why I couldn't leave until Sunday. And I wouldn't have been able to go then if I hadn't turned that darn thing off."

"I think you'd better look at this." He held out the smart-phone.

"Why? I've got a bunch of e-mails marked urgent, don't I? I always do." She crossed her arms and leaned back.

"I think you'd better look at a few of these messages." He eyed the device and clicked a few buttons with the slightly sick but fascinated expression of someone helplessly watching a disaster unfold.

"What does it say? Some idiot forgot their password, right?"

"Sorry, but I think you should read it."

"Fine." She reached over and grabbed it out of his hand. She scrolled down to read the subject lines.

Subject: Problems with DomControl1

FromNoel, the supposedly competent backup administrator her boss had hired against her recommendations because he was his wife's cousin. In the message, he indicated there were problems with the domain controller that processed user passwords and performed a few other critical functions on their computer network. DomControl1 was the heart of everything. He suspected hardware problems.

"Idiot! I told you there were problems with the switch! I told you to plug the domain controller into a different port if you had any problems," she muttered, continuing to read.

The next message from Noel said he was turning off Dom-Control1 because it wasn't acting right.

"No," Cassie moaned. "Don't turn it off, you moron. It's the main DNS server, too! People won't be able to find any of the other servers or get their mail. Oh, my God, what a moron!"

Scrolling up, there were only four more messages, all from FreeMe-mail—not the corporate internal mail system.

The first message turned out to be from Noel again, using the interesting identity of CoolGuy. "No one can get to their e-mail? No shit, Sherlock. Plug DomControl1 into a different port on the switch and turn it back on!"

The next message, the last one from CoolGuy, was not addressed directly to her. She got a courtesy copy that said, "It is my considered opinion that the previous administrator did something to DomControl1 that made it malfunction during her absence in order to 'prove her value' and obtain a raise. As she is not available and has not replied to any of our requests for assistance, I'm going to tear down the systems she set up and start fresh."

"You can't start *fresh* you brain-dead jerk!" Cassie screamed. "And I didn't do anything to the systems before I left. The only mistake anyone made was hiring you." She stood up, her chair crashing back against the wall, and started pacing. "I even wrote instructions, standard operating procedures, disaster recovery plans, and backup plans. Use the plans! You can't ignore everything. And you can't start fresh. Our corporate business runs accounts receivable and accounts payable through the mail system. If you start fresh, you'll lose it all." She stared at the device in her hand.

The final two messages were from her boss, "Supreme-Leader." The subjects said it all.

Subject: If you don't come in today, you're fired.

It was dated Monday. Another e-mail followed it.

Subject: You're fired.

This one was dated today, Tuesday.

"Shit," she whispered. She felt light-headed and confused, as if someone had pushed her out of an airplane without a parachute. Now she was plummeting downward and waiting for the full force of the impact. "I'm so totally screwed."

When she glanced up, Jim was staring at her, his eyes dark with concern and sympathy. "I'm sorry."

"I can't believe this is happening. Noel is completely incompetent. I told them that. I told them not to hire him, that he couldn't handle it, but they insisted." She stalked over to the sink and back. Her stomach gurgled uneasily, and she returned to the stainless steel sink. Her hands gripped the cool edge as she hung over it. "He's a jerk. A total jerk."

She turned around and leaned her back against the counter. She wasn't going to let this make her sick. But she couldn't stop her nervous hands from yanking the ends of her hair.

Jim eyed her like he was waiting for the next piece of bad news. When she simply stared back, he said, "It sounded to me like Noel was looking for a promotion. Did you leave your directions with anyone other than him?"

"Why would I?" A new, more horrifying thought hit her on the back of her head. She stopped pulling her hair and leaned forward, intense. "Oh, my God! Have you got a computer I can use? There isn't one here—at least not one I can use—the one in the lab isn't connected to the Internet. You'd think it would be, but my whacko uncle insists he can use the ones at the library."

"I don't know," he answered uneasily.

She gripped his arm. "If they lose the mail system, they could lose money. What if they sue me? I can see them suing me, even if it's Noel's fault. Noel thinks he's so smart by creating this disaster so he can blame me, but the moron doesn't realize that if they lose enough, no one will have a job there."

"Isn't that a little paranoid?"

"Paranoid? He's already told them I sabotaged it. This could cost them if the billing notifications don't go out. If he messes up enough, they could lose the systems running the financial database. Accounts receivable and payable. Order entry. You have no idea. Please. I need to use a computer. I have a backup plan. I need to send it to them. All of them. It'll bring the systems back up to the date of the last backup, back to Saturday. They won't lose it all. If I was there, I might be able to fix it. They might not lose anything."

He stood. "I've got a computer with a high-speed Internet connection." He reached over and plucked her phone out of her hand. "You don't need this. I'm beginning to see what you meant by stress."

"Not that you are completely exempt from it," she said offhandedly, her attention already focused on work. Her heart rate kicked up. Her mind raced, falling into a problem-solving groove as she started weighing the pros and cons of various recovery strategies.

First though, she'd rewrite her backup-and-restore plan so even a moron like Noel could follow the darn thing. Step-by-minute-step.

Then she'd send it to Noel, their boss, and Gil in finance. Out of all the people working there, Gil was the one most likely to understand and make sure it got implemented. He might also care about his job enough to save it.

CHAPTER THIRTEEN

Although Jim overruled Cassie's objections to sitting in the back seat of his cruiser, he had the uneasy feeling that his offer was a mistake. The investigation was still underway, and Cassie was the niece of a major person of interest.

He drove up the driveway to his house and parked. Even without getting out of the car, he could hear his dog barking. A grin tugged his mouth at the exuberant reaction to his arrival. As he watched, his chocolate Lab raced to the corner of the fence from where it could see the driveway. It jumped against the chain-link fence and let out another volley of welcome barks.

"We're here," he said, unnecessarily, glancing up at his plain white house with its neat black shutters and gray door. Vinyl siding, because as everyone knows, "vinyl is final."

"Isn't this your parents' house?" Cassie asked as he opened the car door for her. She glanced around uneasily and stayed near the car as he strode up the sidewalk to unlock the front door.

"Yeah," he replied. "My parents retired two years ago and moved to Charleston." He had to chuckle at the disbelief on her face. "Not everyone who retires goes to Florida. They like Charleston. It's near enough to still be a pain to my sister and me, and my mom has a sister there."

"I'm surprised Anne moved out."

"She wanted more independence so that apartment over the

diner seemed ideal." He unlocked the door and ushered her inside.

She cocked her head as his dog scrabbled at the back door. "Is that a dog?"

"He doesn't think so, but yeah. Do you mind if I let him in before he destroys the door?"

She looked uneasy, but she said, "I don't mind."

It took longer for him to make his way through the kitchen and let his dog in than it did for the animal to dash past him into the living room. By the time Jim got back, Cassie was hesitantly petting his dog.

"What's his name?" she asked.

"Bosco. He's a chocolate Labrador retriever."

His dog sat on her foot, wagging his tail enthusiastically.

"Oh, I get it. Like Bosco, that chocolate syrup."

Jim whistled, but Bosco simply thumped his tail more vigorously and leaned harder against Cassie's leg, gazing up at her with adoring eyes. "Bosco!" he called.

Cassie smiled, a little uncertainly. "It's okay." She rubbed the dog's ear. "Where is your computer?"

"In the den." He led Cassie down the hallway, Bosco at her heel. When they got to the den, she stopped inside the doorway and looked around.

Over the last two years, he'd built floor-to-ceiling bookshelves from pale blond knotty pine and filled them with a wide variety of books. The volumes ranged from legal and investigative references to his college texts on English grammar, literature, chemistry, biology, and history, which he found surprisingly helpful in his writing. One bookcase was filled entirely with crime fiction. A thesaurus and dictionary sat on the table next to his computer.

"Make yourself comfortable." He snatched away an old shirt that was hanging off the back of his computer chair. "The chair's adjustable, if you need to raise it." He circled around her and turned on the computer. "It'll take a minute to boot up."

She laughed. "I know. Just get me to the Internet. I'll take it from there. And I'll probably be a while, okay?"

"Sure. I've got a few calls to make. I'll stay out of your way."

Bosco placed his head on her lap, tongue lolling in complete adoration. "Is he all right?" she asked, patting his smooth shoulder.

"He thinks he's in love. He'll get over it if you ignore him."

"He's sweet. I think I like this love at first sight thing."

"Then maybe you should get a Lab. They're good at it."

Over the next two hours, Jim made a few phone calls. Then he went over the file he had been putting together for the Gracie murder. They had taken many pictures, collected a box full of evidence, and discussed a lot of theories. But none of the scenarios made much sense to him.

Logically, he could accept Meyers' theory that Frank Edwards was involved in the sale of drugs and had gotten into an argument with his distributor, Nick Gracie. Someone had even shot at Frank, making the drug angle more likely. Perhaps someone was warning Frank to shape up and play ball. Because the shots seemed more like warnings than a real attempt upon his life.

Which made both Frank and Cassie vulnerable since she decided to burn his supply.

He glanced again through the photos and evidence. The condom bothered him. Frank could have snuck in while Gracie was "entertaining" a lady, killed him while his back was turned. And then what?

That's where it started to break down in his mind. If Frank had moved the body, why move it to his own property? Throwing the body into the stream could arguably make sense. The body would decompose and disappear in the woods, gnawed and scattered by local wildlife. The area was private property and posted, so no local hunters would be likely to stumble over it.

If that was Frank's purpose, why go back to it? While some killers were known to return to their kills, that didn't fit Frank's personality, or the proposed reason for the murder.

The more he looked at everything, the more Jim felt that they were missing some important elements. Frustrated, he put everything back into his folder and returned to the den, where Cassie was hunched over the computer, her feet curled around the chair legs.

"You done yet?" he asked.

Nothing.

"Hey!" He moved closer. She still didn't react. Finally, he touched her shoulder.

She yipped and jerked, almost sending his computer mouse over the edge of the table. Bosco, curled up under the table, leapt out and barked excitedly at this new game.

"What are you doing?" she asked, one hand resting at the base of her throat.

"Sorry, didn't mean to startle you. Are you done yet?"

"Just about. I was getting ready to save this document on my personal website and send a copy to the company. I don't think this is as tragic as I initially thought. Even if they can't get into the financial database with their personal IDs, they can get in with the Administrator account. And even if the mail system goes down, they can still send paper invoices and orders. It's not the end of the world, although they may think it is. There's always paper. And they can use the data from the database to keep going." She turned back to the computer. "Give me a minute to send these documents."

He watched as she clicked and typed. Bosco sat at her knee, his head tilted to the side, patiently waiting for her attention.

Feeling a little jealous at his dog's sudden defection, Jim called him. With a wag of his tail, Bosco came over to have his ears rubbed.

If nothing else, this view of Cassie Edwards at work gave him pause for a number of reasons. She was a problem solver and couldn't let go. Even after she was fired.

Which meant she was unlikely to stop interfering in his investigation, even after he warned her.

"There. Sorry I took so long. I really appreciate this." She stood up and turned to face him.

He caught his breath. Her eyes were a deep, brilliant blue. She gazed up at him with partially open lips, scarcely breathing. "I've always had a problem with authority," she whispered.

His hand cradled her neck as he said, "This is a really bad idea."

"I know." Her fingers gripped his collar as her lips brushed his.

Her cell phone rang. She jumped as if she'd touched a live electrical wire, and pushed him away. "You didn't turn it back off?"

"No. Sorry."

She turned it off and shoved it back into the holster on her belt. "It's late," she said, "and I should get back home. I want to make sure Uncle Frank is okay."

"Sounds good to me," he agreed with a sense of relief.

CHAPTER FOURTEEN

When Cassie got home, she searched for her uncle. She felt uneasy about leaving him alone for most of the afternoon. And the fact that she had joined the ranks of the unemployed exacerbated her feelings of inadequacy and impending doom.

Her uncle wasn't in his bedroom or the living room.

"Uncle Frank?" The house felt empty—too empty. "Uncle Frank!" she shouted.

The small glass door to the greenhouse gaped open, letting the humid heat and smell of rich humus waft into the kitchen.

"Uncle Frank?" She ran into the greenhouse, shimmying past the shelves of orchids and other plants, until she reached the corner created by the side of the house and glass wall of the greenhouse.

The computer, Petri dishes, and all the other lab equipment were gone. She stepped forward, on the edge of panic. Something crunched under the soles of her shoes. Broken glass. One of the glass test tubes was smashed on the dirt floor.

Had they been robbed? She backed out, torn between the urgent need to find her uncle and cold fear. What if the thieves were still in the house? What if it was the killer? She hadn't looked in any of the bathrooms or the garage.

She yanked her cell phone out. Trembling, she left the greenhouse and dialed nine-one-one.

"This is Cassiopeia Edwards." Her voice shook. She swallowed, trying to clear the constriction in her throat. "I've been robbed. That is, the house has been robbed."

She gave the emergency operator her address and was told to wait outside the house. Then she heard the sound of a siren and whirled around. "The police are here. I'm going to hang up. Thanks." Before the dispatcher could protest, Cassie cut the call.

A sheriff's car pulled into the driveway. Turning toward it, she felt sudden confusion and disappointment when it was not Jim who stepped out. A tall, thin man walked casually up the sidewalk. She vaguely remembered him carrying a camera and taking photos of the murdered man at the stream.

"Where's the sheriff?" she asked. Her glance bounced from the deputy to the car and then over her shoulder at the house. "Never mind. We've been robbed! And I'm afraid for my uncle's safety. I didn't go through the whole house. He may be hurt, somewhere inside."

"No, ma'am. Mr. Edwards is in custody."

"What do you mean?"

"He's been arrested, taken into custody on suspicion of murder."

Cassie fisted her hands, striving to control the urge to wipe the superior look off his smug face. "Uncle Frank's an old man. He hasn't done a thing wrong, and you know it."

"I'm sorry." He sounded more satisfied than sorry.

"He didn't kill that man. You can't possibly believe that!"

"I believe the evidence, ma'am."

"Evidence? What evidence?"

"I'm sorry, ma'am. I'm not at liberty to say."

"May I go with you to the station?"

He hesitated, the first glimpse of humanity she had seen in his smarmy face. "I suppose that's okay."

Feeling as if she had to fight her way through a pool of cold molasses, she scrambled ungracefully inside the car and steadied herself in the back. The seats were worn and slick. The whole vehicle smelled of rank perspiration and smoke. She shivered and sat forward, trying to keep as little of her in contact with the upholstery as possible.

"What happened, really?" she asked, still unable to comprehend how they could have arrested her uncle.

"Ma'am, perhaps it would be better if you waited until we got to the station."

"My uncle's lab—"

"We had a search warrant and took some evidence—"

"What evidence could there possibly be?"

"You can discuss it with the sheriff when we get to the station."

Had Jim ordered his men to arrest Uncle Frank and tear apart his house and lab? While she had been at his house?

He had made phone calls. She had seen him with the case file. Had he noticed something in the photos or other evidence that made him decide her uncle was guilty?

How could he do that to me?

She felt a strong urge to cry at his betrayal. He had seemed so understanding, so human and warm. She sighed. She'd been a fool because she liked him.

Worse, he knew she was a loser who had been fired. A deep cold coiled through her stomach, sinking into her bones. He had seen her burn the marijuana, and she had as much admitted it to him. At least some of their conversation was recorded.

Her thoughts raced. She'd admitted to tampering with the crime scene. What else had she said? What had she admitted? Shock settled deeply into her bones making it hard to think, as if her brain was slowly freezing solid. Deer-in-the-headlights syndrome.

She had to shake it off and *think*. She was good at solving problems. That's all she did, every day.

Even if they couldn't get Uncle Frank on the murder charge, they could get them on drug charges.

What had seemed so black and white, so easy to identify as right and wrong, now seemed unimaginably complicated. And yet, despite the marijuana, she couldn't believe her uncle was guilty of anything more than stupidity and weakness.

When she looked out the window, she realized with a sinking heart that they had arrived at the courthouse complex. Jail, sheriff's department, and courthouse, all nicely packed together with lawyers' offices in the next block and garish signs for bail-bondsmen across the street.

The deputy sheriff, if that was his title, helped her out of the car and escorted her into the building. He jauntily guided Cassie through the hallway. She could have sworn he was humming happily under his breath. As they passed the first door, she glanced across an open area filled with desks. Beyond that was an office with large windows. She saw the sheriff inside, scowling down at his desk. He glanced up as she walked by, catching her gaze.

She looked away, something hardening inside her.

The deputy guided her into a small room across the hall a few feet from the office area. He waived toward a straight-backed wooden chair that looked like it had escaped from a turn-of-the-century, one-room schoolhouse.

Keeping her voice light but firm, she said, "I want a lawyer for my uncle. How long has he been here?"

"I brought him in an hour ago."

"Did you question him? He's an old man and easily confused. I want to see him."

"I'm sorry, but I need to take your statement first."

"I already gave a statement."

"Yes, but you have so much more to add now, don't you?"

"Miss Edwards?" Jim walked into the room. Cassie tried to

keep her expression neutral, but she could feel the muscles around her lips trembling. She bit the inside of her cheek to forestall a sob.

"I want to see my uncle," she said, her voice choking off in her throat.

"Your uncle?" The sheriff flashed a measured glance at the deputy.

"You people arrested him and he's innocent," she said. "You know that."

"Excuse us for a minute, Miss Edwards." Jim jerked a thumb toward the door. "I'll be back. Please relax."

"Oh, sure. No problem."

Immediately, she regretted her sarcasm. When Jim and his deputy returned, she'd play nice. "You catch more bees with honey than vinegar," Aunt Sylvia liked to say, even if she preferred well-aged vinegar. Unfortunately, experience had taught Cassie to believe you caught more creeps with honey.

CHAPTER FIFTEEN

"Damn it, Bill, what's going on? You arrested Frank Edwards?" Jim asked, glancing over Bill Meyers' shoulder at the closed door and trying to keep his voice down.

The tiled floor and thin walls made voices carry. There was no such thing as privacy in the station. He was tempted to go outside, feeling the urge to emphasize the question in a louder voice.

"Frank Edwards was supplying Nick Gracie with drugs to sell to the kids around here. Nick probably forgot to pay him. Or they were haggling over the price. The killing was drug-related, like I told you. I'm just doing my job." Clearly he also thought that Jim was not doing his job.

While his gut said Frank wouldn't swat a fly, there was no denying that he had been growing a lot of weed. And the sheriff's office had suspected Nick of selling hard drugs as well as marijuana.

"I confiscated an entire lab in Frank's greenhouse," Bill added. "The doc is looking at it. If he finds anything worth more analysis, he'll send it on to the lab in Raleigh. Frank was a chemist—"

"No, a botanist. There's a difference."

"He was growing an illegal substance for sale. And he was so stoned he didn't have the brains to leave the scene after he murdered Gracie."

"Nick Gracie was murdered at least twenty-four hours before

152

Miss Edwards called nine-one-one."

Bill shrugged, his sharp face smooth and slick with arrogance. "Frank went back to the scene of the crime because he thought he was smarter than us, what with his doctorate and all. But it turns out we're not just a bunch of dumb hicks."

The muscles in Jim's shoulders tightened. "And other than the contents of the lab, what evidence do you have?"

Bill raised a hand and folded down his index finger. "One, we have his lawn chair and the photos of the marks it made by the stream. We know he was there and did not report the crime." He folded down the middle finger. "Two, we have photos and physical evidence showing Nick was dragged the last few feet to the stream." The ring finger folded down. "Three, we have an entire file on Nick Gracie, and I ran his prints. He was wanted in Boston for selling crack cocaine and marijuana." The pinkie folded down, leaving his clenched fist in the air between them. "Four, there's evidence that Frank Edwards was Nick's source for that strain of extra-potent 'super' marijuana the kids have been using around here. What more proof do you need?"

"Evidence that he was connected to the murder. We haven't even identified the murder scene."

"That's where you're wrong,"

"You found it?"

"Of course. If you hadn't been so fascinated by the murderer's niece—"

"Where did the murder occur?"

"At the Edwards farm. There was glass in the garbage. We collected it. There was what looked like blood on a few pieces. I sent it to the lab. It could be the vic's blood."

"Did you find where Gracie was killed?"

"No. They must have cleaned the house up pretty good. There was no blood spatter evidence left in any of the rooms, but I figured Frank did it in the greenhouse. The broken glass was in the kitchen trash, through the door to the greenhouse. And that greenhouse has a dirt floor. Easy cleanup with a shovel or more bags off dirt. There's a door to the outside, so it would have been easy to get Nick out of there. I figured the old guy killed Nick and when his niece showed up, she helped him dump the body at the stream. Of course, we can't prove she helped dump the body."

A perfectly reasonable theory that almost fit, thought Jim. They had been watching Nick Gracie, sure he was involved in some of Peyton's drug traffic. But they were missing something.

"You had a warrant?" Jim asked. "You did have a warrant didn't you? Because I don't recall going to Judge Colesford and asking for one."

"I had a warrant."

"What did it cover? Tell me it covered Frank's house. And explain to me how you got that warrant without my knowledge?"

Two red spots stained Bill's sharp cheekbones. He pulled a folded piece of paper out of his chest pocket. "A warrant for the arrest of Frank Edwards on a charge of murder."

"You've got crap evidence, Bill. Instead of building a good, solid case that accounts for all the evidence we have, you've gone off trying to be a damn Lone Ranger. You've probably compromised the case by jumping the gun. Well, this is the last time you're pulling this crap while I'm here. Do you understand?"

"Yes, sir." His lip curled. "But I'm right, and the lab will prove it. The blood on that broken glass will be Nick Gracie's, and we'll have a case. A solid case. And Judge Colesford will know who put it together. He'll know who did the work while the sheriff was playing grab-ass with a possible suspect."

"Bill, I'm going to overlook that remark." Jim leaned forward. His looming presence pushed Meyers into the corner. "But if you ever go over my head again, I'll have you up on charges of insubordination and anything else I can think of. Now we're going to go into that interview room, together. We're going to be polite and treat her as a witness."

"And a person of interest."

"No. We're going to take another statement, a modified statement. Then we're going to allow Miss Edwards to seek counsel for her uncle and see what the judge sets for bail. Though I doubt there's enough to even bind him over for trial."

"Bail? He'll jump bail! His wife's gone. What else will hold him here?"

"Frank is an old man. He's not going anywhere."

Bill jabbed a fist into the wall. He clearly wanted to take a swing at Jim, but he didn't quite dare. And despite Jim's warning, Bill's over-confidence set his mouth in a twisted grin that scraped over Jim's temper like the jagged end of a broken beer bottle.

"I'm going to interview Miss Edwards," Jim said. "Go back to your desk and write up a full report on your activities today. I want it on my desk when I get in to work tomorrow morning."

Bill stalked over to his desk. If there had been a door to his office area, he would have slammed it. He flung himself down on his chair, opened the bottom desk drawer, and kicked it shut.

Taking a deep breath, Jim walked through the office area to the interview room. Hand on the door knob, he paused, sifting through the few facts he had at his disposal.

Bill Meyers had found broken glass, with blood on it, in the kitchen trash. Frank Edwards had been growing marijuana in large enough quantities to sell. Nick Gracie was known to be selling drugs in Peyton, although they had never been able to prove the rumor.

Frank and Cassie had been at the site where the body was dumped. And Cassie had tried to cover up her uncle's presence, although it was nearly twenty-four hours after the murder had occurred.

Nick Gracie's clothing had been hastily assembled, and he'd been dressed, most likely, post-mortem. No man would accidentally leave a used condom in his underwear. And there were the missing socks and the shirt that didn't quite fit.

Had he been dressed in someone else's clothing?

Frank's shirts would have been too long for Nick Gracie. Although Frank was thin, he was tall and had extremely long arms. So he doubted Gracie's shirt had come from Frank.

And what about the damn socks? Why would Nick take off his socks? Had he completely undressed and put on a condom?

Maybe. But why?

Chapter Sixteen

Jim opened the door to the interview room and stood there for a moment, examining Cassie. She sat hunched in her chair, arms crossed, hands clutching her elbows. Her stark profile stood out, palely etched against the dingy wall beside her.

When he took a step, she glanced up, eyes dark and shadowed, face tense.

"May I see my uncle? I want to make sure he's okay." She spasmodically squeezed her elbows until the skin under her fingertips turned white. "He's an old man."

"Cassie, this is a small, local sheriff's office attached to a county jail with a few holding cells. No one's going to rough Frank up." He gave her shoulder an awkward squeeze. Then he walked around the table to take the seat on the other side.

"You've got to let him out!"

"There'll be a hearing tomorrow," he assured her. "Bail will get set, and he can go home. In the meantime—"

"You're not going to continue the investigation! You're so sure you have the bad guy, you'll stop. And the real murderer will have plenty of time to clean up and create an alibi!"

"We're not going to stop investigating."

She sat back so abruptly, the chair scraped backward along the tiled floor with a shriek. "Oh, sure! Tell me about it! Let's say you continue investigating, and start to suspect someone else. How are you going to get a search warrant for someone else's place when you already have someone awaiting trial? Oh, yeah. I *totally* believe that's going to happen. I'm sure you're going to continue this investigation even after arresting someone."

"Relax, Cassie. Give us some credit for knowing our jobs—"

"If you knew your job, you wouldn't have arrested my uncle on no evidence."

He reached over and caught one of her wrists. When she resisted, he dragged her arm on to the table and patted her hand. The action caught her attention as he intended, and she quieted. Then she pulled back to free her arm.

After a full minute, he let her go.

"Now, listen to me," he said. "There will be the hearing tomorrow, and they'll set bail. You have my assurance that we'll continue to investigate. And, as part of that investigation, you're going to answer my questions truthfully and completely. Do you understand?"

"Yes." She stared at him, a mulish expression compressing her mouth. "I understand completely."

"Good. Was your uncle selling marijuana to Nick Gracie?"

"I want a lawyer."

"You have the right to representation," he said, letting the disappointment deepen his voice.

"I'm not going to talk about my uncle. Anything I say will be hearsay. Is that the right term? I have no direct knowledge of anything he may, or may not, have done before I arrived. And I never knew the dead guy, or even heard his name before you arrived on the scene." She deliberately caught his gaze and stared into his eyes. "I want you to understand. I'm not going to contribute to whatever case you think you have against Uncle Frank. I'll answer your questions, but I'm not going to speculate about my uncle."

"Fair enough. You said you never met Nick Gracie before you came here?"

"Yes. I told you that."

"And you had never heard him mentioned?"

"No. Never."

"Your uncle never mentioned him to you?"

"No."

"However, you knew his name when we came to the crime scene."

"Because my uncle told me. I didn't know who the dead guy was until after I spoke to you."

Jim nodded. That part of her story had stayed consistent. "And you didn't come here on Saturday?"

"Is that a rhetorical question? You know I didn't get here before Sunday. Your sister knows when I got here, and you have that fast-food receipt from my trash. And you saw my e-mails. Look, if you have any doubts, and you shouldn't, I can give you my Internet provider. You can trace the calls and know exactly which computers I was using and when I was using them. There will be logs everywhere that can verify what I'm telling you. I was in Raleigh on Friday and Saturday. I was working. I didn't know the dead guy, and although I don't know when he died, if he died while I was working, the logs will prove I didn't have anything to do with his damn death."

"We'll check that, Cassie. In the meantime," he said, pulling out his swab kit. "I'd like to take swabs from the insides of your cheeks."

"Absolutely!" Leaning across the table, she waggled her fingers, impatient for the swabs. "I love science. I have no idea what you think you have that you can compare against my DNA, but I don't care." She rubbed the swabs inside her cheeks and handed them back with a smile. "My uncle's innocent, too. And you know what? I'm going to prove it."

Sealing up the samples, Jim stared at her, his face hardening. "We're going to prove it, not you. Do not, under any circumstance, interfere with this investigation. Do you understand?"

159

"Yes, sir," she agreed. However, her eyes reflected nothing but stubborn resolution.

"Good."

"A few years ago, I worked for a different company," she said. "A really small company. They had this strange problem with a logon script. Never could figure it out. After a couple of years, I quit and got the job where I am, now. One morning I was driving to work, and I realized what was wrong with that stupid logon script. It was one of those obvious things you don't think about. I e-mailed the new systems administrator there, because I knew they were still having the problem."

"Guess they were surprised to hear from you," he commented, thinking about obsessive behavior. And, oddly enough, stubborn Labrador retrievers that wouldn't give up until they retrieved what they were sent after. He admired the trait in his dog. He wasn't so sure it was as admirable in people.

She shrugged. "Never heard back from them. But that's not the point. What I was trying to say is that something in the basement of my brain keeps working on a problem until I solve it." She flicked a quick measuring glance at him as if to calculate how much he understood. "I can't really control it, because it's a subconscious process."

"You can't solve Nick Gracie's murder, Cassie. It's our responsibility."

"That logon script wasn't my responsibility, either. I like problems. I can't let them go. And this one isn't some intellectual exercise. It's my family. I can't walk out on them and hope for the best. Not after I've seen your best. Someone has to do something."

"Someone will. Me."

She eyed him. "And if you're told to stop? Because you have someone in custody?"

"I'm not quitting until we have all the evidence and are

confident we have the right man."

"And you won't let the evidence mislead you?"

"No." He reached across the table and pressed his hand over her clenched fist. Anxiety had chilled her skin and her bones felt fragile beneath his palm. "Trust me, Cassie."

"Find the murderer. Then we'll talk about trust."

Chapter Seventeen

Despite Jim's confident words, Cassie left the sheriff's office feeling lost and more than a little nervous. Uncle Frank would not be released until bail could be set. That meant they thought they had enough evidence to bring him to trial, or they wouldn't have arrested him.

At least that was how she understood the system. Police didn't run around arresting folks without evidence. But she wasn't naïve enough to believe that innocent people never went to jail. And there was the marijuana. They'd be justified to throw Uncle Frank in jail for that.

Hesitating at the corner, she stepped into the alley next to Peyton Place and turned on her cell phone. Uncle Frank might eschew modern communications, but his wife did not. Aunt Sylvia carried a cell. Occasionally, she even turned it on.

"Aunt Sylvia?" she asked, trying to project happy unconcern into her voice. Unfortunately, to her ear, she heard only hear a tentative wobble.

"Cassiopeia? Is that you? What's wrong?"

Her initial relief at hearing her aunt's firm voice faded as Cassie tried to find a way to explain what had happened to Uncle Frank. She sighed and leaned uncomfortably against the brick wall. The rough surface felt cold to her back. Glancing out from the alley, she watched light glittering along the sidewalk and struggled to sound confident.

"Nothing, Aunt Sylvia. I mean, I'm fine. It's not me." Her

aunt's silence made Cassie hunch over, the absence of a response relaying disapproval more quickly than any words. "It's Uncle Frank."

"Are you in Peyton?" her aunt asked in a seeming non sequitur.

"Yes."

"I suppose you went into the greenhouse."

"Yes."

"Did Frank ask you to call me?"

"No. I called because I was hoping you'd come home."

"If you've been to the greenhouse then you know why I'm not home. Frank and I are professional horticulturalists. I've asked him to stop. Repeatedly."

"But he did stop."

"And then he started again. And this time, he didn't smoke occasionally on the weekend. He was growing it. Growing it to be sold! He may have decided to retire, but I'm still working. I cannot be associated with a criminal, not in this field."

"He's got glaucoma," Cassie whispered, staring blankly at the overflowing green dumpster at the end of the alley. She felt like an alien, lost in an inexplicable and ugly world strewn with rotten garbage, rank smells, and decay. "He's scared."

"I'm sorry, Cassiopeia. I know I may seem unforgiving and harsh to you. However, I've been married to him for over thirty years. You were too young to realize how many times I had to give excuses for him or cover up. He went too far, and I'm sorry."

"He's in jail."

The silence crackled and hissed like a hidden fire in the heart of a house. Eating through the walls from the inside and filling the air with poisonous gases.

"I'm sorry, Cassiopeia." Aunt Sylvia said before she hung up.

Cassie stood there, unable to focus. Her fingers strayed over the buttons, sliding back and forth over the seven, the speed dial number for her aunt.

How could her aunt give up on Uncle Frank? How could she leave him alone when he needed her the most?

There was no one left to help him or believe in him.

No one except Cassie.

Chapter Eighteen

Cassie didn't know what to do when she stepped out of the darkness of the alley. She blinked in the sunshine, gazing around Peyton as if she had never seen it before. Finally, spying the library, she turned toward it. The low, brick building was a refuge of quiet and peace. As a child, it had been one of the few places that guaranteed a happy experience.

As Cassie pushed open the glass door, she took a deep breath of relief. Then, looking around at the tall bookcases, she realized there was something else she needed to do.

While she had already sent several people at her previous job all the information they needed to repair their network, she had forgotten about a virtual system she had set up to test their backups. The company hadn't had the hardware to set up a physical system for testing, so she had set up her own "fake" lab. And she had done a test restore last week. With a few simple instructions, they could use that as a stop-gap measure to speed up their network recovery.

Although she had done them all the favors they could expect after firing her so abruptly, she couldn't quite let it go. She had her own sense of integrity, and it had nothing to do with the company and everything to do with her ability to face herself in the mirror each morning.

The problem would gnaw at her until she gave them the best answer she could. She grinned as she looked around for the computer carrels. She'd even offer to fix the problems—for a fee. A very high fee, commensurate with the aggravation factor the situation had generated for her.

And her conscience would be completely clear. She could walk away without any lingering worries, except where she was going to find another job.

She squared her shoulders. Her immediate future would be occupied with proving her uncle innocent. And if she couldn't prove his innocence, she might be arrested for burning his marijuana.

"May I help you?" a round-faced woman asked. She stared at Cassie over the rims of pink-rimmed, rectangular reading glasses. They matched her rose-pink lipstick and picked up the color of her deep fuchsia blouse.

"Do you have any computers available for the public to use? Connected to the Internet?"

The librarian laughed, her plump cheeks flushed. She was one of the pinkest women Cassie had ever seen, and she found herself smiling in return.

"In the back, honey. Over in the far corner. But the Internet connection is dead. Sorry 'bout that. Been dead a few days now."

Cassie eyed the woman's dimpled face. She didn't look like a computer person to Cassie, but you could never tell. "Maybe I can help you? I'm into computers. It might be something simple."

"I don't know, honey. The public isn't supposed to touch that Internet stuff."

"How long did you say it's been down?"

"Two days. There's only one guy to support all the library systems from Raleigh to the Outer Banks. I called him, but he can't get here until Saturday."

"Let me look at it. Maybe it's a loose cable. It would be silly to have him drive all the way down here from Raleigh. I just came from there, and it's a long way."

"I checked the cables and the electricity, honey. He talked me through the regular troubleshooting steps. And he gave me printed instructions, as well. I tried everything. He's going to have to fix it."

"Let me look at it," Cassie coaxed. "What could it hurt? It's not like I can make it worse if it's already broken."

The pink lady opened the top drawer of her desk.

"By the way, I'm Cassie Edwards." She extended her hand.

"Angie." The librarian shook her hand with delicate and powdery-soft fingers.

Cassie bit the insides of her cheeks to keep from grinning. The librarian had painted her fingernails deep rose to match her blouse.

Angie took a deep breath and planted her surprisingly small hands on the top of her desk to push herself up from her padded chair. She was heavier than Cassie anticipated, and she moved slowly as if her small feet had difficulty supporting her weight. Her bottom half was encased in loose, stretchy black pants, and she wore a pair of pink ballet slippers.

Despite her plumpness, she had a beautiful, open face with creamy skin under a short mop of silvery gray hair. When she caught Cassie's gaze, she laughed. "I may be slow, but I'll get there eventually. Gout. The doctor tells me it's from too much red meat and wine."

Her good spirits were infectious, and Cassie could use a severe case of good humor right about now. "Don't bother walking all the way to the back if it's painful. I can handle it."

"I'm already up and moving, honey. Besides, I'm supposed to walk more." She grimaced. "And as you might guess, that advice was given by a man who weighs about ninety pounds wet and would stay in bed for a week if he stubbed a toe."

"Men are such babies."

"Every blessed one of them," Angie agreed. "Here we are. Everything's in the closet here, right behind that computer. We only have four systems. Well, five if you count mine." She gave Cassie an apologetic glance. "We're a small library."

Cassie stood aside, waiting for her to unlock the tiny closet. When the librarian swung the wooden door open, Cassie caught the familiar scents of warm electronics, dust, and heated plastic.

Inside the closet was a gray utility rack with three shelves. A couple of thin metal boxes sat on the middle shelf at about chest-level. Several gray cables ran from the three boxes to a hole cut into the drywall. She studied the setup for a second, identifying a router/firewall combination unit, a small switch, and a modem. A red light flashed on the router unit.

When Cassie glanced over her shoulder, she saw Angie standing next to the door watching her. The librarian had a half-uneasy, half-hopeful glance. She looked like she expected Cassie to start chanting some weird voodoo spell that would magically fix the tiny network.

"Why don't you go sit down? I'll probably be a few minutes," Cassie said.

"Don't you need the administrator password?"

"Not right now. I'll ask if I need it." Feeling self-conscious, she waited for Angie to turn away.

"Did you say your name was Edwards?"

Reluctantly, Cassie murmured an agreement.

"Heard about what happened up at your place." Angie shook her head. "Must have been a terrible shock."

"Yes. Did you know Mr. Gracie?"

The librarian laughed. "Not the kind of man you'd find in a library."

"Oh? What was he like? I never met him . . ."

"Liked to flirt." Angie blushed. "Nice smile."

"Really? Guess he must have been popular. Did he have a girlfriend?"

"Sure." The librarian shrugged and turned away. "A man like that always has a girl. Well, here I am gossiping about that poor man . . . it's a shame, is all. I'm gonna go back to my seat. Let me know if you need anything."

Cassie watched the older woman lumber back to her desk, all the time wondering if Angie knew anything more about Nick Gracie that could help her uncle.

Alone, Cassie turned off all the devices in the closet and re-seated the cabling. After methodically turning on each device, she was rewarded with a shelf full of pretty green lights. When she went to the first computer set up for public use, it let her navigate to her personal e-mail account.

She sent a few more instructions and information about the virtual test system to several people at the company. Then she thought again about what she knew about Gracie. It wasn't much.

"You're back online," she said as returned to Angie's desk. "No big deal, after all."

"Thank you, honey. You were sure working hard."

"I'm just glad to find a computer I could use."

"So you're good with those things?"

Cassie laughed, leaning her hip against one of the half-bookcases in front of Angie's desk. "Sometimes. They're easier than people. If you make a mistake, computers don't hold it against you. And you can redo things as many times as you need to, to get it right."

"I never could get the hang of 'em. To own the truth, I never much cared for 'em." She smiled and waved pink-enameled fingertips through the air in a dismissive gesture. "I like people better."

"A lot of folks feel that way."

"Are you applying for that computer position at the college?" Angie asked.

"What position?"

"I don't know, exactly. Our computer guy mentioned it the other day. You ought to apply."

"What kind of job is it?"

"Fixing computers, I guess."

"Thanks—I'll keep it in mind," Cassie said.

"What exactly do you do, anyway, with those things?" Angie asked, writing down the address of the college website.

"I don't really do workstations, per se. I work on the stuff locked away in big computer centers. Server farms. E-mail servers, and stuff like that. You've been great, Angie. I really appreciate your help and this tip. The fact is, I'm in between jobs at the moment. Maybe I should take this as a sign that I should apply for this job."

"You're welcome, honey. You want a library card?"

"Sure. And I might stop in a little later. I'm on vacation and it's nice to have someone to talk to once in a while." Cassie hoped Angie didn't think she'd been condescending. Most people didn't understand what Cassie did, and when she tried to explain, it came across as patronizing or boring.

It really did make people's eyes glaze over.

And Cassie had seen enough of glazed, dead eyes for a while.

CHAPTER NINETEEN

"Did those lab results come in yet?" Jim asked. "The samples we sent to Raleigh for analysis."

Milt Singleton sat at his desk, frowning with concentration as he pecked at the computer keyboard with his thick index fingers. He glanced up and stared at Jim over the black plastic rims of his reading glasses. "Are you kidding? It's only been a couple of days."

"Have you checked?" Jim asked, stubbornly.

"Ask Mr. Bill." Singleton went back to his laborious typing, breathing noisily through his mouth.

"Where is Mr. Bill?"

"Dunno. Harassing the prisoner, I guess."

"Damn it." Jim turned and walked out, heading for the holding cells.

Halfway there, he met Bill loping toward him. Meyers wore a shit-eating grin, and his long face was flushed with pleasure. Jim folded his arms and waited for the other man to reach him.

"Has Raleigh sent any results yet? For any of the samples we sent?"

Meyers laughed. "Don't need 'em now."

"Didn't I tell you to leave Frank Edwards alone?"

"Maybe so. But I saved us all a lot of work." He waved a yellow legal pad under Jim's nose.

Jim grabbed it and glanced at the first page. It was a solid mass of Bill's too-tight, precise writing.

"He confessed. Frank Edwards confessed," Bill blurted.

Something's wrong, Jim thought. If Frank confessed, it was because he was confused or terrified. And if Bill threatened the old man to elicit a confession and enhance his reputation, Jim would have his badge. He didn't care who Bill knew.

He grabbed the front of Bill's shirt and shoved him against the wall. "I don't care how many confessions you get, we wait for the evidence to be processed. We don't even know where the crime scene is."

"I told you, Nick Gracie was killed in the greenhouse. Frank Edwards killed him when their drug deal went sour." He tried to grab the yellow pad back.

Jim pushed him away.

"I've saved this department thousands of dollars. And I solved the case. Judge Colesford is going to appreciate that."

"We're not cutting short this investigation."

"Oh, really? With the labs backed up and costs escalating?"

Jim thrust the pad back. "Type it up. I want it on my desk before you leave."

"No problem . . . sir."

Unbearably tired, Jim leaned against the wall. Finally, he walked into the outer office, where Milt Singleton was still sweating and leaning over his desk, his gaze flicking between the monitor and the keyboard.

"I want to see you in my office," Jim said to Singleton.

He swore under his breath as he followed Jim. Bill's bright gaze followed both of them. Jim shut the door to his office after Singleton took a seat in front of his desk.

"Shut the blinds," Jim said, pulling out his chair.

"What's going on? What did I do now?"

"Nothing. Sit down. It looks like Bill solved the damn case. He got Edwards to confess."

"Frank Edwards confessed? What did Bill do? Beat it out of him?"

Jim shrugged. Then he felt a twinge of concern. Maybe he ought to see Frank or have a doctor examine him for bruises. Maybe arrange to have a psychiatrist visit to determine if Frank was confused or mentally incompetent.

The confession didn't feel right. In fact, it stunk-on-ice. The condom in Gracie's shorts could not be explained by Bill's half-assed theory.

In an eerie restatement of his own thoughts, Singleton sat back in his chair as if relieved to take a break from the computer and said, "I don't believe it. And if the niece is smart, she'll get a good lawyer. It should be easy enough to build a case to support an incompetence plea."

"No to mention the evidence."

"Don't fit," Singleton said. "How'd he explain the condom?"

"He didn't."

"A man don't go walking around with a condom stuck in his shorts."

Jim grunted. "It'll be interesting to read his report. Assuming he feels I have the right to read it. He seems to think he works directly for old CC himself."

Huge sweat stains darkened Singleton's rumpled white shirt, and the hem was straggling out of his waistband, but despite his sweaty, untidy appearance, Jim preferred it to Bill's buttoned-down air of sleazy, butt-kissing ambition.

"While you were in the hallway, Jim, I checked Mr. Bill's in-box. We did get one report back, at least a partial, although not from Raleigh. From Bolander. I asked the doc to look at that glass Meyers collected. Don't know about the blood, yet, but the glass wasn't the same as the glass embedded in Nick Gracie's skull. Doc said the murder weapon was some kind of lead crystal—something heavy. That glass Mr. Bill picked up was plain old kitchen glass."

"Cassie Edwards had a bandage on her hand. She said she dropped something that cut her."

"There's your glass fragment. And blood."

"But Meyers is right about one thing. CC is going to want to cut this investigation short if it means reducing costs. Particularly lab costs. And I'm going to have a helluva time convincing him to give me a warrant to conduct a search elsewhere when we have a confession." Jim rubbed his face and sat back in his chair feeling pretty much the way Singleton's shirt looked.

After a heartbeat of silence, his deputy picked up a pencil dented with teeth marks. With surprising dexterity, he flicked it between his short, fat fingers, flipping it from one knuckle to the next.

"So are you thinkin' what I'm thinkin'? 'Cause I'd sure like a nice, long look at a few places around here where Gracie hung around."

"Like Nick Gracie's apartment for starters."

"And maybe Howie-the-butt's fancy domicile. It's Gracie's workplace, after all."

"Gracie's is easy." Jim shook his head. "But the Butler residence? I don't know about that. Howie plays golf with CC."

"Maybe, but he was Gracie's employer. And I know we all believe good ole Howie wouldn't hurt a fly if it shit on him." Milt stared at him with wide, guileless eyes. "But we both know that things happen in the best of homes. Rapists and killers break in all the time. Howie-the-butt might not know a thing about what might have happened in his own home. But we'd be downright derelict in our duties if we didn't check to see if that Edwards maniac killed Gracie elsewhere. Like at Gracie's workplace, the Butler residence."

"I can see if CC will go for that."

"Or see if old Howie will let you look around some without a warrant. There's something up there. I can smell it."

"Learned that from your Bluetick Coonhounds, did you?" Jim laughed. "You're right about one thing, though. It's about time—past time, in fact—to go over to Gracie's apartment. That condom? It's as plain as Mr. Bill's ambitions that Gracie was enjoying himself when he unexpectedly shoved his head in the path of an unknown glass object. And what the hell happened to his clothes? Too many loose ends for me."

Singleton rose to his feet, the battered chair rolling backward. It hit the wall, creating another thin crack like a stray bolt of lightning in the rain-blue wall. As Jim watched, a flake of paint fall off and settled on the summit of a small mountain of drywall dust and paint chips built up from previous encounters between the chair and the wall.

If Jim cared, he would have screwed a plate of Plexiglas to the wall or taken the wheels off the chair. He glanced past Milt, through the office window. Bill's narrow, perfectly combed pinhead was bent forward as he studied his computer's monitor and worked on his report.

Although Jim knew he ought to be pleased to see his deputy working so assiduously, it only irritated him further. Bill Meyers was so smug, so sure, such an asshole.

"Give me a minute, Milt." Jim eased back around his desk as his deputy left and picked up the phone. The number for the Raleigh lab was written on the edge of his blotter. He dialed and then turned to open the blinds to the window behind his desk. He stared out at the parking lot behind the building. His conservative, ocean-blue Dodge truck was parked in the closest space. Sunshine and heated air from the surface of the dark pavement shimmered over the smooth curve of the fender, sparkling as if it really was an ocean wave.

Once upon a time, he was going to be a writer and buy a boat. Instead, he was stuck here in Peyton. He was only a few miles from the North Carolina coast, but it felt more like a thousand.

And now he had a murder investigation involving an old man and the first woman he'd found attractive in a long time. More than attractive. He sighed. Cassie was intelligent, too, when she wasn't being a nitwit about her uncle.

She was definitely the exception, rather than the rule, around Peyton. It hadn't taken him long after returning home to discover how few dateable people lived here. He'd gone out with three women he'd known in high school. Their conversations were limited to gossip about other women in Peyton and TV shows. He soon realized he'd moved on after high school and they had not.

The phone at the other end rang several times.

"Hey!" a cheerful voice answered.

"Shantal?"

"Yep. Is that you, Jimmie-boy?"

"Yeah. I've got a favor to ask."

"Sure, honey. Anything you want."

"We sent up some evidence from a murder investigation. I've got to get those results ASAP."

"You and every other cop in North Carolina. You think this is one of them CSI shows on TV? You think we've got an unlimited budget with all them fancy electronic gadgets that can spit out the answers to all your questions in five seconds?"

"No. I sure don't think any of that. I wouldn't ask if it wasn't important. You've got a full plate. We all do. But if I don't get those results soon, I don't think we're going to get them at all. We've got a delicate situation. And time is not on our side."

Shantal's deep, throaty laugh vibrated through the phone. "CC cuttin' the budget on you again, honey?"

"Something like that. I'd really appreciate it if you'd get those results."

"Now wouldn't you appreciate it even more if I told you I already had some of those urgent results?"

"You already have them?" The air around his truck rippled. For one moment, he could have sworn he smelled fresh, salt air.

"Sure, honey. Thought it might be a bit more interesting than the usual."

"What?"

Another laugh. He waited impatiently for her to catch her breath. He could imagine the grin on her luscious, wide mouth. They had met once. She was a beautiful woman with smooth dark skin and deep black eyes. Unfortunately, she was also married with five children.

"Your friend with the condom was a busy man," she said. "As in more than one woman. There was DNA from two women on that lovin' glove."

"Two women?" *Oh, Jesus, don't let one of them be Cassie.*

"I'll write up the reports and send 'em out to you later today."

"Can you email a second copy to my private account? I'd like to read them, even if I'm not in the office."

"Well, sure."

"About the glass—"

"Not there yet, honey. But I can tell you it's not the same as that bit pulled out of that man's brain."

"The blood—"

"Honey, clean out those ears. I haven't gotten to the blood yet. But I'll get you your analysis by the end of the week despite old CC and his budget cuts. And then you'll owe me. Right, honey?"

"Sure." Jim smiled, wondering what he could possibly do for her. "As long as it's not illegal. Or immoral."

"Now honey, you know if I needed anything along those lines, I'd only have to ask your little boy, Bill Meyers. He'd have no problem with either of those things."

Jim body went rigid. "Have you've heard something? About Meyers?"

He swung around to glance out the inner office windows. All he could see was the round, mottled crown of Singleton's head. Meyers was not at his desk.

Across the hallway was another small office, next to the interview room. The door to that room was shut and the blinds were down. Jim's jaw tightened. Obviously, Meyers had gone into the other room to ensure privacy while he made calls to Judge Colesford and pretended not to gloat as he explained how he'd convinced Frank to confess. Meyers had to make sure all the politicos knew that he'd solved the Gracie murder, arrested the killer, and extracted a confession in record time, saving the taxpayers untold sums of money.

Jim was sure that Meyers had it all wrong.

Dead wrong.

Shantal's voice caught his attention. "All I've heard is what everyone else has heard. That boy is dead set on being governor some day. And he's sleazy enough to make it. You're lucky you've got that Singleton boy to watch your back. I sure wouldn't let Mr. Meyers stand behind me. No way."

"I appreciate that, thanks. Send me whatever you get."

"You're gonna have to get me some samples to compare against those females. Doesn't do much good to know your corpse was an active man if you don't know who he was playing with."

"He had a girlfriend."

"He had two girlfriends."

"I'll get a few samples. Somehow."

"Send old Milt out. The ladies can relax around a man like that. He ain't what you'd call dangerous to your well-being. And watch your back."

Jim studied his deputy through the window. For God's sake,

the guy was hunched over his desk, painfully typing with two thick fingers. And although he couldn't see it, he'd bet Singleton's tongue was sticking out, clenched between his crooked teeth in concentrated effort. The man was an old jock gone to sweaty, balding seed and Jim was damned if he could see why any woman would talk to him, much less relax.

"Milt," Jim said, leaving his cramped office. "You ready to go?"

"Sure." Singleton lumbered to his feet, tucking his shirttail into the waistband of his wrinkled khaki slacks.

Jim watched him collect his badge and weapon, noting the heavy, bear-like shoulders and thick neck. He was so wide he gave the impression of being excessively overweight, but there was more muscle than fat on his mammoth frame, and he was built like a heavy, squared-off Hummer.

If Singleton guarded his back, there was no way anyone was going to find an opening large enough to slip even the thinnest knife between Jim's ribs.

"Gracie's place first. Then I'd like a try at the Butler residence. And we need to collect DNA from everyone. If they let us. I wish to God Frank had kept his mouth shut a few days longer so we could have gotten a couple of search warrants. It would have made our jobs a helluva lot easier."

Singleton chuckled. "Did you talk to Shantal?"

Jim gave him a sharp glance as they climbed into the beige Crown Victoria emblazoned with the sheriff's seal. The car canted ominously toward the passenger side as Milt settled into his seat.

"Did you already talk to her, too?" Jim asked.

"Yeah."

"You don't agree with Meyers, then?"

"You young boys may think I've got my head up my ass, but even these old eyes can see that Frank is not guilty of murder. If

179

he's guilty of anything, it's stupidity in growing that damn weed. And in confessing to something he ain't done, of course. Bill must have threatened him."

"Maybe."

"Well, Meyers has never seemed very threatening to me."

"Yeah, but Frank Edwards is an old man."

"Not old enough to be scared of that asshole." Singleton turned his cannonball head to glance out the window. "Frank would do anything for his family. I think Mr. Bill might have said that he'd arrest Cassie for being an accessory if Frank didn't confess. Frank has never trusted the government—no one in that family does. He'd do anything to make sure Cassie isn't involved in any way."

"I have to agree with that," Jim said, remembering Cassie's outburst in the kitchen. The entire family disliked the police and authority of any kind.

Like Thomas Jefferson, the Edwards family clearly believed the best government was the government that governed the least. Ironically, Jim Fletcher believed the same thing.

Who would have thought he'd end up as a heavy-handed sheriff, watching over a town full of sheep?

And one hungry, man-eating tiger that no one could trap.

CHAPTER TWENTY

The distant tinkle of the doorbell chimes woke Cassie up. She glanced around the living room groggily. "Let the Sunshine in" played in the background, sounding mellow despite the repetition and impatience of whoever stood at the door, leaning on the doorbell.

She stumbled to her feet and yawned a few times. The wooden floor creaked, and she noticed a gray puffball of dust drift along the baseboard as she walked. The house needed cleaning and care. No one had been looking after it properly, or looking after Uncle Frank, for that matter.

Guilt burned her much-abused belly. She should never have gone away to Raleigh and left her aging uncle and aunt alone.

Pushing her heavy hair away from her face, she pulled open the door and stepped back in surprise. "Sheriff! What are you doing here?"

"I'd like to talk to you." Jim moved closer toward the door, filling it. His wide shoulders seemed to block out the sun, and his hard, gray eyes glinted despite the shadow cast over his face by his hat.

"I don't have anything more to say," she said in a tired voice.

Despite her nap, her body felt heavy with nervous exhaustion. She wanted to go back to sleep and forget about everything for a few hours. But her mind kept turning over the problems, searching for solutions, unable to rest until she found the answer.

"May I come in?" He took off his hat and strode through the

door before she could answer.

"Why not? My house is your house."

He walked into the living room as if he owned the place, throwing down his hat on the small table in front of the sofa. It landed on a stack of horticultural journals. The magazines spilled over the slick wooden surface and Cassie jerked forward to catch a magazine before it fell onto the floor.

"Sorry." He plucked the magazine out of her hand and collected up the rest of the glossy journals. He stacked them and aligned them at one end of the table before he gently placed his hat on top of the pile.

"No problem," she replied. She remained standing, studying his face. Other than a slight frown creasing the skin between his brows, she couldn't read his expression.

"Has something happened to my uncle?" she asked, his silence making her fear the worst. Her gentle uncle had been beaten, perhaps killed, by some other criminal in jail. She knew it. Her hands clenched. She thrust them into the pockets of her jeans, trying to control her imagination and avoid complete, undignified panic.

"Not exactly," he said in a slow voice. "I'm trying to find the truth."

"You know he didn't do it. You intimidated him, beat him, and—"

"I did not beat him. No one did." He held up his hand when she stepped forward, her body quivering with intensity. "I was wondering if he might have confessed to protect someone else. He may have thought you'd be implicated—"

"I wasn't even here! How could he possibly think I'd be involved unless you suggested it to coerce a confession out of him? How *dare* you do such a thing?" Her heart fluttered while her body flushed cold and hot with panicked shock.

Then the wrenching sensation of falling toward unconsciousness overwhelmed her. She pressed her cold fingers against her burning eyes and tried to concentrate.

"Cassie?" Jim grabbed her arm and gave her a little shake.

She stared into his gray eyes, her mind still whirring uncontrollably like the hard drive in a computer starting up. Slowly, her mind found the boot sector and began to process thoughts again. And she remembered his gentle, wry humor when she knew him as Anne's fascinating older brother.

The skinny guy who wanted to be a writer. He wasn't all bad, was he?

"He didn't do it, and I'll prove it," she said.

His eyes hardened, glowing with dark light. "You're not going to prove anything. I am. I told you, I think he's protecting someone. Rightly or wrongly, that someone might be you."

"No way. He knows I don't need protection. I wasn't even here."

"Your aunt—"

"What about her? She wasn't here, either. Even you should be able to understand that." Suddenly, she realized she didn't know exactly when her aunt had left.

The computer in Cassie's brain clicked and whirred, finally locating all the missing sectors of information. And it assembled a sad and frighteningly cohesive explanation.

She knew why her uncle planted himself near the corpse and pretended to be stoned enough to share a hit of marijuana with a dead guy. And she could explain why her uncle decided to confess to something he obviously didn't, and couldn't, do.

It was all guesswork. Cassie still needed to talk to him to be sure, assuming he would tell her the truth. But Cassie suspected her aunt had left the same day Nick Gracie had been murdered. And knowing Sylvia, she'd probably been upset and angry with Frank for getting involved with drugs again.

She may have told Frank that she was going to speak to

Gracie before she left. It was the kind of confrontational, no-nonsense thing she would do. She'd want to tidy up loose ends and try to help Frank, even if she was planning to leave him anyway.

Because just like Cassie, Sylvia had a hard time giving up on a problem, even a problem she no longer owned.

If true, Frank must have guessed what happened when Sylvia confronted Gracie. Sylvia probably informed Gracie that Frank was not going to grow any more marijuana to sell. And insisted that Gracie stop using Frank, or she would turn them all in to the police.

Then Sylvia left Peyton.

Frank found Gracie's body in the stream, and he came to the inevitable conclusion that Sylvia's meeting with Gracie could have ended in murder.

A shiver of horror went through Cassie at a new thought. Frank may have followed his wife. He may have witnessed the events spiraling out of control, or seen something terrible . . . So he devised a way to prove to Sylvia that he still loved her by shifting any suspicion to himself.

Since he mistrusted the police, he manipulated them. He allowed them to find whatever clues they could and made sure they remembered his bizarre behavior and picked him as a likely suspect. Then, and only then, did he confess.

He had outsmarted all of them in order to divert suspicion away from his wife.

"Cassie," Jim said, interrupting the frightening trend of her thoughts.

"Give me a minute." She rubbed her forehead, aware of an ache behind the bridge of her nose. Her explanation tumbled around in her mouth, but she couldn't bring herself to say anything. She couldn't involve her aunt without talking to her uncle, first.

There was no proof. If she said anything now, it would be supposition.

She needed time to think.

Staring up at Jim, she realized something else. Her uncle might have come to the wrong conclusion, unless he actually witnessed the murder.

Cassie knew her aunt had a temper. And from what Frank had said, Sylvia was at the end of her rope. But there was at least one problem with the scenario. Aunt Sylvia always took honesty to an uncomfortable level.

When Cassie was in school, she quickly learned not to admit anything to her aunt, no matter how much guilt gnawed at her. Because once Sylvia found out, she would take Cassie by the hand and march her over to the relevant authority figure. Then she would ensure Cassie confessed whatever she had done in all its glorious detail. No hiding. No half-truths. Simply the horrible, embarrassing truth.

If Sylvia had murdered anyone, she would have proceeded to the sheriff's office and confessed before they had to come looking for her.

Now, Cassie would rather face a complete computer crash with no backup than give the police any more information they might use against the Edwards family. Even if Jim Fletcher seemed moderately sympathetic and probably hadn't beaten any prisoners. Lately.

"I don't know what to say," she said slowly. "I'm really confused."

Jim stood near her, too near. "I'm sorry." His voice was low, intimate.

His arm wrapped around her shoulders. She leaned against his chest, soaking up his warmth. She rested her forehead briefly against his neck and closed her eyes, wishing she could stay there and forget everything for a few hours.

When she glanced up and found his eyes focused intently on her face, something deep within her stirred, responding to his nearness.

"What happened to you?" she asked, her voice soft. "You were going to be a writer. I had such a crush on you."

He smiled lazily. "I had to eat."

"But why a sheriff? Why law enforcement?"

"Double-major. English and law enforcement. I wanted to write crime novels."

She grew unbearably aware of the warmth of his hand against her neck, the deep thrumming tone of his voice, and the warm scent of his skin subtly intertwined with a slightly spicy, clean fragrance of soap.

She didn't pull away, didn't want to move. A strange passivity clouded her thoughts as she leaned against him, her heart thudding, listening to him, waiting.

His words drifted off. The silence deepened.

She whispered, "Why aren't you a writer?"

"I graduated. Got a job as a deputy while I wrote." He stroked her hair. "They needed someone, and I was qualified. And then they needed a sheriff."

"And you were qualified. So you gave up writing?"

"No. I've written a book, even submitted it, but I have to earn a living." His hand shifted, tilting her face up toward his.

She waited, his mouth inches from hers. His eyes flared with brilliance.

"Okay," she said, barely breathing. "You wanted to write crime novels and being a sheriff gives you experience. But you're still doing it. Why continue?"

He pulled back, his eyes focusing on something in the distance. "And leave Bill Meyers in charge?"

"Isn't there someone else?"

"No. My deputy, Milt Singleton, wants a life. He's not

186

interested in dealing with budgets and politicians."

"You mean he's not thrilled with the idea of idiots trying to knock him down, so they can walk over his lifeless body to grab all the money and cushy political positions?"

His wide mouth twisted into the self-deprecating, endearing smile she remembered. "Right."

"So you're stuck?"

"I wouldn't say that. It's not really that bad."

"But what about writing books?"

"I write in my free time, like everyone else. And I try not to abuse my power. Or authority."

Easy for him to say. His uniform still made her feel vaguely threatened and guilty. She didn't think she'd ever get used to it, despite her perverse and inexplicable attraction to him. Perhaps it was a leftover from her old, high school crush, but she wanted him around. She looked forward to seeing him, or at least she did when he helped her and forgot to be overbearing and ultra-official.

She forced a smile. "Maybe. But are you sure my uncle didn't feel under duress?"

"I doubt it. To be honest, it's hard to know what your uncle felt. I have a question for you, and please don't get all defensive. Would you say he was competent?"

She froze, her heart pounding. "Of course he's competent."

His grip tightened. "Listen to me. We both know he uses drugs."

"A little marijuana. He has glaucoma. It's medicinal." She stopped speaking when he gave her a gentle shake.

"He's getting older, Cassie. And the marijuana has to be affecting him. Maybe I could convince Judge Colesford that Frank confessed because he's mentally incompetent."

"You can't! It would ruin him. And my aunt. They're scientists, and my aunt is still working, still publishing. If Uncle

187

Frank is declared incompetent, it will ruin both of them professionally. Everything they've done recently will be reviewed with an eye toward discrediting them."

"Your aunt isn't here. She's left him, hasn't she?"

Afraid of saying too much, Cassie tried to remember all of their previous conversations. She was nearly positive she had told him Sylvia had gone on vacation alone.

If Jim figured out exactly when Sylvia left, and thought about Frank sitting in a folding chair down at the creek next to a corpse, he might come to the same conclusion she had. Would Sylvia then be incarcerated, trading places with Frank?

One thing was terribly clear. Cassie had to find another suspect for the sheriff to investigate.

She took a deep breath. "I called Aunt Sylvia and tried to convince her to come back. She left long before the murder happened."

"If you don't give us a reason to reject Frank's confession, the investigation will be over."

"Confession be damned! I'll get a good lawyer. You *know* he's innocent, and there must be some evidence that can prove it."

"Cassie, this is a small town. If we have a reasonable suspect and he confesses, we pretty much have to conclude the investigation."

"There's no credible evidence that he did anything."

"There was glass and blood in your kitchen, near the door to the greenhouse."

"My blood! I dropped a glass and cut my hand. Did you test it yet?"

"We haven't received all the results back, but it doesn't really matter. Frank confessed."

"But you get 'fake' confessions all the time. And you saw him at the stream. Something wasn't right with him." She shifted her weight, rocking from one foot to the other.

"If I were you, I'd get a psychiatrist. It wouldn't hurt to raise the issue of his competence."

"His work—"

"Which is worse? Your uncle in jail, or your uncle declared incompetent?"

"Neither is going to happen. I'm going to get him out of jail. And you're going to continue the investigation. You'll find he didn't do it. I'm sure of it."

"I'll do what I can. I may not be as stubborn as you are, Cassie, but I'm not going to let this go. I haven't finished collecting evidence."

Grateful for even that small concession, she leaned forward, grabbed the front of his shirt, and kissed him.

The touch of his warm mouth and scent of his skin sent a shiver of pleasure through her body.

His grip on her neck tightened. Slowly, inevitably, he drew her closer again, holding her against the length of his body.

He kissed her with deep thoroughness, his lips forcing hers open, the taste of him achingly, unbearably right. She took a shuddering breath, almost desperate to soak in the heat of his body, the strength in his arms, and the rush of complex sensations.

He felt like everything she had ever wanted.

Abruptly, he released her. Face flushed, he glanced briefly at the windows.

Her gaze followed his. The drapes were open. Anyone who walked by would see them.

"I'm sorry," she said, studying the empty lawn. "I didn't think."

"Neither one of us can afford that particular excuse. We've both got to think."

"No one saw us."

"No. Not this time." He stepped further away, his hands flexing. "I can't protect your uncle if this investigation is compromised. I'm sorry, Cassie."

"It was my fault."

His lopsided grin almost broke her heart. "I kissed you."

"Yes. It won't happen again. I promise."

"No, it won't. I've got to get going. In the meantime, get a lawyer. If your uncle's confession is false, I'll leave it up to you to decide how far you want to go to prove that."

"Police brutality?" she asked hopefully, pulling down on the hem of her T-shirt.

"Hard to prove, but you can try."

"What about you, if I do?"

He shoved his hat on his head and strode toward the door. As he opened it, he glanced over his shoulder at her. "I'm a big boy. If you want to go that route, do it."

CHAPTER TWENTY-ONE

After leaving Cassie, Jim picked up Milt at Peyton Place, and drove to the Butler residence.

"Did you reach the Butlers?" Jim asked.

Milt nodded. "Talked to Howie-the-butt himself. Said he'd leave us the spare key to Gracie's place under the welcome mat."

"Original."

"Yeah. That's Howie. Original."

The drive from town was brief and Jim parked near the garage. He stared at the building before getting out. Nick Gracie's quarters were in the loft on the second floor. A covered, double-decker walkway ran from the garage to the main house. The walkway on the ground level was a confection of white-painted pillars of wood, complete with elaborate curlicues and chubby little angels peeking out from around the column plinths. A long row of grayish-white plants grew in thick mounds along the walkway. Jim studied them for a moment, struggling to identify them.

"Sage," he said, finally. He had the faint sense that Cassie might not view him so badly if he could at least identify one plant, other than grass.

Milt coughed and wheezed as he climbed out of the car. Standing with a meaty forearm propped up on the door frame, he said, "Culinary sage. Grow some for stuffing." When he caught Jim's glance, he patted his stomach. "Make my own

191

seasonings. Just don't like that dried up shit-in-a-box."

Milt Singleton, the redneck gourmand and horticulturalist. Jim shook his head, feigning disbelief.

"You ready?" Milt asked, moving with a rolling gait toward the garage.

The building had three bays for cars, but all the metal doors were down. Jim didn't want to go to the house yet. He wanted to look around Gracie's place without any distractions.

"Howie wouldn't leave the key under his own mat. There's got to be a separate entrance. Gracie wouldn't have gone through the house all the time." Jim started walking toward the far end of the building.

Long, curving strips of ornamental plantings lined the sidewalk and driveway. More of the silvery sage was interspersed with another dark green plant that had thick, needle-like leaves that reminded him of very short pine needles. He reached down and grabbed one. The air was immediately filled with a fragrant herbal scent.

"Rosemary," Milt said. "Someone here likes their herbs. Rosemary, sage, and a few dill over there." He pointed to a feathery-looking plant near the corner of the garage.

"Isn't that a little strange?"

"I guess. But they're hardy plants, except for the dill. It's a little early to be planting that, but I guess we won't see another frost this late in the year."

The information seemed trivial but it helped Jim build up a picture of the Butlers. It was strange what could be important later. Or irrelevant.

At this point, he had no idea what to include and what to exclude. So he mentally collected everything and let it work its way through his subconscious like water trickling through ground coffee.

What came out might be a decent brew, or one lousy cup.

He glanced around again, trying to get a feel for the place. The silvery leaves of the sage, in contrast to the darker, prickly green of the rosemary, were cool and strangely soothing. When he brushed past them, the plants gave off a rich, mouth-watering fragrance that reminded him of Thanksgiving.

His respect for Mrs. Butler went up a notch. He hadn't expected her to pick, or allow, such an understated and elegant approach to gardening. He would have expected fussy roses or some other gaudy, flowering plant.

As he and Milt walked around the side of the garage, they discovered a wooden stairway that led up to a narrow deck and door on the second floor. The stairway was painted white, but it was strictly utilitarian. No cute, fat angels peered around the supports and nothing but fine, gray crush-and-run gravel was strewn around the base for a sidewalk.

Jim stared up the stairway with a hand on the railing. He felt it move as Milt edged around him and set a heavy foot on the first step.

"Damn, I hate stairs." Milt wheezed, climbing up the steep stairs.

Jim followed. The two men hesitated on the small deck at the top of the stairs, barely having enough room to turn around. Finally, Milt had to step down again a couple of steps to let Jim lift the welcome mat. Sure enough, there was a brass key.

They stared at the solid, white-painted door for a minute before Jim grabbed the door knob. It felt loose in his hand, but didn't turn. He inserted the key and jiggled it for a minute before the lock finally gave way.

Jim pushed the door open and blocked the entrance for a few seconds as he methodically glanced around.

The outer door opened into a kitchen area. Bright, clear sunlight filled the open room, glittering off the chrome components of the sink and refrigerator.

The walls were painted a rich, buttery yellow. White plastic, mock-bamboo shades covered the upper half of the windows. Pale maple cupboards lined the walls, contributing to the overwhelming sense of light and airiness that filled the room. Even the work surfaces, made out of oak butcher-block, glowed. Most of the appliances were understated and very expensive, brushed steel.

He wondered if it spoke more about Mrs. Butler's taste than Nick Gracie's. Jim had expected black leather, glass, and mirrors. Particularly in view of Shantal's report.

"Check to see if he had any video cameras. Or videos," Jim said, moving out of the doorway to let Milt enter.

Once inside, Jim found it wasn't as neat as he'd first thought. The steel sink held an empty pan and a few dirty plates. An old shirt hung over the back of a kitchen chair. Jim nudged the aluminum saucepan in the sink, but there was nothing left in it except a half-inch of scummy water.

A few egg shells were caught on the edge of the drain. Jim opened the dishwasher and discovered it full of clean dishes of the white, generic, truck-stop dinnerware variety.

It looked as though Gracie had eaten breakfast at home the last day of his life. Which confirmed the coroner's theory that he'd died sometime after noon, but probably before five P.M.

After—or during—a little afternoon delight.

Gracie had had an overnight guest because there were two plates. And beneath them was a plastic microwave pan for making bacon. A thick layer of grease coated it, retaining the rich, salty scent of bacon only slightly ruined by a faint musty odor of the mold beginning to grow in the damp, warm environment.

"No sign of blood in here," Milt called from another room.

Jim glanced around, taking in the rest of the apartment. The kitchen flowed into a tiny dining room that contained a small, round butcher-block table and two light oak chairs. The table was bare.

The living room confirmed some of Jim's preconceived notions about the victim. A large black sofa was positioned in front of a mammoth fifty-inch television. A chrome-and-glass cabinet stood next to the TV and held a variety of electronic equipment. The cables from the various components were neatly tie-wrapped with white plastic strips.

As he turned around, he noted a laptop sitting on one of the low glass tables flanking the sofa. He picked it up and traced the electrical cord to the outlet. He unplugged it and coiled the cord.

"He's got a computer," Jim called.

Milt walked out of the bedroom carrying a stuffed pillow case.

When Jim saw him, he felt his face darken with a flush of irritation. Milt had stripped the bed before Jim could see the room. He felt precisely the same aggravation he had when he realized Cassie had smudged the holes left by her uncle's chair.

Why does everyone screw around with my evidence?

If people messed with the scene, Jim found it nearly impossible to build a clear picture of the events leading up to the murder.

It was almost as if everyone was dead set on preventing him from finding the real killer.

CHAPTER TWENTY-TWO

"You should have left the bed alone," Jim said, aiming at lightness. He brushed past Milt and stared into the bedroom.

A king-sized bed dominated the room, stripped down to its pale blue mattress. Apparently, Gracie had liked his comfort. The bed had a thick, memory-foam pad over the extra deep, high-end mattress. Long, king-sized pillows were thrown carelessly against the oak headboard.

The guy had been seriously in love with blond oak.

"Was the bed made?" Jim asked.

"Are you kidding?" Milt held up the stuffed pillow case. "That's why I stripped it. He hadn't been sleeping alone the last night of his life, I can tell you that much."

Jim walked over to the closet and opened it. Two suits hung on the left side, one charcoal gray and the other black with a pale gray pinstripe. Next to the suits were several dark-colored shirts. A series of silk ties in shades of pearl gray to slate were draped over a special hanger.

Nothing that anyone would wear around Peyton. The small town still favored white shirts and blue ties for church and T-shirts the rest of the time.

Built-in shelves lined the right side of the closet. Several pairs of jeans had been badly folded and shoved onto the lower shelves. T-shirts in a variety of colors filled the top compartments, although black still predominated. Gracie obviously preferred the intimidating appearance of a tough drug dealer.

There were no tailor-made shirts like the one they'd found on Gracie's body.

Turning away from the closet, Jim noticed the mirror. It filled the wall above the bed. Pretty much as he expected, considering what he knew of Gracie.

Across the room, a long, low chest of drawers stood against the wall. Jim went through the drawers. No boxers.

"Get in here, Singleton."

Milt wandered as far as the door.

"I don't think the clothes Gracie had on when we found him were his. What about you?"

"You just figuring that out?" Milt started to lean against the door frame. At the last minute, he straightened and took a long look at the flimsy wooden frame before he allowed his shoulder to rest against it.

Jim nearly smiled. Milt had screwed up stripping the bed before Jim saw it. Now, he was nervous about picking up or depositing trace evidence.

As if their budget could afford to collect and analyze any additional findings.

What was important now was the house and surroundings, all the places where Nick Gracie had spent the final hours of his life, before he received the blow to the back of his head.

"I've seen Nick Gracie a few times around town," Milt said. "Black tees and jeans, mostly. And he wasn't the kind of boy to wear those damn loose boxers we found him in. Did you find any in his chest of drawers?"

"No. So it seems unlikely he died here. Whoever re-clothed him had to make do with whatever was at hand. Whoever spent the night with him—"

"Robyn Adams."

"Where'd you hear that?"

Milt smiled and shrugged.

"Check her out when we get back. And get a sample of her DNA. Let's see if we can get it to Shantal before they close that door on us. I want to know who was with Nick before, or when, he died. He must have been killed while having sex, or the killer wouldn't have left a used condom in Nick's shorts."

"If he wasn't killed here—"

"Then he died somewhere else. Presumably a place with a bed. And I doubt he was murdered at Frank's. He was dumped at the stream to confuse us." Jim strode through the apartment, escaped outside, and pulled the door shut behind Milt.

"And point toward Frank Edwards."

Jim glanced around at the bottom of the stairs. "Throw those sheets in an evidence bag and lock them in the car. We need to pay another visit to the Butlers."

Milt lumbered toward the cruiser while Jim approached the colonial splendor of the main house. There was no sign of anyone outside. All the blinds were down to block the brilliant sunshine and spring heat. He waited on the stoop until Milt rejoined him. Then he rang the doorbell.

No one even twitched the blinds. But a quality in the hushed, breathless stillness alerted Jim to the presence of life in the cool shadows of the house.

He leaned against the bell until the door swung open.

Mrs. Butler swayed in the soft gloom. She wore a brief pair of shorts and a thin, pink T-shirt with no bra.

Jim glanced at Milt, then said, "Mrs. Butler, may we come in?"

Her eyes widened. "Certainly."

She drifted back a step, glanced toward the living room, then moved away, clearly not intoxicated enough to invite them into her pristine white room.

"Would you care to join me in the dining room? Howie isn't here," she added belatedly.

"We were hoping to take a look around."

"A look around?" Her wide eyes had a slack look of incom-prehension.

"We don't want to bother you, ma'am," Jim said.

Milt stepped around him and gestured toward the dining room. "I'll tell you what, Ms. Butler. Why don't I keep you company while the sheriff looks around?"

"Do you mean you want to look at the carriage house?" She waved vaguely toward the kitchen. "There's a walkway through there. Search wherever you want."

"Thank you," Jim replied. Adopting the casual tone of friends dropping by for a visit, he said, "I won't be long. Why don't you relax and talk to Milt?"

A drop of perspiration beaded at the hairline of her temple. She swiped at it with the back of her wrist before waving him off.

Milt touched her elbow. She jerked her arm away. Her face briefly twisted into a snarl, then she forced a smile. "Call if you need anything, Sheriff."

With elaborate docility, she let Milt lead her toward the din-ing room. He stopped by the oval table and watched as she moved to the small liquor cabinet next to the doorway.

Jim eased back toward the sitting room, opposite the sterile, monochromatic living room.

After a quick survey of the first floor, he went up the main staircase. At the first floor landing, he hesitated, glancing right and then left. The corridor was empty, stretching out in both directions.

All the guest bedrooms on this floor were clean, but he noticed a slightly desolate air as if they were rarely used. Bowls of potpourri graced identical cherry dressers. The dried flowers and leaves were old and had long ago lost most of their fragrance. When Jim pushed the contents of one bowl around, the disturbance raised the faint odor of cinnamon unpleasantly tainted with dry dust. Sneezing, he left the guest rooms with a determined stride, heading for the master bedroom.

To his surprise, the door was wide open. He paused in the doorway and studied the bed, his gaze running over the coverlet. Expensive but somehow cold. He thought of his own messy rooms filled with magazines, books, and the miscellany of life.

This room reflected nothing but good taste and an efficient maid service. A heavy, crystal lamp rested on the nightstand closest to the door. However, it was the other nightstand that interested him. Given the formality of the room, it should have been graced with an identical crystal lamp.

If Howie was chivalrous enough to take the more vulnerable position nearest to the door, then Mrs. Butler must have recently had an accident with her lamp.

The light on the nightstand farthest away from the door was too tall and appeared seriously out of place. It belonged in a living room, not on a nightstand. The base was made out of the same heavy lead crystal as the other lamp, and both were faceted with static, geometrical snowflakes that glittered in the sunshine from the window, but the taller lamp rested on a pewter collar and had a pale silvery-gray silk shade that was twice the size of the other lamp in its entirety.

It struck him that the light with the pewter base might have been brought up from the white living room that no one used as a hasty replacement for the lamp matching the one on the other nightstand.

However, he had no way to prove it.

But the mismatched lamp pointed to this room as the site of recent, energetic energy. Murder?

Jim unhooked the flashlight from his belt. He turned it on and slowly guided the beam over the carpet around and under the bed. The beam revealed tracks in the thick carpet from a recent vacuuming.

He ran the light over the carpet again, focusing on the far side of the bed closest to the windows, hoping the vacuum had missed something.

And it had. Something sparkled amidst the thick, pale blue woolen strands of the carpet.

Fingers stiff with anticipation, he reached under the edge of the bed and was disappointed to find the glitter came from the gold back of a pierced earring.

Unwilling to give up, he focused the flashlight toward the headboard. There! Nestled in the thick carpet was a shard of glass. Using his handkerchief, he plucked the glass from its woolen nest and swung his light back over the floor. Another, larger shard lay almost directly under the center of the bed.

The two pieces of glass appeared to be heavy crystal, both large enough to retain a small portion of the square-cut pattern adorning the base of the perfect crystal lamp.

There was no doubt that the pieces he held were once part of a lamp identical to the one resting on the opposite nightstand.

Kneeling on the bed, he began a closer examination of the headboard. It appeared clean and undamaged until he identified a slight variation in the color. The fabric looked bleached. And while chlorine bleach effectively eliminated biological trace evidence, it left its own marks behind.

Would it be enough to get CC to authorize a search warrant for his pal's home? And even if the entire team searched the Butler residence, what more would they find? Days had passed; house cleaning and daily living had shifted, disturbed, and probably eliminated a great deal.

Nonetheless, Jim firmly believed he had found the murder scene.

Yanking open a closet door, he was nearly drowned in an avalanche of female clothing. The large, walk-in closet was so full of dresses, shirts, handbags, and shoes that he couldn't even tell how many shelves lined the back wall. He shoved the clothes back inside and shut the door quickly before they could fall back out again.

He eyed Mr. Butler's closet, walked inside, and then checked the shelves built into the rear wall. They contained a variety of very expensive shirts without labels. He picked up a shirt and examined the heavy cotton material and double-stitched seams. It was exactly like the shirt on the dead body. Closing the closet door, Jim opened drawers until he found Mr. Butler's underwear. Large white boxers.

The clothes weren't conclusive. If he wanted evidence that would stand up in court, he'd have to get a warrant. Hopefully, the judge would give him one.

Looking around, Jim was fairly certain that Nick Gracie had been murdered here and then dressed, hurriedly, in Howard Butler's clothing.

The question was, who dressed him?

Downstairs, he found Milt pretending to take sips from a sweating tumbler of ice and a few drops of brown alcohol. Mrs. Butler's glass contained one small, rapidly melting half-moon of ice and a great deal of scotch. She raised it and took a long swallow as Jim pulled out the chair at the head of the table.

He leaned his forearms against the edge of the table, eyeing Mrs. Butler with a growing sense of urgency. Once Frank's confession became common knowledge, the investigation would end. So Jim needed to conduct his investigation as quickly and thoroughly as possible while he still had time.

Unfortunately, he had to admit that Bill Meyers might be right about Frank's drug connection. The shot fired at Frank did suggest a disagreement between the local drug dealers, proving Bill's case.

On the other hand, the shooting seemed so tentative, almost

accidental, as if someone had seen an opportunity to create trouble.

If Meyers was right and it was a dealer intent upon eliminating the competition, wouldn't he have made sure Frank Edwards didn't walk away unhurt?

"Drink?" Mrs. Butler held out her empty glass.

He took her tumbler. The heavy glass was cold and damp with condensation. "What will you have?"

"I'll have another scotch," she said, her voice clear, almost sharp. "And call me Alex." He refilled her glass and handed Alex Butler her drink with the depressing thought that the entire investigation was a mess. And he had almost no hope of straightening it out, not with a tight budget, the crime scene cleaned to a sparkle, Meyers bucking for his job, and Frank's false confession. If he was smart, he'd take the easy way out and close the case.

He took a deep breath and studied his hostess. "Mrs. Butler—"

"Alex." She smiled. "Shit, I hate that androgynous name." Her blue eyes studied him over the edge of her glass. "Maybe Lexy would be better. More feminine. What do you think?"

"I need to ask you a few questions, Mrs. Butler," he said.

She settled back in her chair and smiled as she flipped a lock of blond hair over her shoulder. "Ask away."

"There's evidence that suggests Nick Gracie didn't die at the stream."

"Really?" Her fingers twisted together.

"We found female trace evidence. DNA evidence. It appears that a woman was with Nick Gracie when he died. And he died here in this house, didn't he?"

The knuckles of her clasped hands turned white. She slipped her hands under the table to hide them in her lap.

He waited for a moment and then said gently, "The bleach

didn't wash everything away."

"I didn't kill him."

"But you were there, right? Mrs. Butler, we need to know what happened."

"Ask my lawyer."

"It would go easier if you'd give us your statement."

"Easier for whom?"

"If you're protecting your husband. . . ."

"Howie?" She laughed, then lit a cigarette. Smoking seemed to soothe her. "No. I think you boys had better leave. Talk to my lawyer."

Milt picked up the ashtray. "I'll get rid of this for you."

"Leave it," she said sharply.

He shrugged, hands palm up, before he turned away. He lumbered toward the hallway. "I'll be outside."

"I'd like to get a DNA sample," Jim said.

"I'm sure you would. Ask my lawyer."

The air inside the cruiser was thick and heavy with accumulated heat. Jim started the car to get the air conditioner going. "I'm going to drive down to the curve in the road and stop," he told Milt. "I think I saw their trash can at the end of the driveway. See if you can find any cigarette butts."

"If she empties her ashtrays and doesn't just flush them."

"Do you think she's that paranoid?"

"Maybe. But there may be a few. Who knows?"

When they stopped, Milt climbed out of the car with a wheeze, hitched up his belt, and loped away, disappearing between the thin trunks of the pines toward the end of the gravel drive.

Jim slumped down in his seat and opened the window, letting in fresh air. Frank's confession had been seriously lacking in details. He claimed he had shoved Gracie in an argument.

Gracie hit his head on one of the wooden shelves in the greenhouse and died.

When Meyers had asked about the broken glass, Frank had tacked on the information that there had been glassware on the shelf.

None of it sounded right to Jim, especially since Cassie had offered a different explanation and had the wound on her hand to prove it.

"No cigarettes," Milt said, his face mournful. Then with a grin, he held up an empty water bottle.

Jim grabbed the flimsy plastic bottle. Around the lip were greasy smears of pink lipstick. "You found this in their trash?"

"Yeah." Milt wiped the sweat off the speckled dome of his head. "But the fact is, we can't prove it was hers. I fished it out of her trash, sure. But it could as easily be her maid's."

"I don't care who it belongs to if it matches one of the samples we already have. If we can show that link, I'll get a warrant for an official search, even if I have to go around Colesford to do it."

Milt laughed. "You're not gettin' around that boy. But even old CC can be made to see sense. He may be stubborn about wasting our taxpayers' good money, but he'll see sense if there's sense to see."

Jim tossed the baggie containing the glass shards to Singleton. "I found those under the bed."

"So we know where it happened. That's more than we had this morning."

"Yeah. And Frank's statement is missing a lot of relevant details, including this location."

"Nuisance confession."

"That's how I intend to treat it. We'll see if CC agrees."

When they arrived at the station, they found a boxy BMW in

a rich, subdued oyster-shell white, angled across two slots in the parking lot.

"Shit, what's Dennis Crawford doing here?" Jim parked the cruiser next to the BMW and collected the plastic bags of evidence.

"Looks like that boy could use a ticket for this here great parking job," Milt remarked.

"Don't worry about it."

As Jim opened the door to the office, he could hear laughter and the sound of voices coming from Bill's desk. Jim strode down the narrow corridor, his temper simmering. He stopped at the door to the shared outer office and leaned against the frame.

Bill Meyers leaned back in his chair with his hands linked behind his head. A possum-like grin stretched his face, showing far too many glossy-white teeth, as Dennis Crawford snapped pictures with a small digital camera.

"It was clearly a war between competing drug dealers," Meyers stated. "We'd been watching Frank Edwards for quite some time. So it came as no surprise when he killed Nick Gracie. And when he confessed, I was able to wrap up the case and keep the taxpayers from footing the bill for unnecessary lab and investigation costs."

"A bit premature, though," Jim said.

The muscles in Bill's face contracted, but he didn't change his posture. If anything, he leaned back further in his chair.

With almost comedic finesse, Crawford glanced from Meyers to Jim. The reporter's mouth twitched as he suppressed a grin. "Premature?" he prompted.

"We're looking at the evidence," Jim replied, his attention locked on Bill, daring him to interrupt. "There's the possibility that Frank Edwards may be confused. So we need to review his statement in light of the evidence. Obviously, this office is not ready to close the case at this time." He smiled. "Hope we didn't waste too much of your time, Dennis."

"No." Confusion played across Crawford's face. "Of course not."

Jim forced a laugh. "My deputy was understandably excited. He wanted the public to know that this office is working hard to protect their interests. I'll trust you to show discretion, Dennis. There's no point in ruining Frank's reputation until we can determine the validity of his statement."

"There's the possibility that Frank Edwards is crazy? Is that what you're saying?"

"Not at all. I'm saying that this office is following up on a number of leads and physical evidence, and that we'll continue our investigation until we're satisfied. We need to match the physical evidence to Frank's statement, or the case will never go to trial."

"So you're saying Frank's confession doesn't match the evidence? What evidence?"

"Come on, Dennis, you know better than that," Jim said, guiding the reporter toward the outer door. "We can't discuss that, but I'll tell you this. It's more complex than it appears. And Frank's 'confession' has serious discrepancies."

CHAPTER TWENTY-THREE

As Cassie left the police station, she felt helpless and depressed.

The searing sunshine momentarily blinded her and she closed her eyes, letting the light warm her skin. When she blinked, she was surprised to see Anne and a young girl walk toward her.

"Hey, Cass." Anne draped an arm over the girl's shoulders. "How's your uncle?"

"He's fine." Cassie edged around them.

"Don't worry. I know this is hard, but Jim'll figure it out. You'll see."

"Oh, sure," Cassie said. It took an intense effort to keep the sarcasm out of her voice. "They think they've solved it already. They're going through the motions, but even your brother can't investigate if they've already arrested someone and he confessed." She caught the curious gaze of the little, red-haired girl. "They have no reason to keep on looking." Cassie bent to smile at the girl and terminate the depressing topic of her uncle's confession. "And who is this with you?"

"Megan," Anne said. "Megan, this is my best friend, Cassie Edwards."

The girl gave Anne a sharp glance. "I thought *I* was your best friend."

"A girl can have two best friends. It's not against the rules."

Megan stared at Cassie. Cassie stared back. As near as she could tell, Megan was about eleven and already five feet tall. Her red hair burned with translucent fire in the bright sunshine.

Her long lashes were that same glowing red and made her eyes brilliantly blue. A brilliant but suspicious blue.

Megan's gaze drifted to Cassie's jeans and T-shirt, graced with the words NO RULES on the front and WE'RE TRYING TO ACCOMPLISH SOMETHING on the back. At least Cassie had the sense not to wear the shirt that stated COPS SHOULD POLICE THEMSELVES when she visited her uncle.

"Did you just get out of jail?" Megan asked. Wearing a blue shirt, tailored white shorts, and leather sandals, she looked like a miniature stock broker on vacation at an exclusive resort.

"No, Megan. I was visiting my uncle. He's in jail for a crime he didn't commit."

"If he's in jail he must be guilty," she said with a sniff.

"You can't make assumptions without knowing all the facts, Megan."

"That's true," Jim said, strolling outside. A slow smile seeped across his face and settled into his eyes. "What can the Peyton Police Department do for you today, Megan?"

"It's Henry," Megan said, staring up at the sheriff. Adoration glowed in her face, as bright and intense as her hair. "I think he's under the house."

Jim nodded. "No problem, I'll get him."

"I'm sure you have better things to do," Cassie said. "Like investigating murders."

"I think I have time for this, Cassie," he said. "It'll only take a few minutes."

"Why don't I help Megan with Henry?" Cassie offered. Jim caught her gaze, but instead of anger she saw his slow smile again. It crinkled the corners of his gray eyes.

"Did Megan tell you about Henry?" he asked.

"What do you mean?"

"Henry is a snake," he said.

Cassie eyed him, suspecting a joke. "A snake?"

"A hognose snake." Megan tucked her hand around Jim's elbow with a proprietary air. "They're the cutest. They have darling little faces."

"Do you still want to crawl under the house after him?" Jim asked Cassie.

"No. I don't think so."

"You're afraid of snakes." Megan studied her with disapproval in her bright blue eyes.

"No," Cassie fibbed. "Not really. It's not that. I just realized I've got to get going."

"Yeah. I figured you were busy." Jim guided Megan down the sidewalk, resting his hand on her shoulder. "And this is one thing the sheriff's office can handle."

"Never mind." Anne moved to Cassie. "Come on. How about a milkshake?"

Cassie fell in step beside Anne. "I'm sorry," she blurted.

Anne laughed. "About what?"

"For giving your brother a hard time."

"You should tell him that."

"Oh, sure. The thing is, I see that uniform and I turn into some kind of insane, neurotic anti-establishment hippy-chick. It's like Pavlov's dog. See uniform, start drooling and baring my teeth."

The two women entered Peyton Place. Cassie took a seat at the counter while Anne walked around, pulled down a couple of metal milkshake containers, and began assembling ingredients.

"Why don't you try to see past the uniform? Jim's a good guy. You used to like him."

"He used to be different. He used to want to write."

"He still writes. Ask him."

"Ask him what?" Jim took the stool next to Cassie and winked at his sister. As he propped his elbows up on the cool marble surface, he said, "I'll have a chocolate malt."

Cassie brushed a cobweb off his collar. "That was quick."

"Henry and I are old friends. Megan doesn't like to crawl under the house because of spiders."

"She has a snake and she's afraid of spiders?"

"We all have our quirks. You hate authority figures."

"I don't like people who think they have the right to tell me what to do."

"No one does. But someone has to be around to make sure no one decides they have the right to beat up their neighbor because he has a slight difference in opinion."

"Or arrest him!"

"Look," he said, his shoulders curving forward as he twisted a napkin into a corkscrew. "I don't think your uncle committed murder, at least not on purpose. Cut me a little slack, will you? So I can do my job."

"I'll cut you slack when you do your job."

"Here you are." Anne placed chocolate malts in front of them. "Cassie was asking about your writing, Jim."

"What happened?" Cassie asked. "Rejections?"

"Yes."

"But you're going to keep writing, aren't you? You're not going to give up?"

"No. I probably should, but I'm stubborn, too."

"I'm glad. It's what you should be doing."

"After I finish this investigation?"

"Well, yes."

In truth, he was the only one in a position to perform the investigation.

She took a long pull on the straw. Her mouth filled with icy crystals of chocolate. She had no control over the investigation. Or Jim. Or anything in her life.

Her stomach gurgled and she pressed her hand over it. Even

her body was rebelling.

All she could do was try to behave like a semi-intelligent human being and make sure things didn't get any worse.

CHAPTER TWENTY-FOUR

"But you're not going to give up writing, are you?" Cassie persisted. "I mean, it's what you want to do. Isn't it?"

Jim gave her a quizzical glance before taking a long sip of his milkshake. He focused on the counter and hunched over as if to shut out the rest of the world.

"I probably won't give up writing," he said, "but I like what I do. I enjoy working with the people in this community. And I guess I'm like you. I like to solve problems."

The heat from his leg brushed hers. Cassie held her cold glass up to her cheeks, pretending her flushed skin was the result of the warm air in the diner.

"You were always a funny kid," he continued.

"Funny?"

"Twelve years ago, Mom asked me to pick up a few things for her. I forgot the paper napkins. You were there, hanging around with Anne. And Mom started screaming about those napkins. So you walked into the kitchen and came back to the dining room with a handful of paper towels. You folded them and put one under each fork." He chuckled. "Then you said, 'That will work. Problem solved.' And you grabbed your knapsack and went home. Just like that. While we were all standing around with our mouths open, catching flies. You didn't even care what we thought about it. You didn't even wait to be thanked. It was almost as if you didn't really care what we thought. But the next day I found a yellow sticky note on top of the book I was reading. It said 'Get napkins.' I guess you made a detour on your way out, to make sure I remembered napkins next time."

"I can't believe you remember that," she said with a blush.

"Yeah, you were one weird kid. Princess Valiant."

"I may be weird, but I never acted like a princess. I never wore pink, or any of that frou-frou stuff."

"No, not that kind of princess, more like Prince Valiant. Always ready to leap to someone's defense and right wrongs. I always admired you for that. You seemed so sure of yourself, so positive you were right."

"Is that supposed to be a compliment? Because it doesn't sound that wonderful to me."

"There's a lot to be said for clarity of vision, whether it turns out to be right or wrong. You've never been afraid to let anyone know what you think. And you're always willing to admit it when you're wrong. At least, when I knew you."

"That was a long time ago."

"Something tells me you haven't changed all that much."

Cassie wanted to believe he was telling the truth and admired her, but she knew plenty of others who saw those same traits in a vastly different way. Many considered her opinionated and abrasive and believed she thought she was smarter than everyone else.

Which was so untrue. There were days when she thought rocks showed more intelligence. And lately, she'd pretty much felt that way every day.

"Thanks," she said at last. "I always thought you were intelligent. And cool."

"Past tense." He laughed. "Guess that was when you thought I was going to be a writer."

"No." She stepped out of her comfort zone, despite a deep sense of vulnerability. "Now."

She really did respect him. And although she and Anne often treated it as a joke, Cassie always had.

Growing up, she hadn't been Princess Valiant. She'd been Sam, the trusty sidekick, to his Frodo. He was the one who ultimately came to the rescue and saved the day.

"Really, I still admire you. Even with the uniform. Even if you never publish. I mean, I'd never crawl under a house to get a snake. Even a cute hognose snake."

His gaze intensified, lightning crackling through the dark gray of his eyes. "But you'd like me better without the uniform."

"Oh, yes. Totally. Without it." She locked glances with him. An electric tremor curled her toes. She looked at his hands, her imagination feeding her the sensation of his long, blunt-tipped fingers sliding down her back, leaving a path of warmth against her skin.

He leaned toward her, his broad back separating them from the sprinkling of late-afternoon customers.

"I wouldn't mind seeing you without those T-shirts, either," he said, his voice husky.

A nervous giggle breathed through her lips. The tip of her tongue dampened her lower lip, tasting a sweet drop of chocolate and cream.

"I'm not going to have an argument here!" Anne said, returning to the counter.

Her remark threw a bucket of ice water over them. Cassie and Jim straightened and stared at her.

"If you want to intimidate witnesses, do it at the police station, Jim." Anne's loud voice bounced off the marble counter.

Several patrons glanced at them curiously.

"He wasn't intimidating me," Cassie said. She took a deep breath and grabbed her milkshake to avoid doing something even more embarrassing. Like clutching Jim's thigh.

Anne's face grabbed Cassie's wrist. "Come on. I want to talk to you. And Jim, you can go out the back way to the station. It's shorter."

"My sister's gossip will have to wait," Jim said. "You need to sign your revised statement at the station."

With a sigh, Cassie struggled off the stool, grabbed her purse, and followed Anne and Jim into the kitchen.

"What was that all about?" Cassie asked as they dodged through the stainless steel appliances and work surfaces in the surprisingly large kitchen.

"What is wrong with you?" Anne hit her brother in the shoulder. "You're supposed to be conducting a murder investigation. Everyone in town saw you making goo-goo eyes at each other. At my lunch counter. In public, in the middle of the day! If Bill Meyers hears about this, he'll scream that you're trying to pin the murder on someone else because you're in love with Frank's niece. Can you say 'conflict of interest'?"

Cassie said, "But we were only talking. You know I can't stand uber-macho men who think wearing a gun and a set of handcuffs is some kind of aphrodisiac. And Lord knows what Jim thinks of me."

Even if Anne was her best friend, Cassie didn't want to discuss her confused feelings. She couldn't afford to get distracted by anything, including the sheriff. Besides, she didn't appreciate the princess title, although valiant was sort of sweet in a literary, Sir Walter Raleigh kind of way.

"Oh, yeah," he said, his hands on his hips. "You know I can't stand your friends, Short-stuff. Especially Princess Valiant."

Anne snorted. "All I can say is, turn down the heat before someone else notices and tattles on you two."

"Wait a minute," Cassie said. "You're the one who started screaming. You're the one who called attention to us. We were fine."

"You were not fine. People were staring and smiling. That

kind of fatuous smile people use when they're watching a pair of lovers."

"We're not lovers!" Jim and Cassie said together. They exchanged uncomfortable glances.

"Right," Anne said. "Try to remember that."

CHAPTER TWENTY-FIVE

Cassie and Jim left the diner in sheepish silence. Jim loped down the block toward his office, leaving Cassie alone on the sidewalk. She stared after him, feeling deserted.

"Cassie?" a man asked.

Startled, she jumped. She spun around and found herself almost nose-to-nose with a pudgy, round-faced man.

"Howie?" She took a step back.

He blinked his red-rimmed eyes rapidly. "I didn't realize you were back."

"I came for a couple of weeks. Vacation."

"It's great to see you again. I really mean that." His voice throbbed as if he were about to cry. He waved at the front door to Peyton Place. "I was going to get a sundae. You want to join me? Come on, please. I haven't seen you since high school." He tentatively touched her elbow. "Since the prom."

"Oh, yeah. The prom."

"I'll buy." Howie guided her back into the diner.

When he opened the door, several people inside goggled at them. Howie caught their glances and smiled, seemingly pleased with the attention. Cassie stared down at the floor, trying not to blush. She could imagine what they were thinking.

She was going to end up with an interesting reputation.

"It's been a long time, Cassie. We've missed you around here." He gripped her forearm, urging her toward an empty table at the back of the diner. "It's been what? Ten years?"

"Not that long." She sat down. Surreptitiously snagging a napkin out of the dispenser in the middle of the table, she ran it over her forearm where he had gripped her with his damp hands.

He still had sweaty hands. She remembered his cold fish grip from prom night. Hindsight suggested she'd been lucky to have a case of the flu. Disgusted by her illness, Howie had kept his distance most of the night.

And like a true Southern gentleman to the end, he had walked her up to her door after the prom and given her a firm, but moist handshake while their driver, Jim Fletcher, watched from the car.

Over the intervening years, the entire evening had assumed the guise of a horrible, fevered nightmare. She couldn't look at Howie without remembering that hot, prickling nausea. Or her intense embarrassment as she stood on her porch, knowing Jim was waiting a few yards away to drive her prom date home.

Her life had been one humiliating moment after another. Was it any wonder she had moved away from Peyton as soon as she could?

"It's good to see you." Howie grabbed her hand and held it between his two hands in a death grip.

She tried to gently pull away but he wouldn't release her. He gazed earnestly at her, blinking rapidly and licking his plump lips.

"It's good to see you, too." Cassie finally yanked her hand free, pulled another napkin out of the dispenser, and rubbed her fingers with it. "Sounds like you're doing well, Howie. Anne says you built a gorgeous new brick home."

"Yes." He picked up the plastic-coated menu from its slot in the condiment tray and handed it to her. "I know what I want. What about you?"

"I'm really not hungry." Cassie glanced at the counter, but Anne was still in the kitchen. She thought fleetingly of escaping to the bathroom. Her fingers still felt sticky.

"What about a milkshake?"

"No. Really. Maybe a glass of water."

"A milkshake." He nodded as if she were a child.

Then to her horror, his mouth trembled. A spasm quivered over his face and his frantic blinking increased. "I should never have let you go. You were the best thing that ever happened to me."

What the heck? "We only went out once. To the prom. It was a last minute fix-up." She smiled, trying to make light of her remark.

"Anne did me a real favor, and I told her that. I'd been trying to get a date with you for years." He caught her gaze with mournful, watery eyes. When she placed the menu on the table, he caught her wrist and trapped her hand under his. "Lucky for me that your date ended up in the hospital."

"I'm sure he felt very lucky when he caught the flu the day before the prom." She had caught it from him and ended up being sick in Jim Fletcher's lap. "Good luck for everyone that night, I guess."

"I'm sorry you got sick." His hand tightened on hers. Then suddenly, beneath the table, his other hand gripped her knee.

She jerked her leg away. "I was only sick a couple of days. And then I went to college. I heard you went away, too. Boston, right? And now you're married. So it all turned out great for everyone."

His nervous blink increased. His mouth worked for a moment before he could speak. "My wife," he began, his face crumpling.

"Is your wife sick?" She should never have mentioned the flu. Or his wife.

"She'd be better off sick," he replied.

"Why would you say that?"

"Alexandra—she likes to call herself Lexy—is a cheat and a liar. I've never been more miserable."

Oh God, he wasn't going to do the "my wife doesn't understand me" speech, was he? Cassie's stomach twisted. She glanced over her shoulder, praying Anne would notice them and rescue her.

Howie's hand managed to find her knee again. He squeezed it. She kicked him in the shin. He let go of her leg. She shifted uncomfortably and said, "Sorry, I'm ticklish." She scooted her chair another six inches away. "Anyway, I'm sure Lexy loves you or she wouldn't have married you."

"She loves my money, you mean."

She studied his face, noting the deeply etched frown lines above his brows and bracketing his mouth. His plump, rubbery lips extruded into a pout, and she sensed it was another habitual expression. The spoiled kid had turned into an unhappy, discontented adult.

She knew the type so well. And there was nothing you could do for someone like that, unless you made all the decisions, and took all the blame when things didn't turn out right.

"She won't even sleep with me anymore." Howie tried to recapture her hand.

She leaned back in her chair and kept her hands out of reach. "I'm sorry, I really am. You're a nice guy, but I can't really help you—"

"And if she's not sleeping me, she's got to be sleeping with someone else."

"You don't know that for certain." She remembered what Angie said about Nick Gracie and felt even more uncomfortable.

His Southern accent grew more pronounced as he said, "She's got that look."

"What look?"

"You know. That *satisfied* look. She's getting what she wants."

"Maybe she's in love with you and satisfied that you married her. Isn't that what you're really seeing?"

"I don't know." He pouted and rubbed the tip of his nose thoughtfully. "I made a mistake. I should have married someone like you. You never cared about money."

"We were just friends."

"We could have been more. Should have been more."

"No, I'm sorry. I like you, but I'm sure Lexy loves you. All couples go through bad patches. You have to hang in there, tell her how you feel. Have you spoken to her about it? About your feelings?"

"Of course."

"Well, tell her again."

"Sure. But it won't help."

Hoping to change the subject, she blurted, "Sorry about Nick Gracie."

"Thanks." He cleared his throat. His hands played over the silverware in front of him. "Looks like I needed a bodyguard, after all. I'm glad I was down there at Max Marine Crafters last Saturday when Nick got himself killed."

"Oh? Are you and your wife buying a boat?"

"Maybe. If Lexy stops getting headaches."

"She didn't go with you?"

He stared down at the table and shrugged.

She felt a spurt of excitement and glanced over her shoulder. She finally caught Anne's eye as she came out to the marble counter. "I'm really sorry, but I've got to get going."

"No one wants to listen to me." Howie's frown deepened.

"I'm sure that's not true. But I need to talk to Anne for a minute. Enjoy your sundae."

CHAPTER TWENTY-SIX

"I can't believe it," Cassie said as she slipped around the counter.

"What are you doing in here again?" Anne grinned at Howard Butler and waved.

"Howie caught me outside and dragged me in. And he tried that 'my wife doesn't understand me' thing. Does your brother realize Howie spent Saturday alone?"

"Yes. I think Jim mentioned it. Why?"

"I thought everyone was saying that Howie and his wife couldn't be involved in Nick Gracie's murder."

"So?"

"They weren't together. Howie said he was at Max Marine. Alone."

"I'm sure my brother will figure it out." She punched Cassie's shoulder lightly. "But if it makes you feel better, I'll let my brother know you think Mrs. Butler killed Nick Gracie."

"I'm not saying that. It irritates me that everyone is so quick to jump on my uncle and no one is looking at the Butlers."

"What makes you think no one is looking at them? Let my brother do his job."

Catching Howie's watery gaze, Cassie headed for the kitchen, hoping to slip out the back.

Anne laughed and followed her into the kitchen. "No customers allowed back here."

"I'm not a customer. I didn't eat a thing. I'm escaping."

"From Howie? Poor guy. I don't think he ever got over you."

"Got over me? Be serious. There was nothing to get over. I doubt I spoke to him more than three times in my life."

"You were his date for the prom."

"Thanks to you. And I still owe you for that." Cassie glanced around the kitchen. "When was the last time you were inspected? Maybe I should call the health inspector."

"Don't even think about it. And you were the one who insisted on going to the prom, even with a fever of a hundred-and-two. And when Jim refused to step up to the plate as your escort, you were stuck with last-minute Howie."

Cassie blushed, wishing she could forget the whole nightmare. Sometimes she felt like the flu had changed her entire life. Her boyfriend had gone to Europe after his recovery, and she'd puked on Jim Fletcher, who didn't want to escort her to the prom but was happy to drive her home afterwards.

"I should have stayed home and hung out with the porcelain bathroom goddess like any self-respecting sick person."

Anne elbowed her. "You were hoping you could ditch Howie and Jim would come to your rescue. Come on, admit it. You get dreamy-eyed every time Jim comes into the room."

"That was before he grew up to be a bully and a mindless minion of the authoritarian oppressors."

"You are so full of it. You're afraid someone might try to tell you what to do. That's your entire problem with the law."

"That and fear of unjustified imprisonment." Cassie crossed her arms over her T-shirt. "Which, as it turns out, is a valid fear considering my uncle's situation."

"He confessed."

"Because he's whacked out on weed most of the time."

Anne's face grew serious. "You've got to trust my brother, Cassie. He's doing the best he can."

"I hope his best is good enough," Cassie said as she slipped out the door. This time she was determined to break the continual loop that kept bringing her back inside Peyton Place. This time she was going to make it home. Then she was going to see what she could find in the way of evidence.

CHAPTER TWENTY-SEVEN

Cassie got home in time for a lonely dinner of hot dogs and beans and an even lonelier evening worrying about her uncle. The next morning she was no closer to figuring out what she should do, so she resorted to the old-time solution for a paucity of ideas: she cleaned house.

Scrubbing the bathroom with bleach, she felt a headache forming behind her eyes. She belatedly opened the window and took a breath of fresh air. The intense smell of chlorine wafted around her. Despite knowing it was probably bad for her, she liked the clean, sharp odor.

The distant throb of a car nearing the house caught her attention. She leaned outside the window, trying to see around a pine tree that shaded the corner. The branches waved in front of her, smelling of pine mixed antiseptically with the scent of chlorine. Through the needle-like leaves, she watched a small, lime-green Volkswagen bug screech to a halt behind her car.

A gray-haired, slender woman got out. With swift, impatient strides, she circled the car and opened the trunk. She pulled out a large garment bag and slammed the trunk shut. Then she fussed with the shoulder strap and positioned it carefully over her shoulder before walking toward the house.

Aunt Sylvia? The last time Cassie had seen her, she'd had shoulder-length hair as dark as Cassie's, the gray carefully blended away.

Cassie raced down the stairs. When she reached the bottom,

the garment bag was resting on the bench near the front door.

"Aunt Sylvia?" she called tentatively, moving toward the kitchen.

"Cassie?"

Cassie met her in the doorway to the kitchen. "You've—"

"Changed?" Her aunt nodded. Her hair was still shoulder-length, but her face was framed by gray. Only the hair at her nape remained dark, providing depth and contrast to the silver strands. The lines around her mouth and eyes had deepened, and a permanent groove had formed between her eyebrows, attesting to all the hours she spent focused intently on a microscope. Her blue eyes, however, had kept their youthful sparkle of intelligent curiosity and a glimmer of humor.

Unfortunately, the humor flickered and disappeared, replaced by concern as she studied Cassie.

"I'm sorry. I hadn't meant to stay away so long," Cassie said.

Aunt Sylvia gave Cassie's arm a gentle squeeze. "I understand. Work is important. You've done well, Cassiopeia."

She risked giving her aunt's thin, stiff body a quick hug, trying not to make a smart comment about the prescription medication she was taking to help her mange her successful life. Aunt Sylvia would not approve of that.

"Thanks. I've missed you." Cassie released her aunt. "I thought you weren't going to come back."

Sylvia sighed and walked briskly toward the kitchen. "I realized what that old fool had done after I heard about his supposed confession last night from Katrina." She turned on the oven and pulled out a package of pre-made pie crusts from the refrigerator. With the efficiency of long practice, she threw together a chicken pot pie from a package of frozen vegetables, a can of chicken, and a can of cream of mushroom soup and put it in the oven.

Then, to Cassie's surprise, she pulled out a bottle of red wine.

When her aunt uncorked the bottle and sat down, Cassie touched her shoulder. "You still love him, don't you?" Even to her own ears, she sounded like a child seeking reassurance. "You came back to help him, because you love him."

Her aunt studied her, a serious expression clouding her eyes. "I'll always love your uncle. Unfortunately, he's a weak man. His actions have contributed directly to this situation."

"That's not true!"

"It is true. You'd realize it if you didn't allow your emotions to interfere with your judgment."

"He didn't kill that man. And you know it or you wouldn't be here." She couldn't bring herself to ask her aunt if she'd accidentally killed Gracie. "I've been trying to find the truth. To prove to the police that Uncle Frank didn't do it."

"Then you must know that Frank's activities led directly to his arrest. As I stated earlier."

"He wasn't arrested for that. He was arrested because he was trying to protect you."

Her aunt's brows rose, a mute and subtle expression of disbelief.

"And I burned the plants in the back of the greenhouse. He only grew them because he was frightened. He has glaucoma."

"That's no excuse for growing an illegal substance. And it's not efficacious—"

"I know. But you said yourself that he's weak. He needs your support. If you're here, he won't do it again."

"I was here when he started growing that weed. Again."

"He's terrified. And he's getting old. He's having a hard time."

"Do you think he's the only one with difficulties?"

"No," Cassie whispered. "I know this can't be easy for you, either. Nothing is ever easy."

"Do you know how many times I've listened to his excuses? How many times this type of thing has happened? I love him, but I can't keep bailing him out. Sometimes I'm the one who needs help, and who do I have to turn to? If I can't depend upon Frank, who do I have?"

"Oh, Aunt Sylvia." She hugged her again.

'I'm sorry, Cassie, I really am. But I don't know what more I can do for him."

"Then why come back?"

Sylvia turned sideways and pressed a paper towel to her eyes. "Because while I believe he may deserve to be arrested, he did not murder that man. It's obvious he confessed due to some ill-advised and uninformed desire to protect me."

"Perhaps he also hoped it would make you come back. I know he wants to talk to you and explain. He misses you. A lot."

The timer on the stove dinged. She turned off the oven while Sylvia pulled out the pot pie. She cut them each a slice and gestured for Cassie to pour the wine. The small, domestic duties seemed to calm both of them.

"He could have called me if he wished," Sylvia said. "He knows my number."

"I think he thought you murdered Nick Gracie."

"And ran away?" Her mouth thinned as she carefully set the table. "In all those years, did either of you ever learn anything about me at all?"

"We both did. But you left the evening Nick Gracie died, didn't you?"

"Cassie, I had no idea Gracie was dead. I went to see Howard Butler." Sylvia sipped her glass of wine, then sat down heavily, her blue eyes flat and the corners of her mouth drooping.

"Why did you go to see him?"

"Because of the marijuana, of course. I knew your uncle

would never confront him."

"You went to see Howard? Not Nick?"

"If you wish to solve a problem, you must address the root cause, not the symptoms. You know that."

"But Nick Gracie—"

"Was brought here by Mr. Butler."

"To be his bodyguard."

"Yes, and to help him rebuild his financial situation."

"What?"

"Howard Butler was not the man his father was. He frittered everything away on crazy ideas that never amounted to much. And it pains me to say this, but Howard's first stroke of good luck was his house burning down. He rebuilt and then brought Nick Gracie down here. Purportedly as his bodyguard. However, soon after that, they convinced your uncle to start growing marijuana. And you'd be more naïve than I think you are if you believe that was the only drug they were selling. Howard is doing quite well, I believe. Financially."

"So you went up there? That night?"

"I never saw either man." She glanced away. Her thin skin colored, although the flush was barely visible beneath the light dusting of her pale powder.

"You chickened out?" Cassie asked.

"Yes. I was furious with your uncle. And I wanted to discuss— very emphatically—the situation with those two men. But when I got to the Butler home, I realized how futile it would be. What could I possibly say? I'd only embarrass and possibly endanger myself. I'm not ready to retire yet. I still have my career and my reputation. When my anger died, I realized if I wished to keep those things, I had to make a choice. Frank or my career."

"So you gave up on Frank? After all those years?"

"Yes. After all those years of trying to be strong for him and trying to do the right thing. I left him, because in the end, he was never there for me. Not when I needed him."

Cassie let that sad remark slide, aware of the irony. In the end, Frank had taken the blame for Sylvia. Or at least he thought he had.

"I drove away," Sylvia continued. "I didn't even stop for my clothes. I went to Charlotte and bought a few things to tide me over while I decided what to do."

"But Frank knew you went to the Butler house and never came back. The next day he found Nick Gracie down by the stream, so he assumed—"

"He has known me for forty years. He supposedly loves me. He's supposed to know me better than anyone, and yet he assumed I was capable of killing a man and running away."

Cassie caught her aunt's hands and grasped them, leaning closer. "He does know you. We both know you. We know you wouldn't do that. If you killed someone, you'd march right over to the nearest sheriff's office and confess. He knows that—honestly."

"He told you that?"

"Not in so many words. But have you considered this? He might be afraid someone saw you drive up to the Butler house. Or watched you drive away. He was afraid you might be blamed. I think he felt he deserved to be arrested after being so weak and agreeing to grow weed for Butler and Gracie. I think he wanted to make everything right. He wanted to be there for you, to protect you, because he loves you."

"Why did he confess to murder?"

"Out of love for you. He's probably been as confused as I've been. You know how easy it is to get dragged down deeper than you intended. Or maybe you don't. You've always been so perfect, so squeaky clean."

Sylvia laughed, the sound edged with bitterness. "I was never that perfect, Cassiopeia. No one is."

"You come closer than any living person I've ever met."

"Your experience is remarkably limited. I can be unbending and cruel. And the difference between right and wrong can sometimes be very hard to discern. I've made mistakes. As far as I know, there are no warrants for my arrest, or any unpaid speeding tickets. But all of us make mistakes. I wish Frank, for once, would admit he grew an illegal crop for Gracie and be done with it."

"You know he couldn't. And despite your desire for honesty, it would be the start of more problems. The police would drag your name through the mud, trying to involve you in the murder. Your life would be ruined. At least this way he could get the authorities to end the investigation before they discovered you went to the Butler house. His confession avoided the scandal of being arrested for growing drugs. And he protected you."

"Cassie, I appreciate your support and your belief in my husband, but he has grown—"

"Senile?"

"No. Not senile, just a little vague. I appreciate your efforts to excuse him, but I'd be very surprised if he thought that far ahead."

"Then help me get him out of prison. Help me force the police to continue their investigation. Their efforts have almost stopped since the confession."

Sylvia patted Cassie's arm, picked up her glass of wine and took a few sips, her face composed and reflective. "Then we must act as detectives. Is that what you have in mind?"

"Yes. The sheriff, Jim Fletcher, isn't that bad. He might listen if we find evidence."

"And Milt, of course."

"Milt?"

Her aunt flushed and glanced away, knocking her foot against the table leg. "Milt Singleton."

"You know Deputy Singleton? Don't tell me you dated Milt Singleton."

"For a few months, before I met Frank. I was young, once. I dated. I wasn't born married to Frank."

"Then you can talk to the deputy, right?"

"Perhaps. Although I doubt he'll put himself out for us if the case is closed. But Milt is a good man."

"And the sheriff is still investigating—he's not satisfied. And he's smart." Hope flared. Cassie fiddled with her wine glass. "When you were at the Butler house, did you see anyone out of the ordinary?"

"I didn't get out of the car. Or stare into any windows."

"Did you see anyone drive up? Anyone waking around?"

"No."

"What about cars?"

"There were two cars parked outside the garage."

"Two?"

"Nick Gracie was an employee. He'd hardly be allowed to park in the garage, where the Butlers kept their vehicles."

"So you saw two cars. I suppose one belonged to Nick Gracie, but the other—"

"Could also belong to him. One was a truck. The other was a small, silver car, most likely a second car for him."

"Or someone else? Do you remember the make and model of the car? The license plate?"

"No. Cassiopeia. Be reasonable. It was days ago. I had no reason to record that data."

"So you didn't write it down?" Cassie's brief flare of optimism crumbled.

Before she could retract her dumb question, Sylvia said, "Of course not. I had no way of knowing a murder was about to occur."

233

"I know—sorry."

"Eat your dinner. I'll call Milt and explain to him about Frank's very foolish false confession. And we'll trust that the authorities will, for once, do their jobs."

"Can I ask you an off-topic question?"

"Of course, dear." Her aunt raised her finely arched brows.

"Why on earth did you let Uncle Frank paint the house purple?"

Sylvia laughed. "It's the exact shade of the variety of the orchid, *Dendrobium parishii,* that Frank hybridized for our anniversary last year." Her face softened. "A deep, rich orchid color. I'm surprised you didn't recognize it. We sent you one. He was so proud of it."

And it had promptly died, Cassie thought. "Oh, yeah. I forgot."

She watched her aunt flush with pleasure. "He named it after me."

"And it has a beautiful flower, almost as beautiful as you," Cassie said, trying not to squirm. The plant her uncle sent died well before blooming.

"Thank you," her aunt replied drily. "But you really shouldn't lie. I suppose you still have a black thumb. Don't worry. I'm sure there's another 'Sylvia' in the greenhouse. It may even be blooming. Perhaps a good use of your time would be to take a look at some of the plant labels. It would hurt Frank terribly if he thought you wouldn't know his latest hybrid if you saw it."

"I'll look at them this afternoon," Cassie assured her.

CHAPTER TWENTY-EIGHT

Despite her good intentions, Cassie didn't make it to the greenhouse. The pot pie burned in her stomach and the wine exacerbated it. She was on her way upstairs when the doorbell rang.

Jim Fletcher stood on the front porch, eyeing Aunt Sylvia's VW bug. He wore jeans and a plain white shirt. The sleeves were rolled up, revealing his muscular forearms.

Her heart fluttered. "What are you doing here?"

"I saw your aunt's car on my way home."

"Yeah, well, she heard about Frank and cut her vacation short. Everything is fine. Or it will be when you let Frank go."

"May I come in?"

Without waiting for an answer, he stepped into the hallway and strode forward, pausing at the entrance to the living room. He cocked his head and listened to the sound of Sylvia moving around the kitchen, but instead of turning in that direction, he angled left into the living room and said, "I'm working on letting Frank go."

"Good! Is this an official visit?" Cassie followed him.

"Have a seat," he said, sitting down on the long sofa. He stretched one arm out along the back and glanced at her, clearly expecting her to sit next to him. Just like they were two normal people. Maybe even friends.

While her mind hemmed and hawed, her body took the proffered seat. "This is weird. Don't you think this is weird?"

"No, I don't. And I wish you'd relax." His fingers touched her rigid shoulder. "You're too tense."

"Energetic. I have a lot of energy, that's all. It's easy to mistake energy for tension."

"Look, I wanted to talk to you about—"

"Our kiss?"

"Yes. I don't want to blow this investigation, Cassie. We have to stay focused."

"You have to stay focused. I have to stay out of it. Isn't that right?"

"Yes, it is. What if you tripped over the real killer? Someone who murdered once is not going to hesitate to do it again."

"I know. Sorry."

"I mean it, Cassie. No investigating. I don't want anyone to think he—"

"Or she—"

"Has any reason to fear you. Relax and enjoy your vacation."

"My permanent vacation." Maybe she didn't really need to go back to Raleigh, Cassie thought. Maybe she could stay with her aunt and uncle. Of course, that meant actually dealing with her aunt and her uncle and giving up a great deal of her independence.

As if he'd read her mind, he said, "Have you ever considered staying here in Peyton?"

"It would probably mean a serious cut in pay."

"Maybe, but there's quality of life."

"I'd be living at home. With my aunt and uncle."

"You can always move out," he replied. "Anne moved out."

"She lives above her diner."

"Right. She moved out."

"I don't see any apartment buildings around here, do you? It's houses or double-wides."

"So?" He smiled. "You got something against houses? Or trailers?"

"No. But it makes leaving home a bit trickier. Look at you. Technically, you never left home. Your parents left home."

"Have you asked your aunt and uncle if they're interested in a nice warm condo in Florida?"

"Are you crazy? I'm not even going to consider suggesting that to them. Besides, I'm not sure I want to live in an orchid-purple house."

As they talked, she stretched out comfortably on the sofa, listening to her aunt cleaning up in the kitchen. For once, she didn't feel the need to leap up and do the dishes. Her aunt could handle it without breaking anything. She'd been doing it for years.

With intense gentleness, Jim cupped her neck and massaged her tense muscles. Then he ruined everything by saying, "Do you think Frank confessed to protect his wife?"

"No. I don't." There was no way she was going to implicate her aunt.

"When exactly did your aunt leave?"

"Before I came. Before anything happened."

"Are you sure? There'd be no need for Frank to confess to protect her if she left *before* anything happened. That implies he knew his wife was here when Nick Gracie was murdered. Before she ran away, she may have told Frank enough about it to impel him to make that confession."

"Aunt Sylvia never ran away from anything. She wouldn't do that. And she's come back." Cassie crossed her arms over her chest. "I spoke to her. She had nothing to do with this. Frank's confession was a nuisance confession, pure and simple."

He let her go. "I'd like to speak with your aunt."

"Now? No, Jim. She didn't have anything to do with the murder. Leave her alone."

"You still don't trust me, do you?"

"I trust you."

"Then what are you afraid of?"

"Nothing. But she's tired. She's had a long day, driving back from Charlotte."

Sylvia stepped into the room. "I'm not that tired. Ask your questions, Sheriff."

CHAPTER TWENTY-NINE

When Jim got to the office the next day, he immediately tackled the most difficult task facing him. "Judge Colesford? It's Jim Fletcher."

"How's that investigation going? Wrapped it all up yet?"

"No, sir. The case hasn't even gone to the prosecutor."

"Why not?"

"There's evidence to suggest that Frank Edwards may be—"

"Senile? If you're going to say he's senile—"

"No, sir. But it may be a nuisance confession."

"Nuisance?"

"His statement doesn't match the physical evidence. And his wife, Sylvia Edwards, returned recently. After interviewing her, it appears there's reason to believe her husband confessed because he was afraid we'd suspect her."

"Why the hell would we suspect Sylvia Edwards?"

"There's evidence to suggest that the killing didn't occur at the Edwards place as previously thought. I found broken glass and evidence of a cleanup at the Butler residence."

"What about the broken glass at the Edwards place? Meyers said he collected evidence that proved Nick Gracie was murdered in the kitchen. Or the greenhouse."

"There was broken glass, but it was the wrong kind. Frank's niece, Cassie, broke a glass shortly after she arrived. The glass from the fatal wound was lead crystal, the same kind of glass I saw at the Butler place. And there's more. Nick Gracie had a condom caught on his body with DNA from two women. We found a water bottle in the trash at the Butler residence and it's at the lab right now. In the meantime, I'd like a warrant to get a DNA sample from Mrs. Butler. And another warrant so that the techs can do a thorough search of her house."

"Why the hell didn't you do a more thorough search before making an arrest? Are you boys incompetent?"

"No, sir."

"You damn sure lost control of this investigation. And wasted the State's time and money."

"The evidence doesn't support Frank's confession, sir. It never did. Frank and Sylvia Edwards are well-respected members of the scientific community. We need to be sure before we proceed. When the prosecutor gets the case, he needs as much proof as we can give him. I have to consider why Nick Gracie would have a used condom caught in his clothing if he was talking to Frank Edwards. And his clothes didn't fit. I have reason to believe they weren't his. They might belong to Howard Butler."

"Howard Butler? You'd better have solid evidence if you want to plow that field."

"I'm not going to let politics influence this case, sir."

The judge snorted. "Grow up, boy. Politics influence every case. Take a leaf from Bill Meyers' book. You may not like him, but he's got polish. Make use of him and his instincts—it could save you a pile of trouble."

"Yes, sir."

"Come by my office. I'll sign off on a warrant. Just make sure I don't hear a whisper about harassment. And this had damn well better not be another false lead." The judge paused, then said, "I want this case closed, and all the evidence in front of me by Tuesday."

"Yes, sir." Jim hung up and glanced out his door.

Milt stared back at him. He waved a brown envelope before easing himself up from his desk and moving around the corner.

"We can get that warrant for Mrs. Butler's DNA," Jim said. "And do another search of the house."

"And I got the results of the glass comparisons." He slapped the brown envelope on Jim's desk. "The glass matches the sample from Frank's kitchen."

"How can it? The coroner said it was lead crystal. The glass from the kitchen was plain old glass. I doubt you could hit a man hard enough with a water glass to even knock him out. And that glass from the Butler place—"

"You don't have to convince me. I sure don't understand it. Or that condom, either."

Jim ran a hand through his hair, trying to ignore the uncomfortable sensation of the case unraveling around him like a worn-out sweater. He'd been so sure the glass wouldn't match. "Is it possible the glass didn't kill him? That he fell backwards and hit his head on the counter?"

"Frank could have dropped that glass during an argument," Milt replied. "They could've pushed each other. Nick could've slipped and fallen. Hit his head on the way down and landed on his back, grinding the glass into the wound. Could've happened that way."

"But what about the clothing? The condom? The glass I found at the Butlers' place?"

"Coincidence? Maybe he was so angry about something Frank did, he didn't notice the condom."

"Especially if Frank said he wasn't going to grow any more marijuana."

"You thinkin' our golden boy may be right after all?"

"I don't know." Jim stood up. His gaze fell to the envelope on his desk. He picked it up and locked it in his file cabinet before turning back to Milt. "This could be a career killer if we continue this investigation and it turns out Bill is correct. The judge warned me. I'd understand if you want to let it rest."

Milt's sloping shoulders shook with suppressed laughter. "I'd like to know exactly what happened. If that means I get to retire a little early, well, that wouldn't be so bad."

"Then let's do it."

This time, instead of driving to the Butlers' residence for a third visit, Jim arranged for the techs to go over to the Butler house while Mrs. Butler came to the police station to give her statement.

When she walked in, wearing a blue blouse and white slacks, she looked like the proverbial ice queen. Her face was devoid of expression, her pale skin stretched tautly over sharp cheekbones.

"Why don't we go to the interview room?" Jim asked, politely touching her elbow. The thin bones felt brittle under his fingers.

"Will this take long? I have an appointment at the hair—".

"Lexy! What are you doing here?" Bill Meyers asked, coming out of his office. He glanced at Jim and Milt, then flushed when he realized the intimate, informality of his greeting.

"Making a statement," she said in a neutral voice.

Jim placed a hand in the middle of her back, gently moving her toward the interview room. "Nick Gracie worked for her husband. We're taking everyone's statements, Bill."

"Why? We've got a confession."

"To wrap it up. The prosecutor and judge will want a complete case file, even with a confession."

"There's no need for you to waste your time on this, Jim. I can get her statement."

"Oh, it's no bother. You can work that car theft that came in this morning."

"Car theft?" Meyers snorted. "A bunch of kids—"

"Or the arson. Get with the fire marshal—"

Meyers turned on his heel and returned to his office. Then in a determined show of control, he closed the door with exaggerated gentleness.

"This way, Mrs. Butler," Milt said.

Jim flicked on the lights in the small room and pulled out one of the padded chairs.

Mrs. Butler sat on the edge of the seat and crossed her ankles, resting her wrists against the edge of the table. "Do I have to repeat everything I've told you?"

"If you wouldn't mind." Jim pointed to the digital recorder in the center of the table. "We want to make sure we understand what happened. I'd also like to swab the inside your mouth."

She sat up straighter and glanced at the door. "Why do you need a DNA sample?"

Another person addicted to police procedural TV shows, Jim thought as he pulled on his gloves. "We have a warrant, Mrs. Butler. Would you like to look at it?"

She stared at the swab in Jim's hand. Her gaze flickered over to Milt, leaning against the door jamb. "What's this all about?"

"We're collecting evidence for a murder investigation."

"I know that. I'm not a complete fool."

He leaned toward her, holding a long, cotton-tipped swab.

"What do you want it for? You know I wasn't involved in that murder."

"Then you won't mind if we confirm it."

She leaned away from Jim. "How is a sample of my DNA going to confirm it?"

"We found a used condom."

Her skin turned even paler, if possible. The dark circles under her eyes grew more pronounced, hollowing her eyes.

"He has a girlfriend, doesn't he?" she asked.

"Does he? No one seems to know her name." Milt shifted his weight. "Do you know her name?"

"I don't know. Ask . . ." She dropped her gaze to the table.

"Who?" Jim prompted.

Her hands shook before she clasped them together in her lap, effectively hiding them under the table. She forced a laugh. "Sorry, I was going to say ask Nick Gracie."

Jim leaned forward again, but didn't raise the swab. "Mrs. Butler, one of the females left her DNA on a plastic water bottle found in your trash."

"So what? It could have been anyone in the house. A maid, our cook, even a guest."

"That's why we want the sample. To eliminate you."

"What difference could it possibly make? You have a confession. Why do you care what Nick was doing before he went to the Edwards house and got killed?"

"We have reason to believe he might have died at your residence."

"You can't possibly believe that!"

Jim picked up the swab. "Give me a sample, repeat your statement, and you can leave."

She clamped her mouth shut. Her lips compressed into a thin, angry line before she nodded. "Fine." She opened her mouth and stared at the corner of the room, above Jim's head.

He leaned forward and swabbed the inside of her mouth. "Thank you." He placed the swab in a sterile tube and labeled it in silence.

When he finished, he said, "You know we'll get a match, don't you?"

She shrugged and focused on the opposite wall.

"The police technicians are at your house, collecting evidence. There are always traces, things that bleach can't dissolve. And there is the bleach, itself, considered negative evidence."

"I have nothing further to say. I want my lawyer. You'll get my statement from my lawyer."

"You can certainly do that," Jim agreed. "But suppose we collect evidence that proves you and some other woman slept with Nick Gracie moments before he was murdered? In fact, it's equally possible that you and the other woman were sleeping with him when he was murdered. That could make you an accessory. Even if it was the other woman who killed him."

"We're going to find that other woman," Milt said, "and whoever cooperates with the police first is going to get the best deal."

"Speak to my lawyer."

"Your husband went to Max Marine Crafters on Saturday," Milt said, "so we were wondering what you were doing."

"I was shopping with a friend."

"And the name of this friend?"

"She's a neighbor. I don't think she'd want to get involved."

"Give us a name, Mrs. Butler. If you want us to believe you."

She glanced up at him. Her face remained expressionless, but her eyes revealed an agonizing brew of emotions. "No. I can't. I don't want to hurt him—I never wanted to hurt him."

"You mean Mr. Butler?"

"Of course I mean my husband!" Her voice cracked. "And I never killed anyone!"

"But you know who did?" Jim asked.

"I need to speak with my lawyer." She stood up. "I'm sorry. But unless you're arresting me, I have to go. Am I free to go?"

"Get a lawyer, Mrs. Butler," Jim said. "And think about it. Because if we find the other woman, and she decides to make a deal, you may not get another opportunity."

She nodded. Her thin throat convulsed as she swallowed repeatedly, but she remained silent.

When it became obvious that she wasn't going to say any more without benefit of counsel, Milt stepped away from the door and opened it for her.

"Thank you for coming in, Mrs. Butler," he said as she passed him, hurrying out.

In the hallway, she paused, indecision showing on her face as another woman came into the station. Jim stepped into the hallway behind Mrs. Butler.

The woman standing in the door to the office area was a pretty girl with large brown eyes and pale brown hair. Jim judged her to be in her early twenties, and there was something familiar about her. Perhaps he had seen her hanging around Peyton Place, bent over a banana split. She looked like all the other young women in town. Anorexic and intent on imitating the highly unflattering, tight clothing worn by the latest heroines of video and gossip rags.

When she caught his glance, her shoulders curved forward. She crossed her arms protectively over her nearly concave chest.

Jim moved forward a step, passing Mrs. Butler, his gaze intent on the girl in the hallway. Her face drained of all color. She clutched her cheap, white purse with tense fingers. Her knuckles were almost as white as the vinyl of her purse.

The other woman, Jim thought.

The two women traded quick, flickering glances. Then they each focused with elaborate casualness on other things. The girl, barely breathing, stared at the beige tiles on the floor. Mrs. Butler stared with forced intensity at the glass door of the interview room.

Bill Meyers stepped out of his office into the tense silence of the hallway.

"Robyn? What—" Meyers stopped, noticing the others clustered a few feet away.

The girl glanced at him and clutched her elbows more tightly with her thin fingers.

"It's quite all right, Ms. Adams," Meyers touched her shoulder.

She jerked back as if he had slapped her.

"Ms. Adams," Jim said, hoping to break the tension, "is there something I can help you with?"

"No, I only—" Her brown eyes held his for a moment. Fear flickered in their depths. Then she dropped her head, shutting him out.

"Ms. Adams called me earlier, Jim," Meyers said. "About that arson case." He flashed her a smile. "She thought she saw someone hanging around before the fire. Probably nothing. I asked her to come down and make a statement."

Jim studied Robyn Adams. She wouldn't meet his gaze. Turning toward Bill's door, her hands moved along the hem of her tight pink blouse, tugging the sagging, stretchy fabric. She looked lost, alone, and desperate. And poor. Perhaps abused, without hope of escape.

Jim's gut clenched. This young woman didn't need to make a statement about some arson case. She needed help. He'd seen so many like her in his years as sheriff. And her barely controlled anxiety filled him with a sense of frustration.

You can't save everyone. Anne had told him that a million times. But who else was going to save those without the resources to help themselves?

"Maybe this isn't a good time," the girl said. Her voice was low and hesitant, as if she believed she didn't have the right to talk, or ask for help.

"There's nothing to be afraid of, Ms. Adams." Meyers smiled his best, politically correct smile. "All police reports are confidential. No one is going to find out you talked to us."

Her gaze flew to Mrs. Butler. Jim placed his hand in the middle of Mrs. Butler's stiff back. "Let me escort you to your car."

"That isn't necessary."

"It's no trouble," Jim replied, nodding to Milt.

Milt eased past them and strode to his desk. Jim deliberately caught Bill's gaze and held it while he said, "I'd be interested in reading Ms. Adams information on that arson case. Make sure you get her statement to me today."

"Yes, sir."

Bill's reply was surprising, but only because of the absence of his usual resentment. Jim watched him wave Ms. Adams to the seat in front of his amazingly clean and scratch-free wooden desk. She sat and nervously sipped from a can of soda she pulled from her purse. When she'd drained it, she dropped the can in the trash.

Jim caught Milt's eye and nodded before he escorted Mrs. Butler to the parking lot. She walked in front of him, stiff-legged and straight-backed. When they got to her car, he opened the door for her and braced his arms on the door frame as she climbed behind the steering wheel.

"Are you okay, Mrs. Butler?"

She turned on the ignition, her eyes focused on the sheriff's office. Jim glanced in the same direction. She was staring at the windows to the common office area where Bill Meyers had his desk. But the Venetian blinds were down. There was nothing to see except the grayish glass, set in a plain, red brick wall.

Jim glanced back at Mrs. Butler's cold face. "Are you friends with Ms. Adams?"

Mrs. Butler put the car into reverse, although she kept her foot on the brake pedal. "Please shut the door."

"Did you know her?" Jim persisted.

"I don't have female friends."

"You must have at least one. Because you said you were out with your girlfriend when Nick Gracie died."

"I'm late for an appointment with the hairdresser." She grabbed the door handle and slammed the door shut. Her tires screeched as she jerked the car around and gunned it out of the lot without even pausing to look for oncoming traffic.

He could have given her a ticket for reckless driving.

Instead, when the traffic light at the corner of the sheriff's office turned red, forcing her to halt only a few yards away from the entrance to the parking lot, he waved.

The light cycled back to green. She never turned her head. She took off, this time at a discreet, safe speed. He waited a few minutes, listening to the smooth sound of her engine fade into the blend of traffic noise from downtown Peyton.

There was no doubt in his mind that Alexandra Butler knew Robyn Adams.

The question was, did Nick Gracie know both of them, as well?

Milt was waiting for him in his office. "Did you get anything more from Mrs. Butler?"

Jim smiled. "Well, I learned she's late for a hair appointment."

As Jim sat down behind his desk, Bill poked his head through the doorway. "Ms. Adams didn't know a thing. She saw a few shadows and got scared. So I'm going out to the arson site. I've arranged to meet with the fire marshal there."

"Great," Jim replied. "And check with the insurance agents. I still want that statement from Ms. Adams, though."

"You'll get it."

Milt leaned back in his chair, putting the flimsy wood to the test with his bulk as he propped one ankle up on a knee. Jim winked at Milt. "And Bill, get me your complete arson report by morning."

"Yes, sir." Meyers disappeared, his footsteps meandering to his desk.

"Asshole," Milt commented. He glanced up at Jim and laced his fingers behind his head. His chair groaned as he leaned backward, hanging ominously close to the battered wall behind him.

"What do you know about Robyn Adams?" Jim asked, not expecting an answer.

Milt unlaced his fingers and straightened. "I've seen her around."

"Around where?"

"Just around. She works at that discount store at the edge of town."

"I wonder if Nick Gracie knew her."

"You're thinking she's the second woman?"

"Yes. Get her soda can out of Bill's trash. I'm curious about her DNA."

CHAPTER THIRTY

When Jim left his office late Thursday night, he saw a beat-up truck parked on the side of the road just out of town. A very thin woman bent over the open tailgate. When he slowed down to assist, he recognized her as the girl Bill had called Robyn. Ms. Adams.

He parked a few feet behind her on the shoulder.

"Can I help you?" he asked, climbing out of his vehicle.

"Oh, yes. Thank you." Her smile of relief faded as she recognized him. Her gaze drifted to his nameplate and then down to his sidearm. She crossed her arms over her chest and rubbed her arms as if suddenly cold. "I got a flat. I don't know where the spare tire is."

"No problem." He located the tire under the bed of the truck and changed it for her, keeping conversation to a minimum.

When he was done, she handed him a pack of wet wipes. "I really appreciate this," she said.

"And we appreciated your help today." He leaned against the front fender. "Do you have a few minutes?"

Her smile slipped. She glanced at the steering wheel as if she thought the truck would drive off without her if she didn't immediately climb inside.

"Is it about that fire, Sheriff? Because I already told Bill, I mean Deputy Meyers, everything I know about that. I really didn't see anything helpful."

"Did you know Nick Gracie?"

251

She turned to stone. For several seconds, she even seemed to stop breathing. "Nick Gracie?"

He nodded. "I was wondering if you ever ran into him. Or saw him with anyone. We'd like to talk to his friends."

"I'm not one of his friends."

"Did you ever see him around?"

"No. Why would I? I doubt he did a lot of shopping where I work."

"You're probably right, but Peyton is a small town. There aren't that many single people here. Seems like everyone either gets married right out of high school or they leave. Most never come back."

"Not me." She stared down the road at some distant object. Her face, all sharp bones and tired shadows, was expressionless, but she flashed a quick glance at him, her mouth twisted into a half-smile. "You getting ready to ask me out?"

He choked off a laugh, sensing it wouldn't be the right reaction. "No, sorry, I—"

"Why don't you ask Bill Meyers about single men in small towns?" she interrupted. "I don't fit his view of the kind of girl a brilliant young politician should be seen with, but I'm sure good enough in the dark."

"Maybe he's shy," he replied lamely. Bill Meyers and *Robyn?*

She climbed inside the cab of her truck. "Thanks for helping me. Hope you find whoever killed Mr. Gracie."

He had barely enough time to step away from the truck before she pulled away. The rear tires spewed a shower of sharp gravel and sand into the air. Grit struck his face and bounced off his shoulders and chest as he watched her drive away.

He walked back to his cruiser, wishing life was simpler. It would have been nice if Robyn Adams had been involved with Nick Gracie, but perhaps her lower position in Peyton's social pecking order explained Mrs. Butler's reaction. Her recognition of Robyn might have been nothing more than her distaste of what Robyn represented, which in Mrs. Butler's mind was trailer trash.

If Bill Meyers was her "boyfriend," Robyn no doubt got the same attitude from him.

Jim thought about Frank and Sylvia Edwards with their PhDs. They seemed to lack the underlying insecurity and envy that drove people like Bill Meyers and Mrs. Butler to cling so tightly to their social status and money.

Nonetheless, Jim couldn't help but think Nick Gracie's death had a great deal to do with secrets and the necessity to keep up good appearances. Problem was, he couldn't figure out which secrets and whose good appearance was at stake.

CHAPTER THIRTY-ONE

Although Cassie had hoped that Jim would release her uncle, she waited in vain. There was no word Thursday night or Friday. By 4:30 P.M., she realized it was unlikely he would be released—if he was released—until Monday.

Her aunt seemed equally depressed and spent all day in the greenhouse, taking inventory and pointedly ignoring the empty table where their computer used to sit. By six, both women were too disheartened and tired to do much more than boil a few handfuls of spaghetti.

"I'm sorry, Cassiopeia," Sylvia said with an exhausted smile. "I'm afraid I'm not very good company tonight. Would you mind if I retire? I've got a few journals. I thought I might read for a while in bed."

"Sure. I'll clean up. Maybe later if you feel like it we could go to Peyton Place?"

"Anne Fletcher's diner?"

"Yes. At least it'll get us out of the house."

"I think I'd rather stay here. You go if you wish." Her glance flickered toward the phone.

"You think they still might call about Uncle Frank?"

"I'd like to believe it's possible."

"Did you speak to Deputy Singleton about him?"

"Briefly." Her mouth curved in a smile, but it didn't lighten the shadows in her sad, gray eyes. "They're still investigating. That's a good sign, I believe."

"Very good." She put an arm around her aunt's waist and squeezed. "They'll find out who did it. I'm sure of it."

"I'm glad you're here." She stopped to study Cassie's face. "Would you consider staying a few more days?"

Cassie smiled. "I don't think that'll be a problem. In fact, I was hoping I could convince you to let me stay here for a while. I've been under a lot of stress, and I'm on meds, as well as antibiotics for an ulcer."

"Of course you can stay with us. But ulcers! We had spaghetti for dinner, and you know that's not appropriate. Why didn't you say something?"

"Don't worry about me. Dealing with spicy sauce is what medication is for. I didn't mention it to complain."

"Well, I'm glad you're here. Now if you'll excuse me, I'm going to bed."

Cassie kissed her on the cheek. Her soft skin smelled of baby powder and the faint, vanilla scent of heliotrope. "Don't worry about a thing, Aunt Sylvia."

She watched her aunt leave the kitchen. She suspected she'd lie in bed and listen to Strauss waltzes she loved and catch up on her reading.

The back door slammed open.

Glancing up, she dropped the plate she was carrying to the sink. It shattered on the tiled floor, spilling leftover strands of spaghetti across the polished surface.

Her aunt was upstairs in bed. Frank was in jail.

No one else should be using that door.

Her pulse raced.

"Who's there?" she called as she looked around the kitchen.

Silence.

She grabbed a carving knife from the knife block sitting on the counter. Then she slid along the wall to the hallway. She glanced down the long corridor toward the back of the house.

Evening gloom darkened the corridor and crouched in the space under the stairs. They had always meant to install another light fixture—

"Hello?" Her nervous fingers strayed to the cell phone clipped to her belt. She pulled it out and checked it before pushing it back into the leather holster.

Footsteps creaked on the old wooden floors. A thud shuddered through the house as if someone fell against the wall.

Should she call nine-one-one? There was another thud and she jumped. What about Jim Fletcher? She had him on speed dial. Number four, right after her uncle and Anne.

Her fingers drifted back to the phone.

"Who's there?" She pulled it free of the holster.

Her uncle stumbled into view. He looked ghastly, his face gray and his eyes glittering within deep hollows. When he took another step, he wavered and hit the wall with his shoulder.

"Uncle Frank! What are you doing here?" she asked, pressing four on her cell phone. Something was wrong. She didn't know what, but she wanted the sheriff. "Are you all right?"

Frank shook his head, a dazed expression on his face.

Then, Bill Meyers stepped into view. He pushed Frank toward Cassie with a brutal shove. When he saw the phone in her hand, he pointed a gun at her.

"Drop it. Now! And the knife."

Shaking, her grip on both tightened.

"I don't really care if you want to die attacking an officer of the law," the deputy said, aiming his weapon.

"Wait!" she screamed. She swallowed, trying to control her panic. "What are you doing here?"

"What do you think? Your uncle confessed to murder. Then he got clever and escaped. I followed him here."

"Uncle Frank?" She took a step forward.

Frank shook his head and leaned against the wall, as if he

barely had enough strength to remain upright. His gray hair hung lank and limp around his face and his thin lips had an unhealthy blue tinge.

"I didn't escape," Frank said.

She heard the metallic click as Meyers released his gun's safety. He gestured at her hands.

With a wretched sense of despair, she threw the knife to the floor.

"The phone, too," Meyers said.

She gestured toward her uncle. "Uncle Frank's right there and unarmed."

"Drop the phone!"

She placed the phone on the floor against the baseboard. It showed the call had connected, but she couldn't hear anything.

"Why are you doing this?" she asked, trying to think clearly above the beat of her heart.

"I'm not doing this, Frank is." He pressed the gun against the back of her uncle's neck, pushing him forward. Meyers looked flushed, his eyes brilliant with tension. Angry energy crackled around him. He used the gun like an extension of his hand, pointing it first at Cassie and then using it to prod Frank forward. Head tilting, he paused. "What the hell is that music?"

"Strauss waltzes. I always play Strauss before I go to bed. Do you like music, Deputy?"

"No. Now get paper and a pen," Meyers commanded, maneuvering them toward the kitchen. "I'll bet you keep a pad next to the phone."

Cassie sidestepped the door and continued down the hallway, unwilling to be pushed into anything. Delay was her best ally. Her mind leapt and skittered as she fought back the fear gripping her.

"I'm not sure I have paper in the kitchen." Her voice trembled. She cleared her throat. "I don't remember. You're scaring me!"

He aimed the gun at her, his finger squeezing the trigger.

"Wait!" She sidled back toward the kitchen door.

Her uncle already stood in the center of the room. His shoulders sagged, and he stared around with a puzzled look as if he'd never been there before.

"Sylvia," he said, looking at Cassie. "Where's Sylvia?"

"She's on a trip, Uncle Frank. Don't you remember?"

"Shut up," Meyers said. "Get the paper and pencil, Cassie. Then I want both of you to sit down at the table."

She stalled, hesitating in the doorway. But he pressed the gun into her back between the shoulder blades. It felt like a hard, accusing finger.

The pounding in her chest made her sick. She swallowed, pushing back the feeling of burning nausea and held up her hands. Her shaking fingertips felt frozen, and the chill drained down her arms.

He pushed her forward until her hips hit the edge of the table. She sprawled over the tablecloth, too afraid to move.

"Cassie," her uncle said, reaching over to touch her shoulder. "I'm sorry. This is all my fault."

She straightened. "No, it's not your fault."

She ran trembling hands over her bruised waist and angled away from Meyers. Pulling out a chair, she sat, keeping her back to the wall.

Meyers laughed. Then he shook his head before turning back to Frank. "Take that paper and pen. Sit there."

Despite his pallor, Frank's mouth compressed into a mulish line. "Or what? You'll beat me? That'll put bruises and marks on me. You don't want that."

Meyers swung the gun toward Cassie. "If you don't do as I say, I'll shoot her."

Picking up the yellow pad and a pen, Frank's heavily veined

hands shook. Head bowed, he edged toward the table and took the chair across from Cassie.

"Power corrupts," Frank said. "Those in authority are inherently untrustworthy."

"I know," Cassie replied. "The best government is that which governs the least."

She reached out to touch her uncle's thin wrist. The butt of Meyers' gun slammed her hand. A sharp squeal of pain escaped her as she heard a brittle snap of bone. She jerked back to hide her hands under the table.

Meyers hit her in the shoulder. "Keep your hands on the table."

Cassie complied, protecting her bruised hand under her left arm. Heat radiated from her wrist. A dull throbbing began. Her hand was broken, but she didn't feel the pain—yet. She waited for her mind to catch up with her damaged body.

Then, in the far distance, she heard a dry, cracking sound. Twigs breaking underfoot?

She shifted her chair, scraping the legs against the floor.

"No touching," Meyers said. "Sit there until I tell you to move."

"Absolute power," Frank murmured.

Cassie nodded. She cradled her right hand in the left, intensely aware of every muscle, every beat of her heart. An electrical pulse and tingle zapped along the nerves in her wrist. She tensed. Hot pain flared up her arm. She let out a moan.

Meyers spared her a glance and small, tight smile. "Broken? Sorry. Don't worry about it." Then he returned his attention to Frank. He rested the butt of his gun on Frank's narrow shoulder, aiming the barrel at his throat. "Now write. As long as you write what I tell you, your niece will be fine. And let's not forget your dear wife."

Dear God, Aunt Sylvia. Uncle Frank didn't realize his wife

had returned and was upstairs. She was as vulnerable as they were. Fortunately, the loud waltzes hid any sound from the kitchen.

In her uncle's gaze, she could see his terror. Did he still fear the police would discover sufficient evidence to prove Sylvia had killed Nick Gracie?

Cassie knew Jim would never believe Sylvia was involved, no matter what Meyers said. Uncle Frank was only partially right about power and authority. Meyers proved power could easily be abused. However, Jim's willingness to continue the investigation showed authority could also protect the innocent.

She had to buy more time. She couldn't let Meyers kill them all in a kitchen reeking of garlic and pasta. She had to think of something.

"Go ahead, Uncle Frank," she said. "Do what he says."

"Yes, do what he says, Frank," Meyers mimicked in a high falsetto. He pressed the gun under Frank's ear. "It'll be short and to the point, I promise."

"How do I start?" Frank poised the tip of his pen over the pad. "Dear Sir? To Whom It May Concern?"

"Write what I tell you. Start with 'I'm sorry.' " Then, Meyers dictated a brief note that took very little time to write.

The supposed suicide note said Frank killed his niece when she tried to call the authorities. Cassie wanted him to go back to jail, and he couldn't face life in jail. He couldn't live with what he had done. He apologized to his wife. He said he loved her.

It was all very touching, very believable.

"Sign it," Meyers said.

"Listen, man. Let Cassie go." Frank dropped the pen onto the table.

"Shut up, you damn pothead."

"I didn't kill Mr. Gracie."

"Of course not, you moron! You've never done anything in your pathetic life except grow a better strain of weed."

"Your girl," Frank began.

"Shut up about Robyn!"

"She just did what came natural, man."

"What do you know about it?" Meyers asked.

Cassie stared at her uncle. "Who's Robyn?"

"She's a nice girl, a free spirit. Maybe a little confused."

Meyers stared at Frank, his face flushed. His lips worked as anger consumed him, burning in his eyes. "Robyn has nothing to do with this."

"You loved her," Frank said, sitting back in his chair.

Cassie realized her uncle was controlling the conversation, chipping away at Meyers' confidence and trying to distract him. Frank's left eyelid lowered as he stared into her eyes. Suddenly, the uncle she had known as a child resurfaced, the kind man who would listen and understand anything she told him.

The brave hero who could fix anything.

Then she heard what she had been dreading. The sound of Sylvia's light step on the stairs. Cassie surged to her feet, hands pressed against the wall behind her. She had made a mistake sitting there. With the wall behind her, she couldn't move. She couldn't escape and warn Sylvia.

"Freeze!" A loud voice sounded from the kitchen doorway.

"Jim!" Cassie exclaimed.

Meyers turned toward Jim. Cassie stepped forward and elbowed Meyers brutally in the kidneys. He hunched his shoulders and grunted. Then he turned in her direction, swinging the gun around, his face twisted with rage.

"Drop it! Now!" Jim ordered. He braced his wrists on the kitchen counter, aiming his gun.

Meyers hesitated, swinging his gun between Cassie, her uncle, and the sheriff. His elbow swung up, hitting Cassie on the chin.

Her head snapped back. She hit the wall behind her, but managed to stay on her feet. Then to her surprise, she saw Meyers falling away from her as he tripped over her uncle's long leg.

"Drop it!" Jim repeated.

The rapid, heavy tread of feet pounding over the wooden floor came from the direction of the front door. Meyers squeezed the trigger even as he stumbled.

"No!" Cassie screamed, focused on the direction of the shot. Jim.

But Jim didn't return the gunfire. At the last minute, he halted, raising his gun to point the barrel at the ceiling.

Frank picked up a kitchen chair and slammed it down on Bill's back.

And Milt Singleton charged into the kitchen like a bull smelling fresh hay. He stopped short in the doorway and glanced around. With a grin, he holstered his gun.

"Everyone all right?" he asked.

Cassie stared across the kitchen at Jim. He locked gazes with her as he absently removed a set of handcuffs from his belt.

"What are you doing here?" she asked.

"You called, didn't you? Stay back, Cassie," he added when Meyers rolled over to leverage himself up from the floor.

Before Meyers could stand, Jim pressed a knee into the middle of his back, forcing him down and cuffed him. Then he hauled Meyers to his feet and said, "Take him out to the car, Milt."

"Frank!" Sylvia exclaimed from the kitchen door. "What's going on here?" She walked into the kitchen in a long, flowing nightgown.

Frank gazed with deep appreciation at his wife, and smiled as he edged around the table.

CHAPTER THIRTY-TWO

Relieved and still thrumming with adrenalin, Cassie ran to Jim. She tried to hug him, only to accidentally bang her wrist against his elbow.

She screamed.

He grabbed her shoulders and held her in front of him. "What's wrong?"

"My hand is broken." She moaned and tried to find a way to support her hand and wrist without sending another spasm of pain up her arm. "I think. Not sure."

"Why didn't you say something?" Jim unclipped his cell phone.

"Wait, drive me to Urgent Care. Please? I don't want to go in an ambulance."

He gingerly slipped an arm around her and faced her toward the door. His smelled of perspiration and heated starch from his uniform shirt. The scent of safety. And love.

If only she could enjoy it. She gritted her teeth, starting to feel ill as the adrenalin drained away, leaving her exhausted and in agony.

"Where are you going?" Aunt Sylvia asked from the doorway, her arm around Frank's waist.

Cassie glanced over her shoulder. "Urgent Care."

"How badly are you hurt? Were you shot?"

"No, bruised. Maybe sprained."

"Or broken," Jim said.

She frowned at him and took one step forward before he grabbed her.

With a long sigh, Frank enfolded Sylvia in his arms and pressed his face into her silvered hair. "I thought you left for good." He stroked her hair, his entire body shaking before he pushed her away to stare into her face. Then he pulled her back into his arms.

"You old fool," Sylvia said, her voice vibrating with emotion. "I've never had enough sense to leave you for good. No matter what you did." She laughed and her eyes filled with tears. "Or maybe I couldn't leave for good because you painted the house the color of an orchid named after me."

"Then you'll stay this time?"

She reached up and touched his lined cheek. "Of course I'll stay. Besides, I've got a new project in mind. A pink orchid." She glanced at her niece. "We'll call it Cassiopeia."

He held her at arm's length and said, "I'm not sure I can. I have glaucoma."

"I know. But they have medicine for that, and I'll be your eyes. You're not the only one who can work a microscope. Or use a computer."

Despite her throbbing arm, Cassie couldn't bear to leave. Shocked, she watched tears slip down the furrows lining her uncle's face.

"One condition, though. No weed, my love." She touched her mouth briefly to his. "Only legal drugs. Promise me."

He crushed her against him. "Legal drugs, no problem. I love you."

Cassie let out a deep sigh of relief that ended in a small moan. She glanced up at Jim. "I guess we should go. I'm starting to feel ill."

He stared down at her. "You're not going to get sick are you?"

"No. And I'm not sitting in the back of your cruiser, either. We'll take my car."

"Great." He smiled. "Any cleanup will be your problem."

Behind Jim, she could see the dark doorway into the greenhouse. In the silence, she heard a faint click as the watering timers turned on the misters. The soft hiss of water and the scents of damp soil and vegetation filled the air. The familiar sounds reassured her.

"Here you go." She tossed her car keys to him. "I wish we could keep my uncle out of this nightmare."

"I wish we could keep the sheriff's department out of this nightmare."

She tried to laugh, but strangled with incoherent pain when she stepped outside onto the porch. The jarring motion took her breath away.

"We'll try to keep what happened as quiet as possible," Jim said, closing the door and glancing toward her car. "Unfortunately, I think the drive is going to be difficult, Cassie. You should have let me call for an ambulance."

She shook her head, her mouth compressed into a straight line. With short, ragged breaths, she followed him to the car and climbed inside.

"Distract me," she said as he turned the car around. "Tell me what happened. Meyers—"

"Ah. The fair-haired wonder-boy." He smiled.

"How did you know to show up here?"

"Someone started a phone call and then threw her cell phone on the floor."

"The call went through?"

"Yeah."

"But you got here so quickly."

"I forward my calls to my cell phone when I'm not home.

And I was already on the way here. Milt discovered Frank was missing."

"You came to arrest him again?" She focused on the dark blankness of her window, rocking and trying to control her pain.

"You still don't trust me."

"It's not that. I trust you—"

"You thought I came charging up here to save you?"

"Yes," she whispered. "Stupid, right? I guess I thought you'd rescue me, like you rescued us from driving drunk after the prom."

"That was a romantic gesture, too. Particularly after you threw up on me."

"Why can't anyone forget that?"

"Everyone else thinks it's funny."

"Well, it's not. It was the worst night of my life. Until now."

"People don't always live up to expectations. I didn't become a full-time writer."

"Who cares? *I* acted like an idiot. I thought I could solve any problem by thinking about it."

"Sometimes having a forensics lab and police to investigate helps."

"Hey, it's not like you figured it out. You said you were coming here to arrest Frank. Again."

"Not exactly. How do you think he escaped?"

She shrugged and hunched over. They drove past a few brightly lit houses. In a few minutes, they would arrive at the Urgent Care facility. She let out a long breath, wishing the night was already over. She couldn't think straight. For some reason, instead of gratitude, she felt a vague sense of anger.

"Come on, think about it." He flicked on the turn signal. "I tried to interview him twice, Cassie, to get him to retract his confession. He wouldn't budge. He slept most of the time and showed no interest in anything around him. How was he going to escape on his own?"

"Your deputy helped him escape so he could set us up."

"Correct. I already knew someone had tampered with the evidence. Meyers collected broken glass from your kitchen. Fragments with blood on them. And the lab said the DNA matched the sample from Nick Gracie."

"But I dropped that glass and cut myself when I picked it up. That happened after Gracie died."

"Exactly. And I couldn't see how a drinking glass could be used to bludgeon a man. Unless he slipped and hit his head someplace where there was already broken glass."

"He didn't slip here."

"That was my other problem. Our coroner agreed with you. He took photos of the glass he extracted from the head wound. It was heavy lead crystal. It didn't look anything like the glass Meyers found."

"We don't drink from lead crystal goblets here. That's not what got broken."

"So think about it, Cassie."

"My wrist hurts. I don't want to think about it."

"Sorry."

"Never mind. I told you to distract me. So, you knew the evidence had been tampered with. Switched?"

"Yes. We sent the coroner's photos to Raleigh. The fragments in the picture were not what they received to test."

"How did he get the DNA to match? It was my blood on the glass."

"That's going to be a problem. Most of the evidence is compromised now."

"We more or less have your deputy's confession. That has to count for something."

"It will." Jim turned into the parking lot in front of a long, low brick building.

"Did Bill Meyers whack Nick Gracie with a lead crystal vase?"

"No, a lamp. And there was other evidence that didn't fit."

"For crying out loud—tell me."

"Nick Gracie was having sex with two women when he died. We tracked down the two women. One of them wouldn't talk—"

"Howard Butler's wife." Cassie smiled, although her teeth clenched. "Howie complained to me that his wife was seeing someone else. What about the second woman. Was she married, too?"

"No, but she was involved with someone else."

"Bill Meyers!"

"Yes. Meyers had kept the relationship quiet. He was ambitious, and his flaky girlfriend didn't fit the image he was trying to create. She worked at a discount store and hadn't even finished high school. She was a decent enough kid, but I think she knew Meyers wasn't going to marry her. So it was easy enough for Gracie to take advantage of her frustration—"

"And participate in a threesome?"

"People do a lot of crazy things for love—and jealousy. I think both women were doing it more out of anger with their partners than any desire for Gracie."

"So Meyers killed Gracie because of his girlfriend?"

"Maybe. But I've also been doing a little digging into Bill's finances. Something about him didn't sit well with me. He's done very well as a deputy sheriff. Even better than the sheriff. I found that odd."

"And?"

"Gracie was selling drugs, and he had three partners. His boss, Meyers, and your uncle."

"Frank only grew weed."

"I know. The others were into the harder stuff. But I think Meyers wanted a larger cut. I believe he went up to the Butler house to talk to Gracie about it. Finding him in bed with his girlfriend and Mrs. Butler knocked him sideways."

"So he killed him?"

"He hit him over the head with one of Mrs. Butler's lamps. Then he made the two women help him dress Gracie. From the timing, I gather Butler may have gotten home about that time, so they didn't have time to run all over the house collecting Gracie's clothes. In their haste, they dressed him in some old clothes belonging to Butler. And although they remembered to remove the condom, they must have lost track of it because they left it in his underwear. Frankly, I think Meyers had problems getting the women to help him and clean up before Butler walked in. That's why everything seemed so half-assed and careless."

"And the three of them dumped Gracie in our stream so that could shift the blame to poor Uncle Frank? Then why did Meyers take that shot at Frank? That was him, wasn't it?"

"To make it look like some sort of drug war. Then Meyers tried to speed up the process by arresting your uncle and getting his 'confession.' That should have short-circuited the process and stopped the investigation right there."

"I'm glad you didn't stop."

"How could I?" he asked lightly. "You kept sprinkling fleas in my ear about it until you drove me crazy."

"Oh, thanks. That's a nice image. Fleas."

"The sort of thing a writer would say?"

"More like something a hick cop would say." She eased out of the car and gratefully stood aside when Jim opened the door for her.

There were only a few other people in the waiting room.

After one glance at Cassie's hand, the doctor, nurse, and an X-ray technician pulled her into an examining room and prodded, processed, and developed slides of her wrist. Then the doctor bounded into the room carrying a tray loaded with painkillers, a splint, and cast-making materials.

"You really broke it," he said, ecstatic.

Cassie eyed him askance. "Yes."

"A lot of patients have sprains or a bruise," he confided. "But you have a really nice fracture. Let me show you." He pointed to her X-rays with his pen. "Anyway, I'll fit your cast, and you'll be on your way."

"I'm glad I made your night."

"Sorry." He had the grace to look abashed as he draped a small tent over her arm. "What color do you want? Pink?"

She looked at the rainbow array of fiberglass casting tape. In an inexplicable fit of whimsy, she pointed to the sample in bright purple. "My uncle grows orchids. That color would be great."

"Purple?" Jim asked, catching sight of her cast when she came out.

"It was all he had left," she lied with a straight face. "Frank will like it."

"I bet he will. You ready to go home?"

"Yes."

He opened the door for her and stood aside, studying her as she walked outside. "You look tired."

"If you're hoping to stop by Anne's for a sundae, forget it."

"No." He tilted her head up. His thumb rubbed her full lower lip.

When she didn't pull away, he slowly bent his head, keeping his eyes focused on hers. At the touch of his warm mouth, Cassie closed her eyes, leaning closer, pulling him against her. He deepened the kiss, his hand slipping down her back to the curve of her hip. Her clothing, dampened by the cool, night mist, seemed to melt away against the heat of his body. Warmth soaked through her muscles, easing away the last of her tension.

But before she was ready, he stepped away and opened the

car door. She climbed into the seat, trying to sort through her complex emotions. She leaned her head back against the headrest and closed her eyes. The car jerked slightly as Jim climbed inside, but he didn't comment. He started the car and pulled out onto the deserted road.

"Cassie!" Jim shook her arm.

She sat up and looked around. They were parked in the driveway of her house. She had fallen asleep on the way home and still felt groggy.

"Sorry," she mumbled. "And thanks."

"No problem." He circled around the car and helped her out. "If you give me your prescriptions, I'll get them filled and bring them by tomorrow."

"Okay," she agreed with relief.

They entered the house, Cassie jerked to a stop when the large, hulking shadow of a man stretched across the hallway.

"Sheriff?" Milt spoke from the kitchen doorway. "Thought I ought to come back and wait for you, seeing as how we arrived together. Can't leave my Friday night date to find another ride home, now can I? And I've got Meyers tucked into bed real nice and tight in his own little cell."

"Thanks," Jim said, resting a warm hand on Cassie's shoulder.

"Even got a new statement from Frank. Seems he didn't mean to give us the impression he killed Gracie, after all."

"I see," Jim said.

"Which I, personally, find very believable," Milt continued. "Since he always lacked knowledge of some of the more crucial details, like the weapon that actually killed Gracie. And where he died." He straightened and strode to the open front door. After he stepped outside, he said over his shoulder, "So. You want a ride?"

Jim locked gazes with Cassie. "Do I want a ride?"

"Yes." When he turned away, she caught his arm and smiled.

"Much as it might be nice to have police protection, there's still that old conflict of interest thing. That's the problem with being a cop, isn't it? It must be difficult to date when everyone you meet is either a person of interest or related to one."

"Yeah. And my timing has always been a little off. I should warn you, Cassie. It could get ugly during the trial. Although it's going to be hard for Meyers to explain why he almost shot me."

"There's always the old, 'I was confused' excuse."

"Let the courts figure it out." Jim slipped a hand behind her head and drew her against him, kissing her hard.

"Police brutality," she whispered when he released her. "If you do that again, I want there to be handcuffs. And a bed."

"What? No crystals and daisies?"

"I can't stand that frou-frou stuff—"

"Are you coming?" Milt asked, his back to them. The porch creaked under his weight as he lumbered down the steps.

"I'll be right there." Jim turned to Cassie. "I realize I'm ten years too late to do that prom night favor, but maybe I can make it up to you with dinner?"

"What about 'conflict of interest'?"

"No problem. Got my signals crossed." He moved away.

She caught his arm. "Wait! I'm not saying no."

"But you're afraid for my reputation?"

"I don't want this case to fall apart, Jim. Meyers was ready to kill Frank. And me."

"Are you sure it's not that you can't quite get over the fact that I didn't become the successful writer you imagined?"

"No. I don't hold that against you. I thought you *wanted* to be a writer."

"I do. I write, and I'd even like to publish at some point. But I'm not planning on quitting police work. At first, I told myself that it was a way to get experience, but I like it, Cassie. I enjoy working with people. This case made me realize how important this job is to me." He chuckled. "You're not the only one who likes to solve problems."

"For someone who thinks he's good with people, you're amazingly obtuse. Is it any wonder that I prefer computers? Look, I've never known a sheriff before, not personally, and I've never had to depend on one."

"To save your ass?" His eyes glimmered.

"Yes. So I think we should show a little self-control for a few more days."

"The case will take longer than that to resolve."

"I'm not going anywhere. I got fired, remember?" She tucked her hand into the crook of his arm and walked him outside into the soft, pine-scented evening air. "I'm not sure I want another high-stress job. Besides, I hear there's an opening here at the community college for a computer specialist."

"Is that what you want?"

She laughed. "It may not be as challenging as my previous job, but then again, I won't need tranquilizers." She glanced up the stairs and thought about her purple cast and her purple house with its sagging roof curved like a smile above the porch. "In any case, I want to stay for a while, to make sure my uncle and aunt are okay. I've missed them."

She released him as he stepped through the door. Outside, Milt waited inside the sheriff's car, staring at them through the windshield. She waved at him. "But I'll take you up on that dinner."

"And afterwards?"

She smiled. "Bring your handcuffs. I like the idea of not being responsible. For a change."

"No one can say I'm not a gentleman." He winked at her. "Give me a call anytime. You supply the wine. I'll bring the cuffs."

CASSIE'S HOT DISH

1/2 pkg egg noodles
1 can kernel corn (15 oz)
1 can tomato soup (10 3/4 oz)
1/2 lb bacon, cut fine
1 onion, chopped fine
1 green pepper, chopped fine
Chili powder (1 tbsp, or to taste)
Salt & pepper (1 tsp each, or to taste)
Little sugar (1 tsp, or to taste)
1 c. corn flakes, crushed

Cook the noodles per the directions on the package. Fry the bacon, onion, and green pepper. Add corn, bacon, onions, peppers, and seasonings to the noodles. Add the tomato soup and gently fold together. Place mixture in a buttered casserole dish. Bake at 350° for 45 min (or until heated through), remove from oven and put crushed corn flakes on top, and put back in the oven to let brown for a few minutes.

Please note: If you want to use the whole package of egg noodles, you can use 2 cans of tomato soup and the entire 1 lb of bacon, as well. This casserole is excellent reheated and can also be frozen, so making up a larger batch and saving the extra is a great idea.

ABOUT THE AUTHOR

Award-winning author **Amy Corwin** published her first book, a Regency called *Smuggled Rose,* in 2007. Since then, she has expanded her repertoire to include romantic suspense, and she is a charter member of Romance Writers of America.

Amy lives out in the country and has numerous interests, including writing, bird watching, and gardening. She has been the newsletter editor for her local rose society, won awards at several rose shows, and grows over a hundred Old Garden roses (roses hybridized before 1900). She has written numerous articles on the history of roses, so it's not surprising when roses often show up in her books.